The Secret in the Rubble

Denise Parton

Chapter 1

E lam paled. The last thing he wanted to do was to repeat the word. He looked at the men gathered around the table. All dropped their gaze, none wishing to relay the message. No matter how courageous they appeared, each one held an enormous fear where Abaddon was concerned. The man they once held in high esteem, following his directives without question, had turned into someone they hardly recognized. They watched in horror as he spilled blood with no remorse and boldly wore the white stone that once belonged to his dear friend Ariston. The pendant hung around his neck along with a vial of the murdered Prince's blood. Since his men could not look into his eyes without permission, their gaze always landed on the barbaric jewelry, a constant reminder to them of the lengths to which he would go and to the depths he'd fallen.

It was often rumored as to where he received his incredible power. Some dared to say it came from the Teplem, however it was forbidden to speak of such dark powers. Only ruling authorities knew of this universal evil and the curses one might bring upon themselves for simply discussing it. There were legends, folklore, ancient writings about the Teplem, all whispered in secrecy. It was the one thing everyone feared yet few believed the stories were real, so they balked and ignored any signs that the nefarious influence had preyed upon their perfect world.

Abaddon's outward appearance remained the same, but it was the spirit that gazed from his eyes that immobilized them in fear. It never made a public appearance but always manifested in the secret chambers. It was dark, evil, yet luring, consuming everyone who entertained it with a deep lust for power and admiration. It was that spirit that spawned the notion that Abaddon died some time ago and that the impious one now occupied his body. Whatever the reason, his approval was intoxicating, addictive.

Each man at the table would do the unthinkable to receive the honor of being asked into his elite. None of them would ruin that chance by uttering the message the dead man brought.

Makram had the most to fear. He was supposed to have disposed of Haytham and for six hundred years it was believed he had. No one knew why he didn't. Perhaps it was because he couldn't, yet Elam knew that wasn't the case. He supposed the real reason was because Makram was a noble man in the midst of corruption; and although he compromised, along with the rest of them and chose to side with Abaddon, he did not entirely agree with his directives. Whatever the reason, Makram's secret was soon to be disclosed, and as much as it grieved him, Elam knew he was the one to reveal it.

Elam swallowed hard, his throat constricting in fear. Delaying was no longer an option. It was time to relay the message.

"They're all dead; every one of them. Their slayer left a message inscribed on their foreheads." He stopped and lowered his gaze from the vial of blood to the surface of the table. His heart seized, pounding against his chest. The silence in the room unnerved him; and, for a brief moment he tried to remember what peace felt like.

Abaddon spun the ceremonial dagger lying on the table. It was the same weapon that started the bloodthirsty coup almost seven hundred years ago; the knife that tore into the heart of Ariston, killing the first Prince of Eden.

The blade became invisible as it whirled and then took form again as it slowed and stopped. Abaddon caressed the knife running his fingers reverently across the blade and then back down the handle.

"And how is it that I send ten men over to kill the prophesied scribe and nine of them end up as corpses and you return unscathed?"

Elam swallowed, trying to moisten his dry mouth. His allegiance was in question and if Abaddon thought him a spy, aiding the other side, his execution would be imminent. His stomach grew sick, and he feared he might vomit. When would this end? Could the world ever go back to the way it used to be? Could the name the corpse brought back really deliver them from this pervading darkness? There were rumors of a savior. One who would rise on the scene and put an end to the thickening chaos.

"Your thoughts betray me."

Abaddon's accusation hissed, igniting a terror. How could he be privy to his thoughts? He had not allowed him access. Had the darkness reached so far? Or were the rumors true and the impious one taken residence in a body?

Elam felt the color rush up his neck and into his face, revealing his guilt. His mind searched for an explanation, a quick excuse to give reason for his demeanor.

"No, my Lord. It is not my thoughts that betray you, but the one named in the message. There is a betrayer in our midst and now I must find a way to reveal it to you and my heart grieves in the task."

Abaddon sneered in disgust, "Please spare me your sympathies. Name the apostate and I will kill him."

Elam dared not raise his eyes, yet he could no longer take the image of the repugnant vial; so, he closed them while uttering the forbidden word.

"Haytham."

The silence was deafening save for the sound of Elam's pounding heart. A low rumble erupted as the floor around Abaddon's chair began to shake. Elam opened his eyes and immediately wished he hadn't; for the sight of Abaddon's pupils turning milky white and rolling back in his head burned an image into his memory that he would surely take to the grave. A gust of foul-smelling sulfur swept across the room extinguishing the flame of each candle, casting the room into utter darkness. A hideous shriek ripped into the blackness, the sound of it bringing each man to the brink of insanity. Makram gurgling, gasping for his final breath of air was the last thing Elam heard before icy fingers wrapped around his own neck, forcing him against the cold stone wall. The grasp was so tight he could barely swallow. If it lasted much longer, he was sure to lose consciousness and join Makram in the afterlife. A frigid vapor wafted into his face, no doubt the call of death. His heart seized while he waited for the inevitable. In a way he welcomed the escape, yet he feared his life choices would only transport him from one torture to another. Then to his surprise Abaddon's grip lessened and then he summoned him with his mind so the others in the room would not be privy to their conversation.

Elam drank in the cold air, filling his lungs to capacity, then immediately gave Abaddon permission to enter into his consciousness, "I am listening; my Lord."

"And how is it you survived when the others lost their lives?"

Elam knew he must choose his thoughts carefully. He had one chance to survive, he would take it and hopefully it would be enough.

"I survived, my Lord, because I set a plan in motion some time ago. I have kept connections with friends who believe me to be sympathetic to their cause. I have chosen these contacts carefully, preying on those who are plagued with doubt. It's a weakness I can easily penetrate. Haytham has an elite circle as well. I have infiltrated it, gaining the trust of one. While the other nine attacked, I spent my time collecting information. I left immediately, knowing the report I carried must make it back. I have with me the names of three who could possibly be the scribe. One however, is a writer, she goes by the name Bronwyn Sterling."

The room remained dark and still, not even the men gathered around the table made noise. Had it not been for the feel of Abaddon's fingers curling around his throat, Elam would've thought he'd been sent to the abyss.

"I have a mission for you." Abaddon's thoughts entered his head after an extended silence. "If you complete it with success, I will elevate your status among these men. You will lead my inner circle, and no one will surpass your authority. You will have your choice of the royal manors where you and your family will live in luxury and privilege. You will have any woman you wish to warm your bed. You will walk in significance, and everyone will envy your station in my kingdom."

The thoughts of Abaddon poured into the chalice of Elam's mind like an intoxicating drink, and he swooned at the notion not once considering the price of the prize. And in an instant, his allegiance to the darkness was established.

"I humbly accept the task you require of me."

"Do not accept it in humility," Abaddon's thoughts hissed. "For a humble man will not succeed. Accept it proudly; let arrogance drive your ambition to complete it. I have no use for meek men in my service."

Elam swallowed hard fearing the icy grip once again, "I understand my Lord."

"Listen carefully to your directives. It is up to you to discover the best way to carry them out. It is why I chose you. You possess a scheming spirit that has caught my attention. You have full authority and access to whatever you require to launch your operation. Once you have carried out my directives, you will receive your reward; then and only then can we all celebrate after finally fulfilling the quest we have waited years to complete. Am I clear on this?"

He nodded, savoring the favor of his leader.

Abaddon removed his hand from Elam's throat and then with a snap of his finger, lit a nearby candle bringing light back into the secret chamber. The men seated around the table were shocked to see Elam alive and standing, unharmed.

"Dismiss the men," Abaddon gave the order through his mind.

Pride engulfed Elam, corrupting his wisdom. Dismissing the men meant only one thing. He was now part of the elite inner circle. He could only imagine what they would be thinking. They would be jealous and talk among themselves about how they should have been the one selected instead of him. The thought of their gall in the matter incited bitter feelings. He deserved the promotion. After all he was the one who took the risk of relaying the blood-stained message.

"Leave us."

The dumbfounded expressions on their faces pleased him and once the room was cleared Abaddon continued laying out the devious plot.

"The Scribe opened the book. It is simply a matter of time until the second prophecy is located. Whoever is the first to possess will receive the first clue to the treasure and the precious stone. We cannot lose that. You must prevent them from finding it first. Use your contact on the other side to gain information. Then put together a small army, you will need one. Destroy the book, and then bring Travis, Haytham and the Scribe to me."

Chapter 2

Black Hickory trees circled the two-story home, sitting several yards off the road, like an oasis in the middle of the desert. Storm clouds boiled on the horizon as they did almost every scorching summer evening. The breeze increased, bending the trees, and blowing open the screen door. Madison Sterling took advantage of the chivalrous wind and darted outside. Balancing the laundry basket on her hip, she pulled the clothes from the line, rescuing them from a certain soaking.

I remained hidden, watching from a distance. My parents would welcome my surprise visit and the look on their faces would be priceless. Mother sent numerous facebook messages, all seeped in guilt suggesting I visit more often. Each letter insinuated my dad might not make it another year. That was absurd, he was only sixty-five and in great health. It was my mother's way of manipulating a visit. I loved my parents and welcomed them every time they dropped in but for some reason, I found it difficult to return home.

The wind picked up, pushing harder, shoving against the thick boughs of a massive Hickory growing close to the house. The tree seemed to summon me, trying to catch my attention by scratching its gnarled branches across the top of the house. Its skeletal fingers pointed to the small attic window. I inched closer squinting my eyes. Something was materializing just behind the clouded pane.

A gust of wind swept across the property; shrieking as the sky continued to darken. It snatched a bed sheet from mother's grasp, carrying it across the yard and toppling lawn chairs along the way. The sound of its lament chilled me. The old Hickory slapped against the house, harder this time, drawing my attention back to the small oval window. I pushed against the powerful wind while making my way toward the house all the while I was fixed on the dark porthole. The branches of the black hickory blew aside revealing red glowing eyes watching me from inside the attic.

I gasped and sat up. My room in the Sandalwood Inn was dark and quiet. The only thing that caught my eye was the red glowing numbers 4:34 on the alarm clock. Letting out a long sigh, I ran my hands through my ebony hair and wiped the sweat beading on my forehead. The chilling nightmares of my youth were returning, and I hated it. It had been years since the face with glowing eyes appeared in my dreams.

Shuddering, I turned on the bedside lamp and looked around. The gentle billowing drapes from the open window was the only movement in the room. I climbed from bed, pushed back the curtains, and peered outside. The sun had not risen, yet the sky was changing from a dark blue to deep violet as an early morning fog blew across the ground. Travis's truck was sitting outside, gassed, and ready for my departure just as he said it would be. I looked at the time. 4:37 AM. My alarm was set for five. If I laid back down, I could grab a few more minutes of rest, but I knew that would be impossible. I was much too motivated about my trip. It had been quite a while since I experienced the bliss of solitude. A cross country road trip alone would be therapeutic. I would have hours to think and decipher through all the events of the past week and maybe some repressed memories of my childhood and the old manuscript would surface.

I dressed quickly, pulling on a pair of denim shorts and a soft t-shirt and hurried downstairs with my cumbersome suitcase in tow. The aroma of fresh brewed coffee and muffins greeted my nose. Mavis woke early just to prepare food for my departure. I smiled at her kindness. Veering away from the kitchen I decided to load my suitcase first before stopping for a bite to eat. I rolled the heavy bag onto the front porch and stopped abruptly at the sight of Falcon leaning against the front of the truck; a cigarette hanging from his lips despite the early hour. He climbed the porch steps and grabbed my luggage.

"Morning Scribe. Glad to see you're up and ready, I was hoping we'd get an early start."

My heart dropped into my stomach. Did he say we? Following Falcon off the porch, I watched as he tossed my suitcase in the storage area behind the seat. It fell alongside another piece of luggage that didn't belong to me. My heart sank further. No way! This was not part of my plan! I eyed him suspiciously, "I'm going on this trip alone."

He smirked, "Like hell you are."

"Yes, I am," My mind was resolute as I folded my arms across my chest. "I am capable of making this trip on my own."

Falcon took a draw off his cigarette and blew a long line of smoke, never removing his eyes from mine, "No you're not."

I shifted my feet; uncomfortable at his gaze, "You don't think I can do this by myself?"

He clenched the cigarette between his teeth, "It doesn't matter if you can or can't, which you can't. You're not going alone and that's it."

The two of us engaged in a brief stare down before I ended it by stomping back into the inn.

"Where's Travis?" I demanded of Mavis as I barged into the kitchen.

She gave me a sympathetic smile as she peered over the morning paper. She took a sip of her coffee and then nodded her head toward the screen door. Travis had just left the sheds and was heading to the inn. I stepped outside on the porch and placed my hands on my hips, "Falcon is here, and he says he's coming with me."

Travis mounted the steps, "He is. I asked him to accompany you."

"Well, I don't want him to. I want to take this trip alone."

He walked past me, dismissing my request and headed for the door, "You can't go alone."

Frustration boiled inside of me. Travis wasn't going to fix my problem. He and Falcon were in cahoots, and I realized I had no say in the matter; however, it was not in my nature to give in so quickly. I whirled around blocking the entrance with my body, "Why can't I go alone?"

Travis's eyes smiled at me even though his mouth didn't, "Bronwyn, I know you do not completely comprehend the magnitude of the quest. So, I will remain patient. To sum it up, you opened the book yesterday and now the enemy has been unleashed and will be looking for you as well as the second prophecy. You're not ready for a confrontation with them. Falcon is. He can protect you. That's why you're not going alone. In fact, you're not going anywhere alone anymore. Falcon is your bodyguard. He will be with you all the time."

"And I have no say in this at all?" He didn't respond and by his silence I knew his answer. His mind was set; his words suffocating, so intrusive of my personal space. I closed my eyes and sighed. My two blissful weeks of solitude were now invaded by the rogue Falcon. My heart plummeted at the thought. Falcon still frightened me. If it was so important for me to have protection, why couldn't Travis do it himself?

"He scares me," I whispered my thoughts.

"He is a bit unorthodox…"

"A bit?" My eyes flew open.

Travis gave way to his smile, "He's eccentric and revolutionary to the core, but he is extremely trustworthy, as well as my best friend. And, since I am not at liberty to accompany you, I believe him to be the best there is. Last night you said you would trust me. This is your first chance to keep that promise." His words seemed to be the final say on the matter. Proceeding to move me aside, he made his way into the kitchen.

Mavis exchanged places with Travis joining me on the back porch. She handed me a thermos of hot coffee and a paper bag full of warm muffins which I gratefully accepted, despite the fact my appetite escaped me the moment I realized Falcon was accompanying me all the way to California and back. I gave Mavis a quick hug goodbye.

"He scares me too," she whispered, "But Travis is right, Falcon is good at what he does. You'll be safe with him, and Travis knows that. He wouldn't trust your care to anyone else."

I sighed defeated, "Let's see if I can squeeze these two weeks into one. The sooner this is over the better." She grinned and gave me a loving hug. "You take care. I'll see you soon." I nodded and headed for the truck only to find Falcon leaning against it gloating as he flashed one of his impish grins, "Let's go scribe. You're wasting time."

Walking past him I yanked the cigarette from his mouth, tossing it to the ground, crushing it beneath my sandal. "You want to protect me? Then don't kill me with secondhand smoke. Besides, it's too early in the day for this."

"I knew she was going to be trouble" Falcon directed his words to Travis as he climbed into the cab of the truck.

A smile pulled at the corner of Travis's lips and danced across his eyes.

"You haven't seen trouble yet," I threatened as I slammed her door.

"Seatbelt," Falcon said, instantly meeting my challenge.

"I don't like wearing them."

"I am not moving this truck until you put it on."

"Oh, get real. Don't begin to try and convince me you care about safety. I rode on the back of your motorcycle, remember?"

He shot me another impish grin yet still refrained from starting the truck. "Yep, it's going to be a long, interesting two weeks."

My stubbornness was only delaying the inevitable, so I jerked the seatbelt with such a force that I could have easily pulled it from its encasing.

"Now that's my girl," he mocked, then started the engine and pulled away from the inn.

"Let's just pray those two don't kill each other," Mavis said as she headed back inside.

Travis watched until the truck disappeared down the highway and then made his way into the inn to sound the alarm.

Chapter 3

The morning sun remained low in the sky, offering little light to the winding road. A white misty fog hung in the trees blanketing most of the mountain range. Falcon offered no conversation. Staring out of the windshield, he sped down the narrow highway, taking each curve at an alarming speed. Despite the poor visibility he never let up on the gas. Instead, he tore through the patches of fog like a madman, the tires protesting on every curve. Had it not been for the seatbelt, he insisted I wear, I was sure I would end up in the driver's seat right alongside him.

"Slow down!" At my demand Falcon pressed on the gas, increasing our speed just as the truck rounded another curve. Again, the tires squealed. I peered out of the window and gasped as the truck hugged the edge of the highway. The drop off on my side was at least a mile deep.

"This is your way of keeping me safe?"

He accelerated again, not affected by my protest and I figured one more demand from me would only result in him increasing the speed again. I leaned my head against the back of the seat and closed my eyes. If I were going to plummet to my death, I'd rather not watch. I clutched the door handle bracing for the next curve. Closing my eyes proved to be the wrong decision. It only took a few more turns for nausea to set in. Holding my breath, I placed my head against the window hoping the coolness of the glass would relieve some of the queasiness. The smell of the blue berry muffins was overwhelming in the warm cab. Pushing the metal lever, I lowered the window, welcoming the rush of cool air blowing in.

Falcon took his eyes off the road and for the first time since we left the inn, he looked at me and jerked the truck over to the side of the road, tossing pebbles and stirring up a cloud of dirt. I jumped just as it skidded to a stop and hurled. He took advantage of the opportunity and lit up another cigarette.

I wiped my mouth with the back of my hand and sat in the dirt. Travis would have never treated me this way. I grabbed a handful of grass, yanking it from the ground and tossed it aside. I was pissed. Why hadn't Travis come on the trip instead of Falcon? I looked into the deep ravine that lay before me and was almost inclined to jump, just to rid myself of the two torturous weeks that lie ahead. Better yet, I wondered if I had enough strength to push him over the edge. I didn't want to kill him, just harm him enough to get my revenge.

"Take a swallow." He stood beside me, a water bottle in one hand and a cigarette clutched between the fingers of the other. I had no desire to take anything from him, but I did have a bitter taste in my mouth. Reluctantly, I accepted, drinking the cool water, and sloshing it around in my mouth. I didn't swallow; instead, I spit it out directly on his bare feet.

He tilted his head. "If that's the way you want to play Scribe." He walked closer to the ravine and took a long draw while staring out over the hazy canyon and exhaled a cloud of smoke. I watched his eyes follow a hawk gliding across the vast sky beneath them. The bird let out a lonesome cry as it flew past and, in some way, it seemed to communicate with him. I felt a tinge of shame for my anger.

Taking a final draw, he tossed the cigarette, crushing the butt with his bare heel. He said nothing as he climbed into the cab and started the engine. Grudgingly, I pulled myself up and took in a deep breath of the morning air, filling my lungs with the scent of spruce and pine knowing we would be at the base of the mountains soon and it would be some time before I could smell the pleasing aroma again.

Falcon took off down the road before my door was completely closed but this time, he took the curves at a much slower speed.

The sky was in full light by the time we reached the base of the mountain. The road no longer wound in twists and turns but stretched out before us in a straight line, widening to a broad, populated four lane highway. I glanced in the mirror at the massive mountain range growing smaller as we left it behind. The mere thought of Travis, far away, hidden in the immenseness of the mountains caused my spirit to ache.

Falcon hadn't spoken a word but neither had I. Both of us drew back into our corners waiting for the next round of conflict to present itself. If Falcon stayed on schedule, we would make Texas by early evening. My stomach turned at the thought of how I would explain Falcon to my parents; not to mention how I would explain my impulsive move to Moonshine. Mother was sure to ask a multitude of questions and pry until she wore the truth out of me.

My cell suddenly came alive with notification signals interrupting my thoughts and the stillness of the cab. I startled at the sound. It had been over a week since I used my phone, and now, I was paying the price for my absence. Pulling it from my travel bag I viewed the screen.

"My God!"

Over fifty-three missed calls, forty-seven voice messages and seventeen texts. I scrolled down the call list. Twenty-eight of them were from Ryan's attorneys. I sighed; now that I had closure with Ryan, and offered him the use of the script, the harassing phone calls were sure to stop. Several of the missed calls were from mother; all of them recent. I hoped my parents were well and there was no emergency that would entail so many calls. A couple were from my California neighbor Jamia, and two missed calls from Bethany which I noticed had been placed in the past hour which was a bit strange. The ringing of the cell alarmed me once again, the screen lit up interrupting my review. The ID on the screen said Mother. I sighed, got to face it eventually. "Hello."

"Well, I guess I can call off the search party!"

"I'm sorry mother. I've been out of range."

"No kidding. Your dad and I have been worried. We called The Fiery Dragon, and they said you never made it there."

"We had some car troubles and were stranded for a while. It's a long story. I'll fill you in tonight."

"Tonight?"

"Yes, is it alright? I'll be home tonight."

"Alright!" Mother responded so loudly that Falcon could hear her. "Honey it's more than alright. Your dad will be so happy. What time will you be here?"

"Around seven-ish."

"Dinner will be waiting, so don't eat before."

"Don't go to a lot of trouble momma."

"Are you kidding? I'll kill the fatted calf for this one!"

I laughed.

"I love you hon, you be careful."

"I will. Bye."

I hung up the phone, now more nervous than before. I'd told her I would fill her in, now I had several hours to come up with a story. I should be able to think up something; after all I was a writer. I glanced over at Falcon and chewed my lower lip, wondering how he would fit into my deception.

Another call. This time it was my neighbor, Jamia. She lived in the beach house next door to mine and Ryan's, keeping a close watch on the properties and all the comings and goings of the occupants; eagerly catching me up on the gossip every chance she could.

"Hello Jamia."

"Boy are you a hard one to get a hold of," her cheery voice rang out, "I could call the white house and talk to the president easier than I can get a hold of you."

"Sorry, I haven't had use of my phone in a while."

"I wondered what became of you. I was beginning to worry."

"No need. I'm fine."

"Listen. A couple of men have been snooping around your place asking a lot of questions. They tried to smooth talk me into giving them my spare key and letting them inside. I didn't, of course."

"Did they say what they wanted?"

"Said something about the condo coming up for sale but I know that's a lie. It's a rental. Anyways, I called the owner and he said he has not listed it nor is he planning to. I saw one of them again today. Should I call the police?"

"No. It's more than likely some of Ryan's attorneys, although they shouldn't be coming around now."

"They don't look like attorneys hon. Believe me I've seen my share of attorneys and these two don't fit the bill. They look like a couple of thugs."

My stomach dropped again. It could be paparazzi or reporters from some scandalous grocery store magazine. I desperately hoped the news of my pregnancy with Ryan hadn't leaked out. Lillian had called Ryan, what was to stop him from calling the press? I wouldn't put it past him, especially if he thought he could benefit in some way.

"It's probably just reporters. Don't give them the time of day and don't give them any information."

"I get you honey. I won't say a word. So, when are you coming home again?"

"Actually, I am headed home now. I should be there in a couple of days."

"Great! I miss hearing your stories. You better have some good ones. Don't worry, hon; I'll keep the reporters away. See you soon." I hung up. Falcon spoke for the first time since we left the side of the road, "Someone's snooping around your place?"

"Yeah, probably just reporters or the paparazzi. The condo is actually in Ryan 's name. They're looking for him, not me. They come around from time to time trying to get pictures. They just snoop around looking for anything they can find for a good story. It's nothing to worry about. They're greedy annoying bastards but hardly a threat."

"When are you going to get it, Scribe?" His voice was serious. "What's it going to take for it to sink in that pretty head of yours that you are involved in a war and our adversary wants you dead? Everyone is a threat."

I took offense with his insinuation of my ignorance of the severity of the situation. Maybe Falcon in his revolutionary ways was looking for a fight and over sensationalizing the whole thing. I had yet to encounter any adversary as he called it. The only person I ever saw stalking me was him. Besides, how could anyone know who or where I was? "I just think you're being a little over cautious. After all, no one knows my identity, or where I am. I would have probably done better alone, you with me is a dead giveaway, no pun intended." I felt a surge of confidence in my declaration and grinned at my candor.

He sighed, "I see the need to educate you scribe or we're going to be in some serious trouble."

My exasperation took over. "Oh, by all means, please do. I have been begging for some answers."

He glanced in his rearview and switched lanes, passing a slow-moving Kia before he spoke.

"Abaddon uses dark power. He uses forbidden magic to travel out of his body. His spies do the same. These scouts can't be killed because they are not in physical form. You will never know they are watching you. Sometimes there is a foul smell or a disturbing presence."

I swallowed. I hadn't smelled anything other than the soothing scents of the mountain, but I had sensed a sinister presence from time to time. Like the night at the waterfall. Could they have been spying then?

"Their job is to locate you, and then send the information back. You can bet Abaddon has sent his best through. The second prophecy is vital. Whoever has possession has critical information. Believe me when I say, everyone wants their hands on it. They will stop at nothing to find you because they know you will lead them to it."

I looked out my window at the miles of empty space; nothing but undeveloped land for as far as the eye could see. Only a dilapidated old barn dotted the horizon every now and then... emptiness. It was how I felt about my situation. Empty and void of any inspiration or knowledge of the world in which I was commissioned to write about. All this talk about prophecies. It all seemed like a chapter out of the latest fantasy novel, and suddenly a seed of doubt began to take root.

"They'll be gravely disappointed." I muttered. "I haven't a clue where the prophecy is."

"It doesn't matter if you know or not. All they care about is finding you. The only advantage we have right now is that they have no idea who they're looking for.

"If they don't know it's me. What's to keep them from going after Beth or Lil.?" A new terror began to rise.

"Nothing. It's why two of my best are following them. Just in case."

I sighed and finished going through my voice messages and texts. Bethany hadn't left a voice message when she called this morning. Ryan left a text telling me he had never seen me more beautiful than I was at the cabin. He confessed he'd been a fool to leave me in the first place and hoped that maybe one day our paths would cross, and he would be the man I deserved. He gave his apologies for not being there for me when I lost the child, saying that if he had known, he would have immediately been by my side. I rolled my eyes and deleted the text, hoping he would not try to contact me again. What was done was done. I had not fallen out of love with Ryan; rather I realized I'd never truly loved him in the first place. Travis made me aware of that fact the night in the garden when he told me the true definition of love. True love was a selfless act. A day had not passed that I hadn't relived that evening in my head. And now, sitting in the cab of the truck miles away from him, I had no desire to torture myself with such thoughts. I needed a distraction. I leaned forward and turned on the radio, scanning the channels. All of them offered the same mixture of country music and static; nothing worth listening to. Falcon pressed the button on the CD player. Within seconds the peaceful yet lonesome sound of a folk band led by the husky voice of their lead singer, filled the cab. The melody was haunting but at the same time inspiring. It tugged at the emptiness taking residence in my heart. The lyrics were beautiful stories of love and hope, sprinkled with loss and tragedy, all woven into the most beautiful prose. I thought of Eden and the book I was soon to write and hoped I could pen something as moving. I smiled and leaned my head against the back of the seat. "Who's the band? I love their style." Falcon grinned. "Thank you."

"You're kidding? That's you?" He took his eyes off the endless black ribbon of the highway and looked over at me. "I have a poetic side." I huffed a laugh. "You're serious. This is your band. You have a band?" My eyes danced at the asking.

"Scribe we've been in those mountains for six hundred years, The Moonshine Boys got bored."

"The Moonshine Boys!" I giggled and sucked my lip. "Please, give me one of your CD's. I have to listen to this while I write."

"Done." He smiled a smile that didn't fade for quite a while.

I dozed off and on throughout the day, listening, thinking, and composing a story in my head. Falcon drove in silence, his soothing voice emanating from the radio, allowing me the solitude I had hoped for.

Chapter 4

Bethany dug through her travel bag looking for the letter. It was in there somewhere. She hadn't thrown it away although the thought of ripping it to shreds had entered her mind. Instead, she decided to save it as some sort of evidence just in case the circumstance demanded it. And she had been right. Call it premonition or whatever, but somehow, she knew she would need it.

Frustrated, she dumped the entire contents of the bag on the floor, rummaging through them until the crinkled envelope caught her eye. Snatching it from its hiding place she headed back down the hallway to the front door where the cagey detective was waiting. She was glad to help him in his investigation and felt some sort of vindication in the matter. Her concern over Bronwyn was now justified. She wasn't being a nosey intrusive friend, but rather a true sister, looking out for Bronwyn's best interest whether she realized it or not.

"Here it is," she said, handing him the letter. "It's her resignation. She just up and quit. Not even a two-week notice, nothing."

Elam took the envelope and pulled out the letter, his eyes scanning over the written words. Raising his eyes from the paper he narrowed them in on Bethany, "I'd like to ask you a few more questions if you don't mind."

She swept her hand towards the couch, offering him a seat. She had a few minutes before she needed to leave for another appointment. "If Bronwyn is in any kind of trouble, I'm glad to help. I had a bad feeling about leaving her behind, but she'd made up her mind. She's a stubborn one, that girl."

Elam placed the envelope in his pocket and took a seat. "So, you've known Miss Sterling for quite a long time?"

"We met in the sixth grade and have been best friends ever since. She's like a sister to me. We are both only children, my parents weren't the best; hers were, so I spent a lot of time at her house."

Elam smiled at her, and it lasted longer than she thought it should, so she shifted in her seat and continued talking. "I know her better than anyone, so you can imagine how concerned I've been. And that letter was just weird. It's not like her. I don't know what to think."

Pulling a couple of photographs from his coat pocket, he handed one to Bethany. "Was she ever in the company of this man?"

Bethany nodded, "Once that I know of, she'd been out all night and when she came back to the inn, she was with him. That was the crazy day when Ryan Reese showed up. Oh, did I mention she was engaged to him?"

Bethany's mouth suddenly felt dirty as if she'd spoken out of turn. She had no intention of betraying Bronwyn even though she was upset with her. Now she feared she'd said too much. But to her surprise the detective didn't seem shocked at her disclosure. Perhaps he already knew, after all he was an investigator. She took comfort in the fact that he was a professional and would never allow anything she said to leak out to the press. She handed the picture back. "Except the guy has a scar underneath his left eye."

Elam nodded as if he already knew and handed her the next picture. "How about him?"

Bethany smirked, "Oh yeah, Travis. She did spend an awful lot of time with him. He's married though, so she was kind of disappointed about that. I think he's the reason she stayed up there." Again, her mouth felt dirty. She handed the picture back to remove all guilt.

"Would you happen to have a picture of Bronwyn?" Elam asked. "It would help tremendously for us to have a visual of their latest victim."

"Victim?" Bethany's heart faltered. "Is she in trouble?"

Tucking the picture back into his coat, his face turned grim.

"She could be. Our objective right now is to get her away from these two men, if in fact she is still with them."

Bethany agreed. Bronwyn needed to come back home and get her mind clear. She picked up a copy of her latest novel and flipped it over to the back cover, showing him the author's picture. "This is her. You can take it with you. We have plenty."

If Elam's expression when he gazed at the photograph, didn't bother Bethany enough, what he mumbled did. Pulling his eyes away from the picture, he focused once again on Bethany, asking her for the Sterling's address before giving her his card, promising to be in touch.

"Would you happen to know where she is?" he asked the question as an afterthought while leaving.

"She's staying at the Sandalwood Inn in Moonshine." Bethany offered, still puzzled over his words. "Travis owns the inn. You can find them both there."

"Already looked," He said, "The entire town is deserted. We didn't find anyone."

Chapter 5

At seven fifteen, just as I predicted, Falcon pulled into the long gravel driveway of my childhood home. The wheels of the truck crunched over the rocks, scattering the small pebbles and announced our arrival. I bit my lip and shivered when I saw the house and purposely refrained from looking up toward the attic window. I unfolded my cramped legs and stepped out of the truck. Yawning, I pushed my fist high above my head in an epic stretch. The front door of the house flew open. My mother, an attractive woman in her early sixties bolted outside, her arms outstretched in front of her as she headed toward me, a joyous scream escaped her lips.

"Baby!" She embraced me. I returned the hug holding on tightly. Falcon watched the display from the cab, a slight smile pulling at his lips. My mother was a beauty. Her body fit and slender; her shoulder length hair was adorned in a stylish fashion. Her brown eyes sparkled while her mouth laughed. Dad came out of the door right behind mother. He sported a full head of wavy hair despite his age; and only in the past year had it begun fading from a rich brown to shimmering silver. His blue eyes smiled behind a pair of bifocals that he quickly removed and placed in his shirt pocket.

"You got one of those for me?" He asked. I pulled away from mother and wrapped my arms around his neck. I took a deep breath inhaling his aftershave. It was an aroma I cherished.

The sound of the truck door closing brought all attention to Falcon.

"Oh," Mother's shock revealed itself in her face. "You brought someone with you."

I forced a smile attempting to disguise my nerves. In the twelve-hour trip I neglected to come up with a simple story to explain Falcon. Talk about writer's block. And I was expected to write an epic?

"Yes, I did... This is..."

"The name's Dakota," Falcon approached my parents with an outstretched arm. "I'm Bronwyn's boyfriend. Nice to meet you both."

I stiffened, speechless as Dad grabbed Falcon's extended hand and shook. "Martin Sterling. Nice to meet you, this is my wife, Madison."

Falcon nodded "Pleased to meet you ma'am."

Mother graciously escorted her guest to the front door. However, I was an expert at reading her body language, and from her posture, I could tell she was not thrilled with Falcon's presence.

The delicious aroma of dinner greeted the tired travelers as soon as we entered the door. I smiled knowing exactly what meal was waiting for us on the dining room table. I took another deep breath inhaling the ambiance of the room. There was a comforting familiarity; and yet, there was also a disturbing spirit camouflaged somewhere inside the walls. It was that spirit that kept my visits at bay for some time now. I took a quick inventory of the room. Everything was as it always had been. Only a few subtle changes, such as a smart TV to keep up with the latest technology, new wooden blinds on the windows and different place settings on the table. Mother scrambled to set another place and soon we were enjoying a meal of cedar plank salmon that Dad grilled to perfection.

Falcon gallantly pulled out my chair catching me off guard. He winked and flashed his impish grin before taking his seat beside me.

Dad reached for Mother's hand, "Let's pray." It had always been the custom in the Sterling home to pray before each meal. This ritual was made complete by taking the hand of the person sitting beside you as the blessing was offered. I lovingly took hold of my mother's hand, giving it a tight squeeze. She returned the affection, thankful that I was home safe. The feeling of warmth was interrupted as the rough calloused fingers of Falcon clasp around my free hand. Looking his way, I found his head reverently bowed and his eyes closed. Dad prayed a long-drawn-out supplication, thanking God for the surprise visit from his daughter. He politely offered thanks for the nice man who delivered me safely to them, then gave thanks for the wonderful woman who sat by his side, and eventually got around to thanking God for the food. As the prayer ended, Falcon boldly kissed my hand, displaying affection for the benefit of my parents. I gave him a forceful nudge with my knee and pulled my hand away, placing it in my lap.

The silverware clinked against the China as everyone dug into the delicious meal. Mother passed a basket of warm rolls down the table; starting the conversation, "How long will you be staying dear?"

I took a keen interest in buttering my roll to keep from meeting her inquisitive gaze. "Unfortunately, only tonight. It's one of those in and out trips. We're on a bit of a tight schedule."

She continued to pry, "Aren't you writing a new book?"

I could tell by mother's tone and forced smile that she already knew the answer to her question. I suddenly felt fourteen instead of thirty-three and had a peculiar feeling that my mother was aware of more of my personal affairs than she was letting on.

"Your mother didn't get a chance to read the last one," Martin said, picking up on the charade.

I sipped my iced tea, "I'm glad you didn't. It definitely wasn't one of my best."

"So, you're writing a new one then?" She took a bite of her salad, continuing her strategic questioning.

I paused for a moment, thinking of the best way to answer without causing an uncomfortable interrogation at the table.

"I already finished the new one and am taking a little sabbatical from writing romance for a while."

"So, I heard," her smile was patronizing, igniting a flame of anger inside me. If she already knew, why was she beating around the bush asking questions? Mother had an agenda, and I knew it.

"Really? Who told you?"

Madison took another bite of her salad pleased to have the upper hand.

"I called Bethany when I couldn't get a hold of you. She told me you turned in your final manuscript and said you were leaving the publisher. She said it came as quite a shock to her."

Bethany! I should have known. I could only imagine the conversation she and my mother must have had. Bethany was upset with me and obviously took her revenge by confiding in my mother about my questionable behavior. My stomach dropped. I sincerely hoped Bethany had not mentioned my pregnancy and miscarriage. Yet by the troubled look growing in my mother's eyes, I was certain she had.

"She said she's been pretty worried about you. Said you haven't been yourself lately."

My heart fell while I desperately searched for a sane way to explain the situation.

"She left her job because she is writing a documentary," Falcon came to my rescue. "I have her on contract. We're making a film on the Legends and People of the Appalachian Mountains. I'd say it was providence that led her to us. One look at her and I knew she was the one we wanted to write our story. Her friend Bethany was not privy to this information therefore does not understand Bronwyn's decision to leave the romance genre and write something more meaningful. It's why she decided to remain in the mountains. She is taking the chance as it presents itself. We are headed to California to retrieve some of her belongings. She will be relocating to the mountains to do her research."

Falcon's improvisation left me speechless. I watched in wonder as he effortlessly led my parents in a brilliant discussion of Appalachian history and culture. As much as I hated to admit it, Travis was right. He was good at what he did. A secret agent able to take on any role needed; and as his charade played out, I caught a glimpse of him that was quite fascinating. He hadn't embarrassed me in front of my parents as I feared he would. Instead, he performed as good a role as any actor I'd ever known, instantaneously transforming into an intelligent film maker, the most appropriate character he could have ever improvised. He even spoke of an incredible grizzly attack that had left him with a scar under his eye. I decided to watch and remain silent; allowing him to continue his great fabrication, putting my fascinated parents' troubled minds at rest. The only thing that haunted me in all of this was that if he could spin such a wild narrative and sound so convincing, how did I know he and Travis weren't doing the same with me?

With dinner and the conversation coming to an end, Dad invited Falcon poolside to smoke cigars. Standing from his chair, Falcon triumphantly kissed me on the top of my head, "Need anything dear?"

"I'm good, thank you." I continued the charade but refused to call him anything affectionate. Giving me a sly wink, he headed outside but not before taking our plates into the kitchen. Mother waited until the screen door shut behind them before she spoke, "Well he seems very nice."

"Uh huh," I agreed half-heartedly. The last thing I wanted was to get into a discussion about my love life, and I could tell this was exactly where the conversation was headed.

"I have to admit I'm a bit surprised," she continued much to my disliking. "Bethany mentioned Ryan came to see you recently. She hoped you two might get back together; but she said you turned him down. What was that all about?"

My annoyance with Bethany was rising. It was pretty bold of her to speak out of turn. Besides, how could she possibly know what transpired during my conversation with Ryan, unless she was snooping around asking more intrusive questions. Bethany was only doing this out of retaliation. I would call her the first chance I got and set her straight.

"It was nothing really. He still wants to produce the screenplay we wrote. I finally gave him permission."

Mother wiped down the counter and then hung the cloth over the sink. She dried her hands on a towel and turned to face me. "Are you sure you're okay dear? Bethany is very concerned."

I sighed, "I'm fine mother, really, I am. Bethany is nosey, not concerned. She's just upset that I don't tell her every thought I'm thinking. She's a dear friend but she's beginning to invade my personal space. I needed a change. You understand that don't you?" She eyed me and from experience, I knew the interrogation was far from over. "How long have you known Dakota?"

I dare not mention a time frame just in case father was outside asking Falcon the same question. It would be detrimental to our façade if we gave conflicting answers. "Long enough," Was the only information I offered.

She wasn't satisfied. "Bethany mentioned a married man by the name of Travis. She said you fell in love with him. She never mentioned anyone named Dakota."

My fury rose. How dare she. I was definitely going to have words with her. "She didn't mention him because she doesn't know him. Mother, please, do us both a favor and don't engage in any more conversations with Bethany. I'm really ticked off at her right now. As usual she's jumping to conclusions and talking about things, she doesn't know anything about."

Mother was not completely convinced but knew better than to press the matter. She desired peace more than anything and would do nothing to hinder the happy unexpected visit. I took advantage of the pause in the conversation. "Momma, do you still have all my writings from years back?"

She inspected me a minute before answering. "Yes, honey I do. I have kept everything you have ever written. It's all boxed up in the attic."

"Mind if I snoop and take a few things with me? Being asked to write this documentary has boosted my confidence a bit. I want to go through some of my old work and possibly resurrect an idea."

"Honey you can have whatever's up there. It all belongs to you."

I poured two cups of coffee and briefly told her of the mountains and the beauty of where I'd spent the past several days. She listened intently and for once asked no questions. I neglected to mention the name of the town; for some strange reason I felt the need to protect it. We chatted for some time discussing her friends, her garden club activities, and the house for an underprivileged family father was helping build. I mostly listened hoping the conversation would not veer back toward my personal life. Taking our empty mugs to the sink, I glanced out of the kitchen window checking on Falcon. He seemed content puffing on cigars with dad.

The cuckoo clock on the wall struck ten. A little bird burst through two miniscule wooden doors and tweeted ten cuckoos then disappeared back inside with the cranks and dials. I wished to go exploring in the attic and hunt for the old manuscript; but feared if I mentioned it mother would volunteer to help. Instead, I feigned exhaustion yawning loudly.

"It's been a long day. Road trips can be so tiring. I think I'll turn in since we 're getting another early start in the morning." I noticed my mother's disappointment and wasn't sure if it stemmed from the briefness of my visit or the fact, she didn't retrieve more personal information.

I leaned in and gave her a kiss on the cheek. "I'll spend more time here on our return trip. Maybe two or three days if we can spare them."

"I'd like that," she smiled while giving my hand a loving squeeze. I waited until she slipped out back to join the men and took my opportunity. Despite a looming premonition and incredible fear manifesting inside of me, I stole upstairs to the attic in search of my writings.

Chapter 6

A solitary bulb hauntingly swayed back and forth, casting eerie shadows across the walls, offering a scarce amount of light. I paused, the peculiar heat sensation I had experienced in Moonshine spread through me at an alarming rate, and for once I thought maybe it was my body's warning system, letting me know when I was in extreme danger. The attic didn't sit right with me, it never had. True, it was dark, musty, and housed every old and antique thing my mother ever owned. All children are scared of the attic or basement yet there was something more. Something always drew me here, and yet frightened me to the point where I couldn't bear to look at the door as I passed it in the hallway. Many of my childhood sleepwalking incidents would lead me up to the eerie room. I remembered waking in the attic once, standing on a chair and looking out of the small oval window and screaming for someone to come and find me. That was the dream that unnerved my parents to the point of seeking counsel. I hadn't thought of that moment until now, and with that revelation, other suppressed memories began to surface. I shook the thoughts from my mind, and took a deep breath as I stepped inside, convincing myself I was older now and could do this.

A cool draft crawled quietly across the floor, accompanied by a shiver coiling up my spine. Taking a quick survey, I strolled past years of discarded memories and abandoned dreams. Most every item in the attic was reminiscent of my childhood. All the pieces of my life, now covered in layers of dust, tucked away, and hidden in the black room. I browsed past shelves of trophies, plaques, and ribbons. Some were awarded for my writing skills, others for piano competitions, swim meets and children's theater. I eyed several large rubber bins stacked in the back corner. The light from the small bulb barely reached this part of the room. Nevertheless, I made my way to the bins. Written on the first, in Mother's expert penmanship, was the words Bronwyn's Work. I breathed a sigh of relief. Thanks to my mother's obsessive organizational skills this would be easier than I anticipated. I could locate the manuscript and leave the spooky room.

I blew the dust from the lid and pried it open. Stacks of notebooks lay inside, all school projects. I read through each title, disappointed when I reached the bottom. Nothing resembled an old manuscript written by a ten-year-old. Replacing the lid, I shoved the heavy bin aside. The label on the one beneath it read: Bronwyn's stories. I eagerly dug through the manuscripts lifting them from the bins one at a time. Again, I reached the bottom without finding anything. I continued my search until all the bins had been opened. Disappointed, I paused to think. Barak mentioned my parents taking the book away and forbidding me to continue. If he was right, and my parents had taken the book, perhaps mother would have destroyed it. I hoped that wasn't the case. If I couldn't find it, I would be forced to ask what had become of the book, and that would be a catastrophe. Defeated, I replaced the last bin and was turning to leave when I noticed a small metal container, resembling a safe deposit box, sitting alone in the opposite corner. My heart seized. This has to be it! I stooped down lifting it from its dismal hiding place, when a small key fell from underneath, disappearing as it slid across the dark floor. Desperate, I went down on all fours, feeling my way along the ground, until my fingers touched cold brass. Grabbing the key, I carefully placed it in the lock and turned. A deafening click echoed across the still room, while thunder rumbled in the distance, like the low growl of a beast when awakened. A sudden gust of wind swept through the attic swinging the lone bulb at the opening. I flinched and looked toward the door thinking someone must have entered to cause the sudden rush of air. However, the door was closed. Terror cozied up against me sending a chill through my body. A peculiar sorrow dug at my heart, tears stung my eyes, as my attention was unwillingly drawn to the dark porthole. I gazed out into the black sky, a vague memory trying to claw its way to the surface. Again, I saw the waterfall and Travis standing in the rushing stream. The vision lasted much longer than before but this time I saw another figure running towards us, approaching fast. Urgency tore into Travis's expression and the critical nature of it caused my heart to pound even now. A sudden flash of lightning right outside the window brought my attention back to the box cradled in my lap. Lying in its metal hiding place was a beautifully bound notebook. Holes had been carefully punched into an antique-looking parchment. Blue silk ribbons were woven through the holes binding the papers to the soft leather cover. The word Moonshine was etched in silver calligraphy.

My hands trembled as I lifted the manuscript from its bed. The heat sensation wrapped around my neck as dozens of memories flashed spontaneously across the screen of my mind. My stomach knotted at the vivid pictures of once forgotten events. Despite the intensity of the heat, icy fingers traced a path up my spine while intimidating shadows came alive, emerging from the corners and closing in on my weakened state. The air grew thin as a sinister spirit sucked the oxygen from the room. Could this be the presence of spies Falcon mentioned? Were they watching me now? I gasped for breath yet inhaled scalding wet air. My head felt light; the room began to spin. Another gust of wind blew, an abandoned floor lamp toppled over with a crash. I spun around at the crash and screamed at Falcon who was standing directly behind me, nearly giving him a beating with the coveted book. "Why did you sneak up on me like that?"

"I'm not to let you out of my sight, Travis' orders."

I hugged the soft book against my body to control my shaking.

His impish grin melted into a reverent spirit as his eyes fell upon the manuscript; and his face grew more solemn than I'd ever seen it. His eyes went from the book and back to me. "You found it?" I nodded. He smiled but this time there was nothing impish in his grin. "It's been here all this time."

"Twenty-three years," I whispered, and then, as if I'd just discovered buried treasure, "Want to see if the prophecy is hidden inside?" His face grew grave. "If it's in there and we open it, the enemy will know you have it." I shrugged. "I don't care. Let them know."

Falcon narrowed his eyes; his examination made me uneasy. After a brief stare down, he escorted me to the dangling bulb. Pulling over one of the rubber bins, he offered me a place to sit. I laid the book on my lap and carefully began to unlace the ribbon that held the pages shut. Falcon remained standing, guarding me as I opened the soft leather cover. With trembling fingers, I glided my hands over the papyrus. A smile lifted the corner of my lips as I read the handwritten words, inscribed twenty-three-years ago, in my best penmanship.

"Once Upon a Time, the world was beautiful, perfect, and good. On the earth there existed the amazing city of Eden. All royalty lived in Eden, because it was their home. Everyone lived in beautiful castles with exquisite gardens. There was no need for gates or moats or drawbridges, because no one was afraid. Fear did not exist because everyone loved each other more than they loved themselves. When all you have is love, then there is no reason to fear.

The royalty were beautiful people, strong and wise. They were chosen to rule the earth. There were three princes who were also brothers; they ruled the whole earth as well as all of Eden. Their names were Ariston, Brennun, and Travis. Ariston was the oldest, Brennun was the middle brother and Travis was the youngest. Ariston and Brennan found wives and married. Travis hadn't found his lady until one day..."

The heat continued to rise as I read. The story Barak and the council told me at the Citadel, now presented itself in my own handwriting, told in the innocence and purity of a child. I read over the names of the three princes again. Ariston, Brennun and Travis, and swallowed hard.

"One day Travis met a beautiful young woman. She was a storyteller. Her name was Kenalycia. She was a good and kind maiden, entertaining everyone with her stories. The people loved her because her stories were the best.

Prince Travis traveled far to meet her. As he listened to her story and watched her emerald eyes dance as she told it, he knew he could love no one else from that day forward. When she finished and the people dispersed, Travis called her to himself and asked if she could tell him a story. Kenalycia was honored at his request. They walked for a spell and stopped at a beautiful waterfall. They found a secluded spot behind the falling water, and it was there Kenalycia began to tell Travis a story. Now Kenalycia was clever and knew if her story ended

Travis would go home and she might never see him again. So, she made her story carry on, informing him he would have to come back the next day to hear the rest. Travis was pleased the story was ongoing, for he wanted another chance to be with her. The next night they met at the falls, and again they sat behind the water and Kenalycia continued her story. Again, she made her story longer and told him it would be continued the next night. He was happy. He loved hearing her story but more than that, he loved hearing her tell it and how her voice would change at the exciting or sad parts. He loved watching her mouth form the words and he loved the way her green eyes smiled and danced. Kenalycia's story continued for a long time."

My heart ached as I read my own words. I had read the name Kenalycia before. It was carved into the back of the white stone pendant I found in the small wooden box near Travis' bed. It was no doubt his love's necklace; the one possession he had of hers. Tears flooded my eyes. I didn't want to cry in front of Falcon. I could feel his gaze upon me and knew he was watching. Yet despite what I wanted, a tear escaped, streaking down my cheek and splashing upon the stiff parchment, landing on the word waterfall and smearing the ink. A loud clap of thunder erupted outside shaking the room. I looked up at Falcon, his eyes were locked on me. And then, it happened, another flash, another vision. This time it was Falcon's face plastered across the screen of my mind. The image evoked terror, chilling me as the seed of distrust began to take root. Was this a premonition? He watched me intently, giving me a dreadful suspicion, he might be privy to my thoughts. I looked away from his entrapping gaze and placed my attention back on the book. I would read the rest of the story later. Right now, I wanted to flip through the pages and search for the prophecy.

I paid careful attention as I turned the pieces of paper and skimmed over the words. There was only the story, nothing resembling an ancient prophecy. I flipped through to the last few pages, still nothing. Disappointed, I decided to start at the beginning scanning each page carefully in case I missed it. As I closed the book, my eyes fell upon a small slit in the leather of the back cover. The corner had been turned down just a bit as if to make a hidden pouch. I reached for the soft suede and pulled. It tore away easily, revealing a yellowed parchment. My heart leaped in my throat as I removed a beautifully scripted letter. The handwriting was mine, but the script was in a language unknown to me. I ran my fingers across the page, before turning my attention to Falcon.

"I found it."

By the look on his face, he was more than aware of what I held in my hand. Reverently, he knelt beside me; all the while keeping his eyes fixed on the paper. With quivering hands, I offered him the coveted treasure. "You will have to read it. It's written in a language I don't know." Removing his eyes from the parchment, he gave his full attention to me. His face was somber. "This is an honor I am not worthy of." His words seemed strange and out of place for the roguish guy I knew him to be, and for some reason, his declaration made the quest seem even more vital. If he couldn't read it, then who would?

"Well, the way I see it, you are here, and no one else is. I can't read the language and you can, so in my book that makes you worthy." His eyes smiled although his mouth didn't. My rationalization of the situation must have been convincing. He took the parchment and read it silently. When he finished, he closed his eyes and sat in silence. I waited patiently as he allowed the words to soak in.

Another clap of thunder shook the house in fury while the lighting continued to dance outside of the small octagon window. Falcon remained unnerved, his eyes closed as if he were praying, and it was then I remembered Falcon had no need of a cell phone because his people were able to communicate with their minds. I figured that might be what he was doing so I continued to wait while the wind began to howl outside. After a few minutes he opened his eyes and looked at me. "You ready?"

I swallowed hard and nodded but before he could begin reading, a bolt of lightning hit near the house followed by an intense crackle. The small bulb lost its light, casting the attic in bitter darkness. An ear-splitting thunder clash rocked the room, drowning out my scream. In the blackness Falcon took hold of me, lifting me to my feet.

"Hold on to me, I'll help you downstairs." Without as much as a misstep he led me from the attic and down the steps. His hand clutched tightly around my arm steadying me so I wouldn't lose my footing on the narrow staircase. The strike knocked out the power, casting the rest of the house in darkness as well. Still, Falcon led me through the rooms with ease stopping in the kitchen. My suspicion grew and I wondered if he had the ability to see in the dark. It would explain why he could wear his sunglasses even at night. When we reached the kitchen, I stuck my hand in a drawer; rummaging around for a flashlight, a candle, or whatever would give us a bit of light. Falcon gently removed my hand and withdrew a tall slender candle. Grabbing a holder off of a nearby shelf, he removed the lighter from his pocket, and lit the wick bringing light into the room.

"You can see in the dark, can't you?"

The flame lit his infamous grin confirming my suspicion. He picked up the candle, lighting our way to the bedroom.

The rain pounded against the roof, and the wind rattled the glass in the windows like an angry intruder demanding entrance. Falcon closed the door and placed the candle on the nightstand. Kicking off my shoes, I crawled up on the bed and grabbed the soft blanket draped across the antique footboard.

Falcon removed a gun from the back of his jeans and laid it on the nightstand. Before I could protest, he removed a knife and placed it underneath the pillow.

"What if my parents see those?"

He smirked, "The door's locked, besides, they're in bed."

Peeling my eyes off the weapons, I returned my attention to the prophecy he held in his hands. "Okay, let's hear it."

He gave me a final glance before reading.

"Listen inhabitants of Eden and all people of the earth, you who have been misled and mistreated, whose lives were stolen by the one you called friend. Traces of deliverance have come! The spirits are whispering. They whisper words of remembrance, words of resurgence, and words of rebirth. The scribe has returned home to the land of protection and has opened the first two books.

Draw your battle lines and prepare for war! The doorway is open, and all dominions are released. Be diligent to know the truth and do not be swayed by what you know to be right. For some among you will be influenced by the darkness and join forces with the enemy, threatening your redemption. The betrayers have crept in unaware and are living among you. Wolves in sheep's clothing are eating at your tables, and then spying upon you when your backs are turned. Be careful that you are not deceived. Their words will be convincing, they will offer pleasing and beautiful promises of knowledge and power, yet in the end, the only thing you will get for your allegiance with them is death.

To the Scribe, pen your story. The beginning is yours. Follow your heart and you will preserve life. All depends on your ability to make the right choice. In time you will be led to the secret place. Enter without fear, it is there you will find the third book, and the third prophecy.

Falcon rolled the parchment back into a scroll, clicked on the lighter and held the flame to the end. My eyes widened, "You're burning it?"

"I've committed it to memory, and I read it to Travis. If I burn it, then it can't fall into the wrong hands. "A small red flame began crawling across the scroll. Falcon made his way over to the fireplace and tossed the burning parchment inside. The tiny flame consumed the entire document, and within seconds the long-awaited prophecy was gone. Thunder protested in anger, rattling the windows, and shaking the house. The wind howled a lament, sweeping through the trees in search of something it would never find.

Feeling the need to protect the book, I held it close fearing that Falcon may burn it as well; or, that the wind would crash through the window and rip it right out of my hands. Strange as it may seem, my book felt like an old friend. Despite the terror, it also brought a great deal of comfort along with a strange connection to something or someone, I didn't know exactly what. The mysterious bond created a desire to read more; consuming every word just in case the book was taken from me again. However, the scarce bit of light emanating from the dancing flame was hardly enough to make out the aging words, so I closed the book, holding it close like a child hugging a teddy bear.

The branches of the black hickory scratched against the window-pane bringing back the nightmare of early this morning. I shuddered trying to erase the mental image. Falcon came back over to the bed and sat on the corner. He lifted my chin, so I eyed him directly. "Don't lose confidence. Remember what I told you before. I will give my life to save yours. You have nothing to fear as long as I am with you. But if anything should ever happen to me..."

I shook my head in protest. I wasn't a plan "B" type of girl and didn't want to discuss that turn of events; but Falcon was all business at this point and continued on in spite of my protest.

"Scribe," His words were firm. "We just read a prophecy stating that all dominions had been released and you can bet they are roaming earth looking everywhere for you. If anything should happen to me, make your way back to Travis. And, should the worst happen, and you end up in Abaddon's keep, do what's necessary to stay alive, for if anything happens to you, all hope will be lost."

I shook my head, pouring out my objections. "I'm not sure I can do this." Falcon nodded in frustration and lifted my face to his again. "Well if you can't then I guess we're all damned, aren't we? There's no room for doubt. You're the scribe now get your act together."

His unsympathetic remark appalled me. I wasn't asking him to coddle me, only to understand the overwhelming burden placed on my shoulders. "The prophecy said it all depended on my ability to make the right choice. I'm sorry if I disappoint you, but that is a huge burden to bear. I'm not afraid as much as overwhelmed at a task I don't think I am good enough to accomplish."

The thunder applauded my confession while the wind howled in delight. Falcon shook a cigarette from the carton and lit it up. Taking a draw, he looked toward the window and the dancing lightning outside. "It's who you are that matters Bronwyn." His tone was soft, the sarcasm gone. "True there are many scribes who are masters at prose, who studied their craft at great universities. However, there are some things that cannot be learned no matter the brilliance of the mind or the prestige of the school attended. Those things are a part of the soul and are the very essence of the person's identity. You are someone special Bronwyn; believe that. The private ponderings of your heart have cried out and captivated their attention. You were chosen because they saw the most hidden parts of you, parts you don't know exist as of yet ...and they were pleased." He took another draw and brought his eyes to mine and then with a crooked smile, he continued, "You have forgotten who you are."

Something in his announcement stole the breath from my lungs and for a brief moment I sat frozen, my eyes locked on his. A feeling of familiarity swept past.

"Who am I then?"

The thunder resounded outside as the tiny flame on the candle flickered and then diminished altogether, and from the darkness he answered.

"You're a storyteller."

Chapter 7

The rain continued through the night and on into the next morning. The fierceness of the storm subsided, leaving a drizzle falling over the city. I woke to the sound of the steady rain tapping against the window. My mind re-engaged as I gradually began to recall the events of last night. The attic, the book, the prophecy... My heart sank, remembering I was sharing a bed with Falcon. Rolling over I found him sitting up beside me, reading the coveted book.

"Morning, Scribe."

I pushed my hair away from my eyes, leaned up on my elbow and glanced at the flashing twelve o'clock on the alarm. "What time is it?"

"Around seven."

I groaned and laid back down. "You can sleep longer if you like," he turned a page and continued reading. We aren't on schedule."

As much as I would have liked to go back to bed, I forced myself to get up. The sooner we made it to California the sooner I could get back to Moonshine and write. I dressed in the privacy of the bathroom; then met my parents in the kitchen for a quick breakfast while Falcon showered. Dad commented on the unexpectedness of last night's storm and mother lambasted the weatherman, accusing him of not correctly forecasting the entire summer.

Before I could pour a cup of coffee, mother asked if I would take a quick ride with her to the pharmacy, to pick up a prescription. My stomach fell. The last thing I wanted was a one on one with her. I knew from experience that a barrage of questions and opinionated advice was what the quick trip to the pharmacy was really about. Despite the inner urge to deny the request, I found myself in my mother's Buick, heading down the driveway. Just as I had expected, she immediately voiced her concerns over Falcon and the impulsive decision of leaving my job and relocating to Moonshine. Without warning, she turned and asked the question I had hoped she never would.

"Honey, did you lose a baby?"

I clenched my fist. This had to be Bethany 's doing. I turned away and watched the misty rain blow against the window. "I wasn't that far along, just a few weeks." Mother was quiet but only for a moment, "Just for the record, Bethany and I are both hurt that you didn't trust us with the information. We would have loved to help you through it."

I pursed my lips. "Bethany had no right to tell you."

"Don't blame her honey," she jumped to Bethany's defense. "She assumed I already knew. One would think a mother would know about things like this." Her words were biting.

"There are some things I would rather deal with on my own. I can manage my disappointments. I'm doing fine."

"Are you really?" Her tone turned to sarcasm. "That's not what I've heard. Bethany is really worried about you, and to tell you the truth, so am I. Honey, she said you have been staying out all hours of the night with a married man. Is Dakota married? I sincerely hope he isn't!"

"Who's Dakota?" I growled before remembering it was the name Falcon used when he introduced himself to my parents. It was too late to retract the question. Mother's eyes were locked on me. "Dakota is the man you arrived with yesterday. I believe that is what he called himself, although Bethany has never heard of him either."

My anger rose. "You talked to Bethany again last night?"

"Honey I'm concerned!"

I sighed, there was no way of defending myself. Any truth I could tell her would sound even more bizarre and would only confirm that I was definitely losing my grip on reality.

She pulled the car into a spot near the front of the small pharmacy.

"Well... Is he married?"

"No! He's not married, mother. As usual Bethany doesn't know what she is talking about."

Covering her head with her purse, she made a quick dash into the pharmacy leaving me fuming in the car. I stared out of the window, wishing Falcon and I were in the truck, heading far away. Despite our biting at each other, we shared some sort of camaraderie.

In no time at all mother climbed back into the car and offered me the small paper bag in her hand. "I had my doctor call these in for you. They will take some of the stress away, help you relax, and put things back in perspective."

I folded my arms in front of me, refusing the package. "Send it to Bethany. She can use it more than me."

Mother sighed and drove back to the house without saying a word. The truck was missing when we pulled into the driveway. I figured Falcon must have left to gas it up, and I hoped he would hurry back. I'd grab a quick cup of coffee and my travel bag, so I'd be ready to hit the road as soon as he returned. Now that I had recovered my book, there wasn't a need to stay and hang around. I hated to leave with a rift between us but knew no amount of persuading would convince mother of what she had already believed to be true. Dad sat at the table drinking his coffee; his expression informed me something was wrong.

"Where's Falcon?"

"Who the hell is Falcon?"

Damn it! Why couldn't I remember the script? I really needed to pay attention.

"I mean Dakota. Where is Dakota?"

Dad sat his mug on the table.

"He left to go look for you. He's pretty upset. He didn't like the idea of you going somewhere without telling him."

My face flushed. This looked bad, and I was sure I wouldn't be able to explain.

"What? Are you kidding me?" Mother's voice elevated with her concern. "Is this the kind of relationship you're in? You can't take a quick trip with your mother to the store? Oh, this is scary! I have heard about men like this, over possessive and controlling. They always end up as abusers. Honey, we're concerned. How well do you really know him? Bethany said it's only been a week."

Falcon entered the kitchen on the tail of her last words. With his jaw clenched, he lowered his sunglasses, looking only at me.

"Say your goodbyes we're leaving."

Aghast, mother looked over at my dad, wanting him to intervene. "Martin?"

Dad peered over his bifocals. "Are you ready to leave hon?"

Although I would have liked nothing more than to defy Falcon for embarrassing me as he did, I wasn't up to the challenge. All I cared about was removing myself from my mother's suspicion and the awkwardness of the moment.

"Yes. I'm ready to leave." Giving my parents a quick kiss goodbye; I left them standing on the porch, more concerned than ever.

"Don't ever do that to me again," My words were ice as Falcon backed out of the narrow drive. "As if I didn't have enough explaining to do. What you did looked really bad."

He jerked the truck onto the road and then checked the rearview.

"Scribe, I am only going to say this once more so listen well. You are never to leave my side. Not for a minute, not ever. You do something like that again and you'll be sorry."

All my anger toward Bethany and my mother was nothing compared to the fury I felt for this smart aleck I'd known for less than a week. And then, a feeling of empowerment engulfed me, readying me for the challenge. I wasn't going to take anything else.

"Are you threatening me?"

"Yes."

"I don't like being threatened."

"I don't care what you like. Do what I tell you and I won't have any reason to threaten you."

I sat back hard against the seat crossing my arms in front of me. "Why make such a big deal about running a quick errand with my mother? You're being ridiculous. Nothing happened. I refuse to live in fear—"

His sarcastic chuckle interrupted my tirade.

"You think I'm kidding, I'm not!"

He checked the rearview again, "Scribe, you don't know fear."

"Oh really?" I met his challenge. "I'm beginning to believe you use scare tactics as a means of control. Funny, I've yet to see the enemy.

Everything up till now has been all talk. Maybe you give your adversary more credit than he deserves."

Even though Falcon said nothing, I could see my words annoyed him. I smirked, pleased at myself for not backing down. Giving a final huff, I turned to watch the falling rain. I wasn't going to waste my time worrying if he was mad or not. I didn't care. The person causing me the most trouble right now was Bethany. I would give her a call and tell her what I thought of her meddling but figured it best to wait until I had calmed.

The rain continued all morning with no sign of letting up. We drove along in silence; the only noise was the repetitious song of the wipers slapping against the misty windshield.

Falcon hadn't spoken since our squabble. I sighed loud enough for him to hear my frustration. Must every day of this trip start out with us at odds with each other? If this was the way it was going to be, then it would be a long excruciating ride.

I opened my travel bag and removed the old book. I was interested in knowing more of the story, yet feared with my emotions running amuck, I might cry if I learned more about Travis' lover, Kenalycia. Still curiosity got the better of me and I opened the aging book with reverence, to where I last read.

"Read it aloud if you don't mind." Falcon broke the silence. I didn't want to read out loud, because I was certain he would hear the quiver in my voice if I became emotional. Still, I had no reason to deny his request, so I took a deep breath and began.

"After many weeks of meeting behind the waterfall Kenalycia decided to tell Asa the truth about her story. When he arrived, she lowered her eyes in shame and spilled out her confession. She admitted purposely making the story with no ending, so she could be with him night after night. She promised to end her story and he would be free to do whatever he desired with his evenings. Travis smiled and told her that he also had a confession to make. However, he did not lower his eyes. He looked right at her and admitted that as much as he enjoyed her stories, they were not the reason he came night after night. The reason he came was to be near her. He asked her to never end her story. From that night on Travis and Kenalycia were inseparable.

The familiar ache of a broken heart flared up again. I held my breath and pressed my lips together, fearing my voice might tremble at any minute and then Falcon would know of my desire for Travis. He would belittle me and make fun, just for sport. Besides, it was difficult to read about this woman that intrigued him. I pictured her to be a flawless beauty, hidden away somewhere in Eden, waiting for Travis to come and rescue her. My heart weighed heavily in my chest, so I took a deep breath before turning to the next page. Before I could read, the truck jolted, spinning violently across the rain slick highway, sending the manuscript flying out of my hands. Everything was a blur as the truck skidded sideways off the road, sliding backwards down a shallow embankment. Despite my seatbelt, I banged my head against the window as the truck came to an abrupt stop. We sat in silence as the wipers swiped furiously at the pounding rain.

"You alright Scribe?"

"What happened?"

"The tire blew."

I picked the beloved manuscript from the floorboard. "Need help?"

He smirked. "You stay put. I can do it myself." Opening his door, he ventured outside, disappearing into the blinding rain. I took advantage of my privacy, realizing now would be a great time to try and soothe some ruffled feathers. I'd calmed down quite a bit and hoped mother had as well. Since I hated leaving things the way I did, I decided to call and give an impromptu performance convincing her that everything was okay. Tapping the mom icon on my phone, I waited. A surprised Madison answered. "Everything alright honey?" The concern was evident in her voice.

"Everything's fine, mother." I forced a cheery tone. "I hated the way we left things. I wanted to call and let you know I'm fine and that I love you. It was really good seeing you and daddy."

Her voice softened. "I love you too honey. That's why I worry about you so much. You'll always be my baby."

"I know mother. We'll have a better visit on the trip back. I promise."

"Will Dakota be coming with you?"

"Yes..."

There was a noticeable silence before she spoke again. "Honey, please don't get upset, just hear me out on this. I just spoke with Bethany; and she said a detective came to her home very late last night and asked a lot of questions about you and Dakota."

My sigh was loud enough for mother to hear on the other end. "Momma, please. I am sure the detectives were hired by Ryan to find me so he could ask for the rights to the screenplay. Maybe he forgot to call off his guard dogs. I'll check into it but don't worry, Falcon's not a criminal."

"So, Falcon's his name huh? Why is he using a pseudonym then?"

Damn it! I did it again.

"Honey, we're concerned. These detectives weren't hired by Ryan. They are conducting a serious investigation into illegal activity taking place back there in the mountains. Your dad and I would feel so much better if you didn't travel with Dakota or Falcon or whatever his name is. Seriously honey, you just met him. How well do you know him?"

I closed my eyes and massaged my temples, all the while wishing I'd never placed the call. I should have known better. "Momma, there are things I can't tell you, and if I could, you'd never believe me. You just gotta trust me on this one."

This time it was Mother who sighed. "Well, whatever it is you can't tell me, you're gonna have to tell the detectives. It's just a matter of time until they catch up with you. Your dad and I told them where you were headed and what vehicle you were in."

"Mother! Why?"

"You can't expect us to lie to the authorities. I answered them truthfully and you'd be best to do the same."

"Okay mother," I cut her off before the conversation turned sour again. "I'll tell them whatever they want to know. I have nothing to hide." Even as the words slid from my mouth, I felt guilt for lying. I had everything to hide. My only comfort in the matter was that we were doing nothing illegal. Saying a quick goodbye, I hung up the phone; wishing I'd never made the call.

The driver's door opened, blowing in the misty rain. Falcon climbed in. His t-shirt clung to his sculpted chest and water dripped from his hair and face. He hit the power locks securing both doors before starting the engine. The back tires spun in the wet grass trying to find their traction. He pressed down hard on the gas. The truck swerved a couple of times before it shot out of the ditch roaring back onto the highway.

He drove with intensity, his agitation was evident, yet he kept focused on the road ahead. Within a few minutes we entered the city limits of a small town. Taking the first exit ramp, he turned into the parking lot of a nearby truck stop. The highway oasis provided every comfort for any cross-country travelers, allowing them to pull their rigs in for any needed maintenance, while they enjoyed a nice home cooked meal in the small diner. Afterward, they could shoot a game of pool in the dimly lit arcade, shower in the locker rooms and replenish any needed supplies at the market before hitting the road again.

Dozens of semis sat parked in rows in the back of the lot; some were at the pumps refueling, along with other smaller vehicles traveling the long stretch of highway.

Falcon parked the pickup directly in front of the mechanic's garage. The sound of idling engines and diesel fuel filled the cab as he opened his door. "Stay put and keep the doors locked," he ordered before slamming the door.

I watched him enter the garage and approach one of the mechanics on duty. Stay put? Rebellion began rising inside of me. I was tired of everyone dictating their demands; my mother, Bethany, and worst of all, Falcon. I hadn't forgotten his little charade this morning, or his idle threat. I would meet his challenge. If I obeyed his every command, then I would allow him to set the precedent of how things would be. I would not wait in the cab like a pathetic puppy waiting for my master to come back and throw me a freaking treat. Besides, I was feeling the effects of driving for five hours without stopping. I needed a restroom break and to be able to stretch my legs and make a quick trip to the inside market for water. I locked the doors as he instructed. I'd give him that much, besides, I wanted to make sure the book was safe. Dodging the rain, I ran inside of the small diner. The cashier pointed the way to the restrooms located past the arcade in the back with the showers and lockers. The smell of country cooking reminded me how hungry I was. I didn't eat breakfast because of the quick trip to the pharmacy and our hasty departure. I hoped the tire would take a while to repair so we could sit at a table and dine instead of getting a meal to go and eating in the cramped cab.

The restroom was rather large, with dozens of stalls and showers in the back. It was surprisingly empty save for a woman sitting on the floor, leaning against the wall. No matter the cleanliness of the place, I shuddered at the thought of someone taking refuge on the floor. I skirted past, making my way to a stall when the woman reached out to me. Her eyes were glassy and her voice so feeble, I could hardly hear her.

"Are you okay?"

The woman was trembling, as she struggled to speak.

"I need my insulin."

I looked around for a bag.

"Where is it?"

Although her words were slurred, I was able to understand the insulin was in her truck. My heart fell. There were hundreds of semis outside. How could I find this woman's rig not to mention retrieving her medication? I also knew firsthand how serious her condition was having a friend in high school who suffered from diabetes and nearly died several times due to a lack of insulin being administered at the proper time.

"Maybe I should call for help?" I reached for my back pocket but realized I had left my cell in the cab. "Do you have a phone on you?"

The woman shook her head, rolling it against the wall.

"No, help me to my truck. My husband is there," she managed to say.

With no other choice available, I assisted the woman to her feet and slipped outside into the blinding mist.

Chapter 8

Although the mechanic was accustomed to dealing with intimidating truckers, there was something menacing in Falcon's demeanor that persuaded him to put all other work aside. Falcon hadn't responded favorably to the fact that it would be a couple of hours before someone could get to the job. He pulled the dark glasses away from his eyes and insisted the work be done immediately. The mechanic felt a strange sense of dread when he looked into Falcon's eyes and decided it would be best to get the work done and send this delinquent on his way. Satisfied, Falcon went back to get Bronwyn. They could grab a quick bite to eat. His eyes fell on the empty seat.

"Damn it!" He banged his fist against the window, whirling around, scanning the parking lot. He bolted into the small diner, figuring she would be easy to spot in the sea of overweight bearded faces. He scanned the room, his eyes inspecting every table.

"Hi handsome!" a gaudy waitress greeted him while balancing a tray of food on her shoulder. "Have a seat in my section honey and I'll bring you whatever you need."

He pushed past her, heading into the convenience store. Not finding Bronwyn in there, he bolted down the narrow passageway into the dimly lit arcade. Nothing but a couple of men shooting a game of pool, and another fellow placing quarters in an old pinball machine, illuminating flashing lights and ringing bells. The men glanced briefly at him and then returned to their games. He continued down the narrow hallway pushing open the door to the women's locker room. A hefty woman wrapped in a towel stretched to capacity startled at his abrupt entrance.

"Scribe!" He called out ignoring the woman while walking through the room kicking open the doors to every stall and pulling back the plastic curtains hanging in front of the showers.

"There aint no one in here but me." The plump woman bellowed while holding one hand on her towel and another on her hip. "And unless you want an eye full you better get the hell out of here."

Falcon left the room disgusted at the thought. He entered the men's room. Nothing! Dread grew inside of him as he retraced his steps. Again, he scanned every room he passed through, all the while knowing every second was monumental. If the enemy had grabbed Bronwyn from the truck, they could be miles down the road by now. He bit down hard on his lower jaw at the thought. He exited the diner pushing past the cheap looking waitress who called after him offering a later rendezvous. Back in the falling rain, he scanned the gas pumps and rows of parked rigs in the back lot. Suddenly, he caught sight of a beautiful brunette, drenched from the rain and walking alone amongst the semis. His eyes narrowed in fury. It was time to make good on his threat and show her just what their adversary was capable of. After today, she would never doubt him again. He slipped quietly into the alleyway near rows of trash dumpsters and waited patiently.

Chapter 9

Dodging the rain, I made my way back to the diner. I hadn't meant to be gone for so long, and for that matter, I never intended on taking a walk in the blowing mist. Now my clothes were soaked and clinging to me. It would be a miserable ride in the frigid cab, wearing wet clothes, so I decided to grab a change, hoping the truck wasn't on the jack just yet.

A bolt of lightning zigzagged across the sky giving a warning to veer to the side of the building instead of walking out in the open. When would the rain end? I'd had my fill of it.

Picking up my pace, I made my way toward the diner, staying close to a long row of dumpsters lining the way to a back alley. Just as I was questioning the wisdom of walking near metal dumpsters during an electrical storm, A hand reached from the shadows and yanked me inside. Before a sound could escape my lips, a forceful punch to my stomach knocked the breath from me, stealing any cries for help. Strong hands dug into my arms and pushed me against a trash dumpster. The cold dirty steel slapped against my face. I swung my leg out behind me, struggling to kick my abductor but he was fast, and anticipated my next move. He worked quickly, yanking me off the dumpster with great force, and before I could get my bearings, he slammed me against a neighboring bin. He repeated this move several more times, all the while dragging me deeper into the alleyway. Every slam against the hard metal dulled my senses, which along with the blowing rain blurred my vision, stealing my focus on my abductor or a way of escape. Panic rose at the thought of being raped by some roadside serial killer and I wished I had heeded Falcon's repeated warnings not to venture out alone. Then, a thought...what if my captor was one of Abaddon's men? It would explain the crushing strength. If that was the case, maybe Falcon noticed I was missing and was looking for me, after all he'd left my parent's house this morning searching for me.

Realizing the air had returned to my lungs, I decided to try yelling again; hoping that amidst the pouring train and diesel engines he might hear me. Feeling my chest rise he quickly covered my mouth, smothering the call for help. He drug me a few feet further before pinning me to the dumpster. Moving in close, he pushed against me so tightly it was difficult to take a breath. The lack of air, combined with the sheer terror, depleted my energy. I wanted to fight but there was no strength left. The adrenalin rush I felt earlier departed, depleting me of any strength to break free. I was growing faint, my legs wobbled. The only thing keeping me upright was the man's hip pinning me to the metal wall. Keeping his hand firmly over my mouth, he pressed his lips against my neck and whispered.

"Where were you scribe?"

My heart thundered. Falcon? The sound of his gruff voice frightened me.

"I told you to never leave me, didn't I?"

Remembering his threat, that if I went off on my own again, I would be sorry, filled me with rage, vanquishing any fear that may have manifested during the attack. With renewed strength I hoisted my leg, thrusting my knee violently in his groin. He pulled me off the trash bin and threw me to the wet ground and pounced on top of me, yelling over the rain. "What were you doing over there among the semis?"

My eyes flared in anger while staring at him in defiance. "None of your damn business." I bit.

He raised his arm, striking me across the cheek with the back of his hand. My jaw rang in pain as the copper taste of blood exploded in my mouth. My heart faltered, not believing what was happening. The seed of distrust growing inside of me was now in full bloom. I grabbed a fistful of mud, and slung it in his face, fighting back, and knocking the dark glasses from his eyes. He grabbed hold of both my arms, pinning me to the ground; and leaned in close. "How long do you want to do this Scribe? Let me warn you, you are no match for me. I'm going to win. The question is how much pain are you willing to endure? Now tell me, what were you doing over there?"

I curled my hands into fists, struggling to pull up against him. My efforts were futile. He raised his hand to strike again, but my words stopped him. "I was helping someone."

"Who?" he asked, not letting up on the force in which he held me.

"I don't know, some woman who was sick asked me to help her to her truck."

His hand fell across my face again, this time my lip split open.

"I told you to trust no one but me."

I spit the blood in his face. "You expect me to trust you after this? You 're crazy!"

He leaned over practically lying on top of me and placed his mouth directly on my ear. "Just so you know, that wasn't a simple blowout we had back there. Our tire was shot out. I left two men on the side of the highway dead. One got away and he is looking for you. Better I rough you up a little, than they kill you or do worse things, things that will make you beg for death."

I turned my face away from him, wanting to cry but wouldn't dare give him the satisfaction. Not that he would notice, with all the rain spilling onto my face. Deep inside I wasn't sure I believed him. All the talk about the enemy and still I had yet to see them. Right now, the only person who posed a threat was straddling me. I wondered how Travis would have handled the situation, and if he would agree with Falcon's aggressive lesson. He had referred to him as a little unorthodox, but this behavior was far more than just eccentric; and even though Travis trusted Falcon I wasn't sure I did. But for now, I had no other choice. I would watch and wait; time would tell, and if I needed to take off on my own, I would plan it in a way where he would never find me.

I let my body go limp, no longer resisting him. He pulled himself off and sat on the ground beside me, then offered his hand. I refused it, stubbornly sitting up on my own. I wiped the blood from my lip; it stung and felt twice its normal size. We sat in silence like two junior high boys who had just fought it out. He gave me a slight smile.

"You're filthy Scribe. Let's get your things; you can shower up before we leave."

Falcon's presence in the locker room accompanied by a very muddy and blood-stained me sent the hefty woman along with a couple other ladies flying out the door. Falcon sat on the vanity waiting outside the stall while I showered. His menacing appearance prompted anyone who entered the restroom to change their plans. Once I was done, he took his turn cleaning up, then we agreed on a quick lunch while the mechanic finished up on the tire.

I decided on a bowl of soup and a cornbread muffin since my lip was beginning to swell. Even though I was in dry clothes I continued to shiver and hoped the warmth of the meal would remove the chill.

The adrenaline rush of the attack left me weak. That, combined with my wariness of Falcon cast a greater pall over an already gloomy day. To add insult to injury, we ate in silence, forced to listen to a talk show host interview Ryan about his latest movie, from a television in the corner of the diner. Falcon shook his head in disbelief as Ryan prattled on about refusing to use a body double, insisting on doing all his own stunts. And just when I thought my day couldn't get any worse, the local programming was interrupted by a breaking news report. A grave-looking reporter stood under an umbrella, speaking into his microphone.

"A grisly discovery on Interstate 40. Two white males, stabbed to death, were discovered in a small ravine seven miles off the Briarwood exit..."

Murmurs from the diners sounded throughout the cafe as they realized the closeness of the gruesome sight. Grabbing a remote control, the gaudy waitress, turned up the sound, so all could hear the ghastly report.

"No vehicle was found at the site; however fresh tire tracks were discovered in the grass. Authorities are speculating the victims may have been killed elsewhere and dumped at the scene. Local police are combing the area, beginning with several truck stops and rest areas nearby. Anyone with information should contact the local authorities immediately."

I pushed my bowl of soup aside. Falcon had told me the truth, which also meant he was the killer the authorities were searching for.

"Should we leave?"

Keeping his head low, he cut his eyes up to mine. "Not yet. Getting up now will make us look suspicious. We need to leave pretty quick though. This place will be crawling with the police soon."

My stomach dropped. I played with the saltshaker, in an attempt to calm my nerves, and leaned across the table, lowering my voice.

"Why didn't you tell me what happened back there? We could have bypassed all this if you'd just told me."

Falcon scanned the diner again before locking eyes with me.

"In order for you to survive this quest, Scribe, you need to trust. Your ability to choose wisely will be our salvation. Believe me, you will meet up with the enemy, it's just a matter of time, and he will not be anything you're expecting. He will appear kind and good. If you trust in only what you see, you will die." He leaned across the table before delivering the next few words; "I know you don't trust me and I'm warning you now, there will come a time when you trust me even less. If at that time, you react to what you see, all could be lost. So, get over demanding answers, and start trusting."

There was no time to decipher his ambiguous words, for Falcon was looking past me, into the large parking lot, at the two police cruisers pulling in.

"Time to move."

Chapter 10

The cheap looking waitress squinted at the photograph before grabbing the reading glasses dangling from a chain around her neck. Lifting them to her eyes, she examined the picture more carefully. "Yep, he was here, handsome fellow, looks just like him, 'cept he had a scar under his left eye."

Elam smiled as he replaced the photograph in his jacket pocket. "Was he traveling with someone?"

"A woman, 'bout the same age as him, thin, pale, but pretty."

Elam retrieved another picture, "This her?"

The waitress replaced her glasses once again.

"Sure is. 'Cept she wasn't smilin' much. Didn't look so happy to be with him though. I think they were fighting. I noticed she had a swollen lip. She ordered soup but hardly ate any. I don't care how hot the guy is, in my opinion, if he's beatin' on you... leave, ya know?"

"Definitely," Elam agreed. "I wish all women thought the way you do."

The waitress reveled in the handsome detective's approval, not knowing he thought her capable of taking down any man that looked at her crossways.

"How long ago did they leave?"

She pulled a pile of receipts from her pocket, fumbling through a few before stopping at one.

"By the time on their receipt, I'd say 'bout an hour and a half ago." She grinned, revealing a gold tooth. "He left me a big tip."

Elam thanked the waitress, leaving her to tend to the hungry diners and headed for his car. Next stop, California.

Chapter 11

Needing a breath of fresh air, I lowered my window, inviting the night breeze inside. I loved the outdoors at nightfall. The scents of the earth always seemed stronger in the evening. Man-made sounds diminished, giving way to nature's orchestra, it was always peaceful, and I certainly needed peace. The events of the day had me on edge; starting with my mother's quick trip to the pharmacy and ending with Falcon's surprise attack. All the thoughts rambling through my head were tormenting, doing nothing to calm my troubled spirit. I had tried sleeping, hoping to escape the onslaught of questions and conspiracy theories crowding my mind. Despite Falcon's instructions in the diner to quit demanding answers, I found myself looking for a logical explanation of it all. Mother's call telling of detectives looking for Falcon haunted my thoughts. What if I were part of some elaborate illegal scam? What if I'd let my guard down because of my infatuation with Travis and was actually being duped. The farther I traveled from Moonshine, the easier it was to second guess it all. But there was the fact of my old manuscript, and the cottage in the mountains, and the book with my handwriting. It had to be real. I leaned my head toward the open window and inhaled. The rush of air stirred through the cab and must have stimulated conversation from Falcon.

"So, tell me about your pretty boy."

His topic choice surprised me, and I wondered if he noticed my troubling thoughts and was trying to distract me, trading one turmoil for another.

"He's not my pretty boy anymore."

Falcon smirked, "You seem to be an intelligent woman, what was the attraction to a guy like Ryan Reese?"

I laughed, not believing I was actually having this conversation with Falcon.

"First, it was his looks. I happened to find him quite handsome as do most of the female population in this country. After all, he is considered the sexiest man alive according to all the magazines."

Falcon laughed, "That's what made you love him?"

"It wasn't only that. We had a lot of fun together too."

Falcon nodded in disbelief, "I have a lot of fun with my friends, but it doesn't mean I want to marry them."

I felt foolish. My past engagement suddenly resembled a junior high crush.

"Well, I am not with him anymore, so I guess it doesn't matter." I hoped my declaration would be the final say in the matter, ending the unwanted discussion. Falcon had different intentions.

"And why is that? Didn't he come to Moonshine and beg you to take him back?"

"Yes, he did," I was smug, feeling a bit vindicated in the matter.

"And why didn't you?"

"Because Travis made me realize that I never really loved Ryan."

"Oh, so you're in love with Travis, now, are you? Good luck with that."

My face went as crimson as the setting sun before us.

"That's not what I said. I meant Travis allowed me to realize that I was only in love with my created version of Ryan."

"And how did he make you see that?"

"He accused me of not really knowing what love was. Then, he explained true love to me."

"He did, did he?" Falcon seemed amused. "Please, tell me what he said."

I could quote word for word what Travis said that night. A day had not passed since I had not replayed that scene inside my head. As the sun disappeared on the horizon, I took a deep breath and recited Travis' words:

"If I say I love you, do I love you in the same way I love the mountains, or the smell of the earth after a good rain, or the way I love music? Do I love you because the way you look ignites a passion inside of me? Is my love for you only contingent on the way it affects me, how it makes me feel? If this is so, I only truly love myself, and I only love and want you for how it affects me. Do I love you, despite the times you are angry, bitter, and unlovely? Do I continue to love you, although your heart belongs to another? Can I send you away, knowing I will never experience you, but you will experience all you've ever dreamed of? I can if my love is for you and not myself."

The long silence that followed was awkward, so staying true to form, I broke it. "I hope I can love someone like that one day, but I am afraid I'm too selfish." For the first time since we left the truck stop, Falcon took his eyes off the road and smiled. There was nothing impish or wicked in his grin.

We drove all night. Falcon thought it best not to stop, saying that the further away we got from the crime scene the better our chances of not being detained. I volunteered to drive but as usual he refused. He did allow me to stretch my legs, so around eight-thirty he pulled off the main highway. We traveled a few miles down a secondary road before stopping at an overgrown field. In the middle, an old, abandoned house sat in solitude. Of all the places, I wondered why he would stop here. It looked haunted and spooky; I had experienced enough fear lately. I didn't need to add to it.

Falcon climbed from the cab, immediately lighting up a cigarette. It had been hours since his last smoke and I figured he was desperate. I stretched my legs, but quickly recoiled in pain. The little bout at the truck stop was setting in, leaving me sore.

Falcon blew a line of smoke into the evening breeze, "Sorry about that."

I rolled my eyes, "I'm sure you are."

He took in another draw, locking eyes with me.

"You don't trust me, do you?"

In light of our surroundings, his question seemed threatening. Had he asked it at the truck stop, or while we were eating in the café, it wouldn't have frightened me as much. But here, in the black of night, in the middle of nowhere, standing helpless in the overgrown yard of an abandoned house, it sent a chill. "Not entirely."

Clenching the cigarette in his teeth, he stepped toward me. Not wanting to appear fearful, I stayed my ground, determined not to move away. He pressed in close, still, I didn't move. He was taller, so I found myself staring into his throat, wondering what his intentions were.

He placed his hands on my shoulders and turned me to face the dilapidated house. We'd left the rain and storm the further west we drove. Now standing in the open field the moon showed bright in the sky overhead, spotlighting the ram shackled home.

"What do you see?" he asked.

I shrugged, confused and somewhat apprehensive about the moment.

"Just a run-down old house."

"Is that all?" he kept the cigarette clenched between his teeth.

I looked around, "Well, there are some dried out decaying trees, a broken-down fence, some busted windows but that's pretty much it."

He sighed and when he did a gust of smoke enveloped my face. I pulled away from his grasp, coughing.

"It's a pathetic shame." He said, crushing his cigarette with the tips of his fingers and tossing it into the tall grass.

Anger began to boil inside, at his condescending attitude. I still hadn't forgiven him for what he did at the truck stop. I refused to take any more.

"Really?" I bit back. "You're referring to me?"

"That I am. At least you got that one right."

I wanted to punch him, to give him the thrashing he inflicted on me; however, it would only result in him laughing at my lame attempt.

"How am I a pathetic shame?" my voice quivered with the words. I wasn't sure if the quiver was born out of anger or the haunting truth inside me that my life was pretty pitiful.

"You aren't the pathetic shame," He corrected me, leaving me feeling a tinge better. The shame is in the fact that you are our redemption, and you are not ready to be. Not now, anyway."

"Well, I could have told you that," I began to laugh at the thought of it. Me, Bronwyn Sterling, the savior of a world I knew nothing about. The thought was preposterous. Maybe it was extreme exhaustion or perhaps the anxiety I felt being with the cad Falcon; whatever the reason, I couldn't stop laughing. I took a deep breath, but the laughter continued. Falcon shook his head in disbelief and lit up another, staring at me while he smoked.

"You know what I could use right now?" I asked between breaths. "I could use a drink. I just realized I haven't had alcohol in almost two weeks. I was trapped in Moonshine and never even had a swig." I threw my head back, hysterical at my own humor.

Falcon flicked the ashes from his cigarette. "Strong drink isn't for the noble, who hold the lives of others in their hands. It's for the common, so they can drink and for a while forget their misery."

"Then fill 'er up!" I laughed again but allowed it to trail off when I noticed he wasn't smiling. This time I stared at him, narrowing my eyes in deep inspection. I had to admit his words were interesting, and it surprised me that such insightful words could come from a man like him. Since he was being philosophical, I decided to ask him the question but couldn't resist a bit of sarcasm.

"What do you see then? Is that night vision of yours illuminating something I can't see?"

He let out a thin line of smoke and looked towards the house.

"I see what once was. I see a man coming home from work and his children running to meet him. I see his wife standing in the doorway smiling, thankful he's home and that their children love him. I see a fireplace with a welcoming fire and a dinner table with a family gathered around it. I see beds where the children dream. I see a tree with a swing, and a dog wagging his tail and barking while the kids play. I see a woman hanging clothes out to dry and stopping for a moment to chase her kids through the trees." He took another draw and expelled the smoke slowly as if he were lost in memory.

"I see time marching through; an enemy they couldn't stop no matter how hard they tried. I see what once was, and not the shell of what is. I see what can be again if a renovator would come and see the potential. I see something that, if given the proper care, could bring happiness to a family again." He took one last draw before he finished. "You don't need night vision to see these things, just a heart."

I was ashamed. I should have seen all of that. After all, I was the writer; I should have seen the story in the rubble. Falcon was right, it was a pathetic shame. When did I lose my wonder? When did I start existing, and quit living? I gazed at the house, bathed in the glow of the moon, and tried to imagine what it was like in its prime and then my eyes fell on Falcon, and suddenly wondered why he had stopped here. What was he trying to show me? Was he the house? Did he want me to see who he once was, to look past the rough chain-smoking façade to who he really is. I felt the same about myself, hoping he and Travis could see past the bitter, heartbroken woman I'd become. I wanted a do over, a remote control where I could rewind life to the place where I began messing up and start fresh. And then it hit me. Tonight was my do over, a fresh start. And as I stood in the overgrown field, under a sky filled with stars, I knew someone, somewhere, in the great expanse of it all was renovating my life; because they saw potential, they knew who I really was and who I was destined to be.

Chapter 12

I took a sip of the strong coffee, thankful for the morning brew. I'd intended on sleeping much later than I actually did seeing we drove nonstop, after our visit at the ram shackled house and arrived at the condo sometime around seven. After Falcon staked out the place, making sure no one was hiding in the shadows, we collapsed in bed for a well-deserved rest. But our peaceful slumber was interrupted two hours later by Jamia's persistent rapping on the patio door. She'd woken to take her three Bichon's for their walk when she noticed a strange truck parked outside my place. Being the one person who constantly kept an eye on the beachside condo, running off Ryan's attorneys and nosy paparazzi, she banged on the door determined to have it out with whoever was trespassing.

Falcon reached the door first, shirtless, and with his hair a wild mess. He was in no mood to be interrogated by the neighborhood watch. I could hear his verbal assault from the bedroom and bolted down the stairs just in time to hear Jamia threaten to call the police unless she saw me. The two looked as if they were ready to have an all-out brawl when I appeared at the door, my presence diffusing the situation. After answering an onslaught of questions from Jamia, I realized there would be no returning to sleep anytime soon.

She insisted on cooking breakfast, for which I was thankful. I was hungry and since I had been away, there were no groceries in my condo. Within minutes Jamia returned with a basket of goodies. She brewed a fresh pot of coffee, poured ice cold orange juice, laid out a spread of croissants and muffins while she fried up some turkey bacon, and eggs.

I yawned, sipped my coffee, and went through the mail, while Falcon disappeared upstairs to take a shower, figuring I was safe in the company of militant Jamia.

"He sure is a handsome one." She commented, refilling my mug. "He looks like he could beat the shit out of that pussy Ryan."

I gave a slight smile in return, which prompted Jamia's next probing question. "He didn't give you that busted lip, did he?"

Her question teemed with skepticism. Jamia was smart and attentive. Her discerning abilities always amazed me, and I knew I wouldn't be able to fake my way through this conversation without being found out. I continued to thumb through the mail so I wouldn't have to look her in the eye.

"Come on Jamia, do you really think I would be with a guy who hits me?"

"Definitely not, you'd kill the bastard. But you can 't blame me for asking. He does look like a bad boy."

"That he does, but his bark is worse than his bite. He's rough on the edges but once you look past it…" my voice faded off as I came to an ivory-colored envelope, addressed to me in aged Calligraphy. There was no return address, no stamp, and no postmark, yet it was delivered with all my other mail.

Jamia kept rambling on, but her voice seemed far away, the mysterious letter had captured my utmost attention. Grabbing the letter opener, I slit through the envelope and pulled out an aging piece of parchment, unfolding it carefully.

Crossing the room, I retrieved a Bible from the bookcase. My hands trembled as I thumbed through the table of contents trying to locate the book of Habakkuk. Another cryptic message, just like the one I received the night of the ice cream festival. The message in the mysterious letter read; Habakkuk 2:2-3.

With trembling hands, I thumbed through the pages. I wasn't much accustomed to the Bible but knew from my childhood days in Sunday school that Habakkuk was in the Old Testament. Obadiah, Jonah, Micah, Nahum...Habakkuk. I turned to the second chapter, the second verse, and with a trembling finger, underlined the words and read.

Write the vision and make it plain, that he may run who reads it. For the vision is yet for an appointed time; but at the end it will speak, and it will not lie. Though it tarries, wait for it, because it will surely come.

Although the enigmatic message was from the Bible, I knew it was for me. Lost in my own sea of thoughts, I looked past the patio, across the sandy beach, to where the ocean meets the horizon. Write the vision and make it plain. What vision? I hadn't had any other than a few nightmares and a couple of brief flashes of me and Travis standing in the falling rain. Was I to write them down, or was there a foretold vision I was to see in the future?

That he may run who reads it. I was at a complete loss to the meaning of this phrase, so I moved on.

For the vision is yet for an appointed time. Was this meaning the vision was yet to come or what I see in the vision will be something that takes place in the future? I thought it was probably the latter.

But at the end it will speak, and it will not lie. Though it tarries, wait for it, because it will surely come. Something about the last phrase caused a dread to rise inside. The message was urging me not to give up hope, which meant only one thing...suffering.

I was so lost in my thoughts; I never heard Jamia go back into the kitchen, rattling on with endless advice and stories of past hurts in living with an abusive man. Nor did I hear Falcon return to the room and ask me what was wrong.

"Scribe!" His voice interrupted my thinking. "You alright?"

I nodded and handed him the envelope. He read the passage on the letter and as he looked back at me, I handed him the Bible, already turned to the assigned page. Taking the heavy book from me, he read the passage, and then with a nod of his head motioned me to the outside on the patio, out of Jamia's earshot.

"You've had a vision?"

"No, nothing worth writing down anyway. Just some small flashes, mostly of Travis." I blushed at the confession, and quickly turned my face toward the ocean, hoping he hadn't noticed the color flooding into my cheeks. He seemed surprised at the disclosure.

"Really? What kind of flashes?"

I leaned on the railing, continuing to watch the waves collapse on the shore. The breeze coming off the ocean moved my hair away from my face and cooled my burning cheeks.

"They're always the same. He's standing in falling rain, he looks distraught. Then I reach for him, and when I do, I start to fall, and then it's over."

Falcon said nothing and I had no desire to turn and look at him even though I could sense he was watching me.

The delicious aroma of bacon and eggs tickled my nose, enticing me from the awkwardness of the conversation to a satisfying breakfast inside. But as I was deciding to go inside and grab some food, Falcon's disclosure stopped me cold.

"He lost her." His statement pulled my eyes off the incoming tide and onto him. My heart skipped and I prayed it didn't show in my face. He was referring to Travis's love, so I lifted my brows along with my chin and hoped he would continue.

"She went through the portal first. Travis was supposed to travel with her, but he got captured, and she went through alone. Then years later, when we all came through, he went searching for her. He searched the entire globe, spent enormous amounts of money but never found her."

I didn't know what to say. I had a million questions but wasn't sure which to ask first, or if Falcon would even answer them if I did. He looked at me so intently that I shifted my feet in discomfort.

"She is beautiful, like you. In fact, you look like her."

Another shocking statement. For starters, I never knew Falcon thought of me as beautiful, which caught me off guard. His admission that I favored Travis' love may have explained Travis' attentiveness to me back in Moonshine. That, and the fact I was his ticket home. I couldn't let myself forget that painful part.

"She was fearless, exciting, adventurous, she had no enemies. Everyone loved her, even Abaddon." Falcon paused and pulled a cigarette from his pocket. I watched him, wishing he would hurry and continue. He was revealing secrets and I desired to know them all. Holding the flame to the end of his smoke, he inhaled, keeping his eyes fixed on me. He placed the lighter in his jeans before blowing a long line of smoke over the railing.

"Abaddon launched his upheaval on their wedding night, preventing them from marrying. Travis lost his brother, his love... his entire world in one night."

I thought back to the night of the festival, being overcome when I realized it would have been my wedding night, had Ryan not broken off our engagement. Travis took me out on the lake to watch fireworks, comforting me. Yet my loss was nothing compared to his.

Falcon watched me as he exhaled another line of smoke.

"His greatest fear is that Abaddon's men found her and took her back through the portal. If so—"

"Breakfast is ready." Jamia announced, interrupting his story, walking out onto the balcony with two plates of food. "Lets' eat before it gets cold."

I sighed, my portal to information was closed for now.

Chapter 13

Jamia cleaned up after breakfast, left a tray of muffins on the counter, and headed home leaving me to sort through my belongings. It was pretty easy to decide what to take to Moonshine and what to leave behind. Ryan and I rented the condo furnished; only a few pieces actually belonged to me, and those items, I decided, would go into storage. The kitchen utensils such as plates, silverware, pots and pans, coffee maker, and the like, all belonged to me. Those would go in storage as well, because as I remembered correctly, my cottage in Moonshine was completely stocked.

September was only a couple of weeks away. The weather in the mountains would be cooling off soon and I would need my winter clothing. Pulling out a suitcase, I tossed sweaters and boots inside. A feeling of excitement began to grow. I reveled in the idea of sitting in my mountain cottage, sipping hot cider, penning an amazing story, while watching the leaves turn shades of amber, bright orange and yellow, before saying their last farewell to the tree and falling to earth. As I thought of these things, my mind turned to Travis and I pictured him, imparting life to the people of his world. As their time passed without him, they would grow old, falling away from his nourishment, left to decay and die on the earth. Barak said they had three years left before they began to age and start the process of death. I wondered if my thought on this matter was the vision I was to write down, but figured it wasn't. In my opinion a vision should be something you see, like a huge movie screen, playing out a story that no one else is privy to but you. A vision wouldn't be a simple thought in the head; it had to be much grander than that.

Each time I filled a suitcase, Falcon would take it downstairs, and place it in the truck, to hasten our departure. He remained quiet most of the day. He seemed to be in deep thought or better, yet he was more than likely communicating with Travis or his men. I was sure his conversations were important, still I was disappointed, hoping he would continue the story he began on the patio before Jamia interrupted us.

There was an anxious spirit within him, as he kept his vigil, watching the beach, scrutinizing the people walking by, glaring at them if they ventured too close to the condo.

As the day wore on, my body reminded me I was existing on only three hours of sleep. But as tired as I felt, I wouldn't stop. I was as anxious as Falcon to leave this place. Everything I touched was a reminder of mine and Ryan's time together. True, I was no longer heartbroken, but still there was pain of a lost relationship and I desired nothing more than to move on, burn the bridge, and leave it in the past.

I took a break from packing to enjoy a delicious meal Falcon ordered from a local restaurant. He set a nice table for us outside where we could dine and watch the sun set. Most of the beach goers already packed up and headed home for the day, only a few remained gathered around fire pits, roasting hot dogs, and s'mores. I sipped my ice water watching the sun disappear into the ocean, surprised Falcon hadn't opened one of the many bottles of wine in my kitchen. I guessed he wasn't kidding when he said strong drink wasn't for those who hold the lives of others in their hands. I appreciated the fact he wanted to be alert and in control should this supposed enemy, he continually warned me of, decide to strike. Come to think of it, I'd never seen him drink. Other than his chain smoking he seemed to be one of the most disciplined men I'd ever known. A warrior, always prepared, always one step ahead of the adversary and ready to run into battle. Ready to give his life for the cause, which meant he was driven by a passion, because all discipline is rooted in desire. And then, I had a thought, so I decided to voice it audibly.

"Do you have someone special waiting for you in Eden as well?"

He smirked, "Why? You interested?"

I laughed. I couldn't help myself. I walked right into that one.

"Hardly, I think we'd kill each other. Although, last night you did reveal a rather tender, poetic side."

He leaned back in his chair, "So you're saying I have a chance?"

I laughed again.

By the time we finished dinner, the moon was high in the sky, reflecting its silver light upon the water. Falcon lit up a cigarette and perched himself on the railing, keeping a careful watch over the surrounding area. The fire pits along the beach were ablaze leaving a line of small fires as far as the eye could see. Friday night beachgoers gathered around the warmth, dancing to the music flowing from their phones. Couples walked hand in hand near the water's edge, a few straying near our condo, coming closer to the deck than Falcon liked.

I looked out over the black waters. "I love the ocean at night. It's so dark out there...so black...so mysterious; I always wondered if the roar was a foreign language, telling me of something I should know."

Falcon took a long draw, expelling the smoke and studying me. I let him look. I had nothing to hide. I would look back, but I feared being locked in his gaze seeing things in his eyes that might frighten me. I kept my focus on the blackness and allowed it to hypnotize me with the rhythmic sound of crashing waves. My heart ached for a reason I didn't know. There was an all-encompassing emptiness enveloping and suddenly I felt alone. True, I'd recently made a life altering decision, leaving my job and my best friends behind, not to mention rejecting Ryan after he came back. Still, the loneliness didn't stem from any of those things. My soul felt as empty as the great black expanse I was staring into.

"Abaddon and Kenalycia had a special love too..."

Falcon picked up where he left off. "Some people did not understand their relationship and assumed they would end up together, but it wasn't that kind of a love, at least it wasn't for her. Some say Abaddon truly loved her more than he showed and hid his true feelings. There were many rumors, but once Kena fell for Travis and he fell for her...well, I think it was the most powerful love ever. I have never seen two people more in love than they were."

I kept my gaze over the ocean so Falcon could not see the pain of his statement reflecting on my face. Although I wanted to hear more; any mention of Travis loving another only caused the loneliness I was feeling to expand. I hoped time away from him would ease the pain, but with each day that passed, I found myself longing to be near him. Now I must endure Falcon disclosing how much Travis loved another, and as much as it hurt, there was an insatiable desire to know more. Falcon paused and looked out over the black ocean before continuing the tragic tale. "They confessed their love for each other and set the date for their marriage." He took another draw, expelling a cloud of smoke. "In our world there is a week of celebrating that takes place before the actual wedding. The night before the ceremony is sacred and intimate. The couple meets at a secret location and give themselves to each other for the first time. Sex, for our world's Royals, is the ultimate gift, given only to the one person who truly holds their heart. Royals save their gift, and when it is presented in that way, it is the height of ecstasy. The pleasure never subsides because it has not been cheapened and used for selfish gratification. Neither do they give it to multiple people because then it loses its significance and desire."

I could feel Falcon's gaze on me and wondered if he was intentionally accusing me with his words, knowing I had already given myself to Ryan. But I wasn't royalty, so it wasn't a rule I was bound to. I supposed Travis was still saving his gift for Kenalycia. Another reason he never made a move back in Moonshine.

"Abaddon launched his rebellion the night Kenalycia, and Travis were to give themselves to each other." Falcon took another long draw and as he continued, bitterness laced his voice. "His men were strategically placed all over Eden, poised and ready for his signal. One of his spies followed Travis to the secret location while some of his men kidnapped Kenalycia. Travis waited at the waterfall, but she never came. Instead, Abaddon showed up. As soon as Travis saw him, he knew something was horribly wrong."

My heart raced; although the night breeze blowing off the water was chilly, it did nothing to lessen the heat flooding through me. And despite the intensity of the warmth, I shivered.

"Abaddon showed Travis his knife, informing him the blood stain on the blade belonged to his brother Ariston. Travis flew into an uncontrollable rage and being a man of incredible strength, he took out ten of Abaddon's men immediately. He overpowered Abaddon and was ready to kill him when Abaddon warned him that unless he surrendered, he would give the order for his men to kill Brennun and Mavis. Travis surrendered. He was taken as a prisoner and escorted back to the citadel and placed with Brennun and the rest of the ruling royalty taken captive that night. Travis searched for Kenalycia only to find out she had been placed in Abaddon's care."

Falcon swung his legs over the railing and jumped down upon the deck. He crushed the butt of his cigarette and tossed it in the trash. "Want to go for a walk?"

His invitation sounded nice. I had been tired early and would not have agreed to a moonlit walk on the beach, but the story had brought me fully awake, and I hoped he would continue as we walked.

"I will if you finish your story."

I wrapped my arms around myself as we walked near the breaking water and wished I had thought of bringing a light jacket. Falcon noticed my shivering. "You, okay?"

I nodded, "Just a little cold."

"We can go back,"

I nodded again, "It's alright.

We walked in silence further down the beach until we stumbled upon an abandoned fire and decided to take advantage of its warmth. We sat in the cold sand, watching the burning bits of embers rise with the breeze, and blow away from the pit like fireflies back in moonshine. Falcon sat near me, silently, staring off into the dark expanse. I watched him, not caring if he noticed my deep inspection of him. The dancing flames cast eerie shadows across his face, and I wondered what he was reminiscing of after all this time, and if the pain was just a hollow memory or if his wounds still bled.

"Where were you when all this was going on?" My question sounded accusing and when he cut his dark eyes to mine, I wished I'd worded it differently.

"When Abaddon launched his revolt, everything turned to chaos. No one knew who was siding with whom. Abaddon's inner circle was top secret and although he and I were very close he never included me in his elite, so the entire rebellion came as a shock. After the initial uprising he asked me to stand with him, joining his regime. He promised me a lot. I figured I could do more to help Travis and the others if I was on the inside. So, I accepted his offer, making him think I gave him my allegiance. Unfortunately, everyone else thought I had as well. Some even believed I was part of his elite and helped him plan the entire revolt. I could see how they thought such a thing seeing I lived in the main house of the citadel and had considerable authority. What Abaddon and the others didn't know was that I had plans of my own."

I kept my eyes locked on him the entire time he spoke, captivated by his words as he recounted the wretched event.

"I saw Kena every day because we were both living in the main house. She assumed I was in league with Abaddon and had betrayed Travis. I knew Abaddon was planning on implementing some dark schemes. I couldn't let it happen. I came up with a plan and tried to tell her, but she refused to have anything to do with me. I finally caught her alone and forced her to listen. Once she heard me out, she realized my allegiance was still with Travis, so she trusted me, agreeing to go along with the plan. We snuck away from the Citadel. The plan was for Travis and Kenalycia to escape through the portal. When we arrived, I hurled a surprise attack on Abaddon's men. I was able to hold them back long enough for Travis to send Kenalycia through. He didn't go with her. Instead, he stayed back to help me." Falcon swallowed, his throat bulging as if he blamed himself for their separation.

"Abaddon was outraged when he learned what had happened. He had me beaten for my betrayal and when I was too injured to fight back, he sliced his revenge into my face."

My teeth chattered, and although my arms were still wrapped around my chest, my trembling wouldn't stop. My shuddering was not caused by the breeze blowing off the water but rather the fury raging inside me as vivid pictures of Falcon's bloody, beaten body flashed through my mind along with the sound of his anguish ringing in my ears, overpowering the roar of the ocean. The story grieved me with such sorrow. Yet at the same time it inflicted an all-consuming anger. The kind that could prompt me to kill and not regret taking a life. I had never felt such hatred before and at the same time there was love and forgiveness mingled in, battling against my wrath. The sensation was disturbing, much like the night at the falls when the opposing forces fought. Then suddenly the roar of the ocean was overpowered by the mournful cries of the oppressed. Falcon did not seem to hear the lamenting as I did. Instead, he sat staring out into the expanse, unresponsive to the pain searing a wound into my heart.

Just when I thought I couldn't endure the weeping any longer, the song of the woman began to surface, overpowering the sorrowful howling. The peaceful haunting song flooded my soul and brought with it a renewed sense of strength, calming my spirit, and empowering me with an unexplainable courage. The melody brought with it a realization that I was endowed with the power to write the redemptive story and make right all that Abaddon had wronged. This sanctioning filled me with great inspiration, destroying the blockage that had long since closed off my ability to write. I felt it dissolving inside, freeing my imagination from its captive state. I lay back in the cold sand, staring at the night sky. The roar of the ocean became audible again as the song of the woman subsided. The salty night breeze cradled me, cooling the intense burning heat.

Falcon's story ignited a passion inside of me, an outrage at injustice, and a strong desire to love unconditionally. I realized the pain true love would bring. If I wrote the story the way it should be, then I would be reuniting Travis and Kenalycia. I would be sending Travis away, never experiencing him, but knowing he would experience all he ever dreamed. My heart nearly broke with the thought, yet I knew it was what I must do. One single tear escaped, rolling off the side of my face onto the sand and simultaneously, a star shot across the night sky, leaving a fiery trail. At that moment, I felt the universe was grieving right along with me.

Chapter 14

Although I was existing on less than four hours of sleep, I had no desire to go to bed. After spending the past hour listening to Falcon unfold the events of Eden's uprising, my mind was alive. The inspiration that had been foreign for so long, was back with a stimulating vengeance. So, after a quick shower, I grabbed the leather-bound book, unlocked the latch with the miniature key, and settled down to write. I didn't inform Falcon of my plan, so when he passed through the living area checking the doors before turning in, he stopped cold.

"You're writing?"

"I am," I gave him a soft smile, confident in my ability to do so. "I know you're tired, don't feel like you have to wait up."

His face took on a respectful expression I had yet to see amidst all the sarcastic looks he'd thrown my way over the past couple of days.

"This is a sacred moment for me. What providence to witness the foretold story at its beginnings. To be in the very room as it is composed. Sleep can wait."

He took a seat across the room, and for the next three hours never removed his eyes from me. He watched as my hand moved rhythmically across the blank pages, filling them with life. My body swayed as I wrote, as if my spirit was dancing to a melody that only I could hear. Every so often my lips would curl into a smile and a couple of times; a tear escaped my eyes and trickled down my cheek, splashing onto the dry parchment. I wrote for nearly three hours without stopping before laying my pen aside and closing the book; locking it with the small key. I looked at Falcon, my lips forming a satisfied smile.

"It begins."

He swallowed hard; his throat parched. He remained unmoved; his eyes locked on mine.

"You're pleased with what you wrote?"

"Yes, it begins well."

Standing from his chair, he extended his hand to me, "Then we had best get our rest my lady scribe. We have an enormous battle ahead."

He was right, I needed sleep. The lack of it combined with the intense emotion of the night was taking its toll and suddenly I couldn't wait to fall into bed.

He escorted me upstairs and into the master bedroom. I placed the treasured book into my travel bag, zipping it shut."

"Should we set an alarm for the morning?" I asked, but before I realized what was happening, he lunged for me, knocking me to the floor, blocking the shards of broken glass showering down around us, shattering the stillness of the room.

"Stay down!" He ordered, grabbing the small travel bag, and pulling me toward the doorway. Terrified, I followed him, crawling on my hands and knees, feeling the jagged fragments of the shattered balcony door cutting into my skin.

Once in the hallway, Falcon pushed me flat against the wall, shoved the bag into my hand and motioned for me to stay put. My heart raced. Surely, he wouldn't leave me alone. He bolted down the hallway stopping at the top of the staircase, flattening himself against the opposite wall. To my horror I heard footsteps rushing up the stairs. Someone was in the condo! Riveted in terror, I watched as the dark outline of a man topped the stairs and entered the hallway. Falcon stepped forward and with one swift move the man slumped to the ground. A slight shaft of moonlight drew a line across the hard wood of the hallway, illuminating a significant amount of blood pooling from underneath him.

I leaned against the wall, unable to take my eyes off the gore. I grew dizzy and felt as if I would retch.

"Stay with me Scribe," Falcon was matter of fact, pulling me off the wall. I stepped over the corpse, gagging as the sticky fluid oozed between my toes. Once we reached the base of the stairs, Falcon stopped and scanned the dark room. It was quiet and empty.

Hugging the wall as well as we were able, we edged our way across the room toward the garage, stopping at the massive picture windows. Falcon pulled me low to the ground as we inched our way underneath the glass panes. Taking advantage of our crouching position, a dark figure leapt from the upper loft taking Falcon down immediately. I screamed at the unexpectedness of the attack, drawing immediate attention to our whereabouts. The room came alive as shadowy figures manifest from the upper loft and dark corners. Within seconds, three men stormed the room. Falcon sprung to his feet, forcefully throwing the attacker off, tossing him through the plate glass window. Wasting no time, he pulled his knife. Spinning around he kicked the approaching aggressor out of the way, while burying his knife deep into the chest of the second man. The front door burst open, splintering the hinges as another assailant bolted in heading toward me. Horrified, I stood frozen, watching everything unfold.

"Get out of here Scribe!" Falcon yelled, jarring me from my petrified trance. The man dove for me, but I whirled around heading back up to the bedroom all the while keeping my bag and the precious book close. I bolted up the stairs taking two at a time. My adrenaline was on overload as I dashed down the hall jumping over the slain man. My bare feet slid in the sticky blood, still ebbing from the lifeless body. I hit the ground hard, biting my tongue and sliding across the unyielding floor. I swallowed hard to keep from vomiting and took a quick glance over my shoulder. The man was topping the stairs. I had to place my hands in the warm blood to get the traction I needed to stand. I scrambled to my feet and loped into the room slamming the door behind me, pressing my body against it in a feeble attempt to keep it closed. My bloody fingers trembled, slipping off the latch, making it almost impossible to lock.

Please! I could hear the heavy footsteps of the ruffian moving fast down the hallway. I wiped my wet hands across my t-shirt hoping to dry them enough to grab hold of the lock without it slipping. Please God, I prayed again. The lock clicked into place just as the man slammed his body against it. Excruciating pain detonated inside as the door shook violently, buckling under the force of the blow. It would only be a matter of seconds before it was knocked completely off its hinges.

Dashing across the room, I knelt beside the bed, and with shaky hands, I lifted the heavy mattress. With one trembling arm I held it up as best I could and with the other, I desperately searched the empty space underneath. Please be here... Please.

After hearing disturbing reports about psychotic fans stalking celebrities, Ryan purchased a handgun, despite my protests. He figured it might come in handy with his newfound fame. I hadn't thought of the gun until now and hoped Ryan had forgotten about it as well and left it behind when he moved out.

Bam! The man threw his body against the door, intensifying my desperate search. The wood facing splintered, buckling the door. The next blow would surely force it open. I continued my blind hunt; the fear surging through my body, zapped my strength. My wobbling arm wouldn't be able to hold the mattress up much longer. Then, my fingers touched cold hard metal. It was still there! I pulled the gun from its hiding place, hoping it was loaded. Thanks to all the times Bethany insisted that I go to the shooting range with her, I had learned how to shoot.

The sound of splintering wood drowned out my thrashing heart as the door came crashing open. My hands shook uncontrollably, nearly causing me to drop my only protection. Squatting down, I hid, crouching behind the king-sized bed. My heart smacked against my chest, the intense fear choking the breath from my throat. The bedroom was a rather large suite; and I hoped it would take a few seconds before the brute made his way to my side of the bed, giving me more time to familiarize myself with my weapon. The shadow moving across the wall however thwarted that idea. The man rounded the corner. He stopped suddenly when he saw me, but it wasn't the gun in my hands that immobilized him. He stared at me, giving me a curious expression before his lips curled into a smile. He laughed.

"As I live and breathe. They weren't kidding." He stretched out his brawny arm. "You're coming with me."

Scooting away from his reach, I raised the gun, aiming at his chest.

A deafening explosion pierced the quiet of the early morning hours as the handle unexpectedly kicked back into my face. A flood of pain erupted inside my head, blurring my vision as blood began pouring from my nose. And despite my hazy vision I watched the man's eyes go manic as he lunged straight for me.

Chapter 15

The explosion of gunfire upstairs caused Falcon's heart to sink. Pulling his knife from the chest of his last attacker he rushed up the stairs, hurdling over the fallen man, nearly losing his footing on the blood covered floor.

Could it have ended so quickly? After all the years of waiting and anticipating their redemption, and with only one small section of the book penned, could all hope of deliverance be gone?

His heart ached as he thought of Bronwyn. He couldn't bear the thought of her dead. He believed her to be truly innocent, totally oblivious to what was really going on. A pawn in a game she didn't remember playing. True he'd been hard on her, giving her no slack, but his actions were for her own good. He knew the enemy well and must prepare her for the inevitable encounter. For all the good it had done. He would grieve later. Right now, fury raged inside of him. He would find the one who took her life and mutilate him.

Replacing the knife in his jeans, he pulled his gun and stepped into the room. No need to kill in silence, the deafening blast had more than likely woken the neighbors. It would be only a matter of time before the police arrived.

Picking up on movement behind the splintered door, he kicked it off its hinges, and found himself staring down the barrel of a gun.

With a twist of his wrist, he snatched the weapon from its owner, hurling it across the king-sized bed. Grabbing Bronwyn, he buried her bloody face into his chest and kissed the top of her head.

"Let's get out of here." He whispered.

Stepping over the corpse one last time, we descended the stairs. I glanced about my once peaceful living room, stunned. Four dead bodies lay scattered across the room, each one's lifeblood splattered across the furnishings and draining from a gash across their neck or chest. Shards of shattered glass lay beneath the large picture windows. This time instead of stealing across the room slowly, we raced through it, heading to the garage.

Fortunately, Falcon had already loaded the truck for departure. He grabbed the bag from me, tossing it into the cab. I ran to the passenger side and was reaching for the door when a dark figure jumped from the open bed and grabbed me by my hair. He yanked my head back and placed the cold blade of his knife against my neck. I swallowed and closed my eyes, choking at the sting of it. I had seen enough killings tonight to know it would only take a fraction of a second for the blade to rip across my throat and end my life. A small surge of air passed near my temples as a warm liquid splattered across my face. The man's grip lessened, and he slumped to the floor. Falcon's aim was impeccable, missing me by a fraction and landing a bullet directly in the forehead of my attacker.

"Get in." He yelled.

We sped away, the peaceful sound of breaking waves was drowned out by barking dogs and approaching sirens.

Elam

walked briskly through the beautifully landscaped corridor of the palace estate, making his way past the marble pillars. Lush floral vines snaked their way around the columns and up through the overhang, mingling with the massive ferns offering ample shade to cool him from his hurried pace. Making a sharp turn, he walked by the way of the sparkling fountain, making sure not to make eye contact with anyone. He had no intention of wasting time in idle conversation. Besides, he was of the elite inner circle, and no one should dare engage in conversation with him unless invited. He wished to speak with only one man, the crowned head, Abaddon.

He carried news that would shake the very foundations of his world. He was certain to be rewarded even more. More than likely, he would be swiftly promoted within the elite to the position of Abaddon's right hand.

Rounding the corner, he pushed open the grand doors of the palace hall, purposely turning his head to avoid looking into the courtyard lying to his left. Despite his own malevolent ways, he feared the place. It was on the grounds of that majestic courtyard that the first blood was spilt. He witnessed what the dark desire for power could accomplish. To this day he could not relieve his mind of the image of the fallen Prince Ariston. If by chance, he dared to glance that way; he feared he would see the whole traitorous coup d'état play out. It was his own fear that imprisoned him and lured his allegiance to the darkness. It was that weakness that caused the inhabitants of this earth to loathe him as one of the most murderous traitors since the legendary Judas

Iscariot from another dimension. Today, however, he felt a renewed sense of purpose and inner strength emerging, overpowering all doubt and fear plaguing him since that night. Times had changed, and the encompassing power was different. It offered more options, yet there wasn't much freedom as each choice seemed to enslave you further into its purpose. Still, there were so many options. Things that had been forbidden in the previous establishment were now laid open to experience. It was a new world and you either embraced it or ended up merely existing hanging on to a feeble hope that could never stand against this certain kingdom. The only price for these new alternatives was peace. Chaos was growing, not necessarily in the city or the world for that matter but it was growing in the mind. At least it was in his. There was unrest, a murkiness that swirled inside his being. It drove him, promising the more he immersed himself the sooner it would settle. But it hadn't, so he continued to serve, no matter what it cost.

Approaching the entrance to the secret room, he gave the attendant an arrogant nod. The guard immediately pushed open the door, allowing him entrance. His determined walk through the room accelerated his steps, pumping the adrenaline through his body. Just as he expected the inner circle was there, awaiting his return and the news of the capture of Prince Asa, and the death of the Scribe. They waited with great expectation, prematurely congratulating one another on the success of the mission. Confident they would be partaking from the tree of life soon, stopping imminent death, allowing them to continue living forever.

"You're alone?" Blaine taunted from the table, "Where are the others?"

"With war there are casualties," he spit his venomous words back on the viper. Blaine was resentful of his new position and would revel in seeing him demoted so he could slip into his place. Blaine wasn't worth his time; it was he who was crossing the portal, taking the risk, doing all the work. It was his brilliant plan that was playing out; landing him the information he carried in his coat pocket. He focused his attention on Abaddon. The conversation at the oval table quieted as Elam approached.

"Your Liege," He bowed. His heart thundered inside of him as if it would suddenly leap from his chest.

Abaddon cast his fiendish eyes on him. A malicious calm gave expression to his face as he reclined.

"I only see you. I was expecting Travis and a corpse."

Elam swallowed hard more than anxious to deliver the news. He had no fear of not bringing Travis, for it was only a matter of time, considering the update on the situation, before Travis was in their midst.

"I am afraid it's only me at the moment. Nine fell and the others have remained behind for the time being. Travis is unaccounted for at the moment."

A roar of inquiry erupted from the oval table as the men hurled a multitude of questions upon him.

Abaddon raised his hand. A quiet hush fell across the room while Abaddon contemplated Elam's words. "I bestowed upon you the honor of guiding the council in how we were to acquire valuable information allowing us to locate the Scribe along with Prince Travis and the remaining heirs. In your scheming, you were to gain access to the second prophecy, as well as the hidden treasure, delivering the information to us before our adversary lay hold of it. So far, you have done nothing but lead our men to their deaths. I am pressed to believe you may be aiding our enemy more than us."

Elam's hand trembled with excitement as he pulled an item from his coat, passing it to Abaddon. "Behold your Scribe."

Keeping his cold stare upon Elam, Abaddon took the item from his hand. "You offer a picture when I have asked for a corpse?" A rumble of laughter echoed among the men at the oval table, Blaine's was the loudest.

Elam could care less what the ignorant men thought. Once Abaddon looked at the photograph, he would be placed over their charge then they would suffer greatly for their insolence.

"Take a look my Lord. I believe you will be pleased with what you see." Abaddon removed his threatening stare from Elam and glanced down at the picture in his hand. A disturbing smile curled at his lips, then turned sinister as his eyes swirled into milky white pupils. It was those moments when Abaddon himself seemed to disappear while something else took over. None of the men wanted to be in the chamber during these interactions, yet fear paralyzed them, fixing them to their chairs with no strength or courage to remove themselves from the nefarious presence.

"Do you know her whereabouts?" A voice that did not seem to come from Abandon, hissed through his mouth.

"I have someone on the inside. I have laid a trap." Elam's throat was dry, bulging as he spoke.

Silence.

Although fixed in their seats, the men shifted, uncomfortable with the looming presence. A spirit of chaos swept through the room, weaving amongst the chairs where the men reclined, yet they could not rest. Not with the manifestation of this heinous force, stirring their minds, and scrambling their thoughts. The feeling was torturous making them contemplate the notion of peeling the skin from their bodies, just to rid themselves of the oppression. Death would be a welcome relief. Still, they ground their fingers into the arm of their chairs and held their breath, waiting for the essence to pass. Seconds seemed like hours, minutes like eternity. And then, Abaddon's eyes returned, the emerald, green, dispelling the milky white pupils. Abaddon appeared different after each encounter. Sometimes he became weak, other times more empowered, and Elam wondered what power entered Abaddon in these moments and where it originated from. He had heard rumors, tales of primordial evil, that swept the universe, hunting for a host. He shuddered at the thought.

Abaddon recovered and motioned to the coveted chair beside him. "You have served me well. Come and sit. We must talk." Giving his attention to those gathered around the oval table, he addressed his elite. "Men, your directives have changed. There is a new assignment. Listen carefully to Elam. He is your superior, take heed of his instructions."

Chapter 16

WHO is it?" Jamia asked, pressing her ear against the door, trying to hear over the three Bichons yapping at her feet.

"Police."

Sliding back the bolt, she opened the door, welcoming the two officers into her home.

"Are you the woman who phoned in the emergency?"

She nodded, pulling her robe tight, "I am."

"You heard gunshots?"

"Well at first, I heard breaking glass. It woke me from a sound sleep. I was terrified." She placed a trembling hand over her heart. "We're not talking about a few dishes; it was loud, like several windows shattering all at once. I jumped out of bed hoping it wasn't one of mine and that's when I heard what sounded like a gunshot coming from next door."

"Just one?"

"No, there were two. I'm really worried." Jamia twirled the end of the sash around her fingers. "I've called my friend several times but she's not answering. Please go check on her. She is in the company of someone she said was her boyfriend, but I don't believe her. He's not her type. Plus, I noticed several bruises on her along with a fat lip."

"Okay, we'll check on your neighbor. What's her name?"

"Her name's Bronwyn, Bronwyn Sterling."

Jamia peered through her window watching the two officers disappear around the corner, hands poised on their holsters, their flashlights flooding a path, making their way over to the rental.

Nearing the condo, Officer Cook pulled the radio from his utility belt.

"We've got a homicide." He reported, his beam spotlighting a body lying motionless in the sand. "We're heading in and could use some backup."

Drawing their weapons, the officers mounted the steps. Cook rapped on the door, "Police!" All was silent. Keeping his gun held high, he pushed on the door, it opened. He cast his light around the room and groaned. "My God, it's a massacre."

Back up arrived almost immediately. Cook's superior stepped from his unmarked car, wanting a report.

Cooke shook his head. "Seven body count, one outside, three in the living room, two upstairs and one in the garage. All males, no ID on any of them and no sign of Miss Sterling anywhere. We found a gun on the bed and a car in the garage. Ran the plates, the vehicle belongs to Miss Sterling. The neighbor reported a man visiting her. I'm headed over there now to get more information."

Jamia waited, taking a break from her nervous pacing to peek outside, hoping to see Bronwyn walking up her path. The continuous howl of sirens frightened her, as more emergency vehicles appeared on the scene, their flashing lights pierced through her curtains, pulsating inside her condo like a discotheque. The sound of a helicopter joining the madness filled her with alarm. What could possibly have happened? Pulling back her curtain, she watched its high beam searchlight sweep across the beach. Her heart fainted within her telling her something dreadful had happened. Feeling helpless she sat quietly on her sofa, twisting her hands, and over petting her three dogs. Leaning against the soft cushions, she dozed off while she waited for news.

It was daylight when a quick rap at the door woke her from her restless sleep. She bolted nearly tripping over the three dogs. She swept her hand across the room inviting Officer Cook inside while quieting her Bichons. He took the offered seat on the floral sofa.

"My God it sounds like the end of the world out there," she said, holding her hand across her heart. "What happened? Is my friend okay?"

Officer Cook removed a small notebook from his pocket, "We're concerned about her safety. I need to ask you some questions, which might help locate her, if you don't mind?"

Jamia covered her mouth with her bony fingers, "She's missing?"

Officer Cook clicked open his pen, "Not sure if she's a missing person, however she wasn't at the condo. When was the last time you saw her?"

"Last night. She and her boyfriend, Dakota, I don't know his last name, were having dinner on the deck. I saw them walking down the beach, they got back home right before I went to bed."

Officer Cook scribbled down everything Jamia was relaying to him and nearly dropped his pen when she disclosed the information that the home was actually rented by the mega star Ryan Reese.

"Yes," her excitement grew; pleased to share the intriguing information that they were actually engaged and lived there together until Ryan broke it off last December.

Officer Cook looked skeptical, "I thought he was with Gabriella Mendez."

"I'm talking about before Gabriella." Jamia savored the fact that she was privy to such information. "He was engaged to Bronwyn. I can't imagine why he would trade such a sweet girl for the likes of that home wrecking whore Gabriella Mendez."

Officer Cook suppressed a smile, "What was the cause of their break-up?"

"Fame went to his bull head."

"Tell me about the man she is with."

Jamia began twisting her hands in her lap. "Between you and me, I didn't think he was her type at all. He sure was handsome enough, but there was something about him that didn't sit right with me. He was overly protective, and I noticed he kept his eye on her constantly. She seemed different too, like she was hiding something."

"What do you mean by that?"

"I don't know I can't put my finger on it but there was just something. Maybe she was hiding the truth about her boyfriend. She arrived with a swollen lip and bruises on her arms and legs. When I asked her about them, she blew me off." Jamia leaned forward and scooped one of her Bichon's in her lap. Her fingers trembled as she stroked the white hair. "She was going through her mail, and I noticed she became sort of overcome with a letter. We were talking and when she opened it, she lost all train of thought. She headed for her Bible and then showed it to Dakota, and they walked outside on the balcony and talked in private." Jamia blushed, "Now don't get me wrong, I usually don't read people's mail, but I snooped some, you know, to protect her. The letter was a code of some sort. It was from the Bible, the book of Habakkuk. I think the letter may still be lying on her desk."

Officer Cook wrote fast, detailing all of Jamia's information while she sat patiently, stroking her pet. She waited until he stopped writing and then asked. "So, can you tell me what happened over there?"

Clicking his pen closed, he replaced it and the notebook back in his shirt pocket. "There was a shooting."

"Oh," she paled, "Who was shot? Did she shoot Dakota? If she did, it was probably in self-defense."

"That's what we're trying to figure out." He paused a moment and then scooted closer to her before delivering his next piece of news. "Actually," he said tenderly so as not to upset her, "We discovered seven bodies in the condo."

"My God!" Jamia panicked, covering her mouth with both her hands. "Seven?" Her voice quivered with her words. "But I only heard two gun shots."

"The others had their throats slit," he spoke softly, attempting to downplay the grisly news. "If you feel up to it, I would like you to take a look at the bodies and see if you can identify any of them."

She nodded. Grabbing a tissue from the box, she dabbed at her tears, and continued to fill officer Cook in, telling him of the publisher Bronwyn wrote for, and how she recently resigned. She mentioned the White Ram Pickup they arrived in, saying she didn't know the plate number, but remembered the tags being from North Carolina. When she finished, Officer Cook led her outdoors.

The scene outside astounded her. Red and blue lights flashed against the lavender of the early morning sky, calling attention to the myriad of emergency vehicles surrounding the scene. Several vans with news station logos sat parked nearby. Reporters gripped their microphones, attempting to get an exclusive interview from one of the uniformed officers, as well as one of the plain clothed detectives, who were busy entering and exiting the condominium. Yellow tape surrounded the exterior of the home barring the entrance to the many onlookers standing around outside.

Jamia cinched the belt on her robe tighter and clutched officer Robison's arm as he led her through the frenzy, to view the seven fallen men.

Jamia shook her head in disbelief, "My God, seven people murdered...who in the world could they be, and what on earth does sweet Bronwyn have to do with it all?"

Chapter 17

I tried to clean up amid the filth and grime of the service station restroom. It was a futile effort, trying to remove dried sticky blood with thin paper towels and diluted liquid soap. Besides that, the only water temperature the dump restroom offered was ice cold. I glanced at my reflection in the faded mirror and nearly fainted. Blood from my busted nose covered half my face not to mention, the flesh and gray matter from the man Falcon shot. My knees buckled beneath me at the sight, I grabbed hold of the porcelain sink to keep from falling.

Pulling clean clothes from my suitcase, Falcon glanced my way, and then bolted for me before I fell. Grabbing hold, he turned me around to face him.

"Come on Scribe. You can do this, Stay with me here." He plucked off some of the remains of my assailant, flinging it across the dirty room. It was too much, I turned away hurling the remaining contents of last night's dinner across the floor.

Wasting no time, he pumped a handful of liquid soap and smeared it across my face. He followed with the rough paper towels removing as much of the gore as possible. Satisfied for now he tossed me some clean clothes, my toothbrush and toothpaste.

"Change into these and brush your teeth. You'll feel better. Make it quick, our ride should be here soon."

We'd driven for nearly two hours after leaving the condo, finally stopping at the deserted gas station. It had an outdoor restroom that could easily be broken into. Falcon grabbed my suitcase from the truck intending for me to discard my blood-soaked garments in the trash. He placed my phone, wallet, and the book into my travel bag. That was the sum of what we would be taking with us. The rest would stay behind along with Travis' abandoned truck.

He respectfully turned away as I peeled off the blood-soaked t-shirt clinging to my skin. I shivered in the coldness of the restroom and quickly dressed in a pair of jeans, a clean tank, and an oversized hooded sweatshirt of Falcon's he told me to wear. Once he heard the sound of running water, he turned back around, and while I brushed my teeth, he pulled my hair away from my face, fastening it in a sloppy ponytail. We accomplished our tasks quickly, and then sat on the suitcase, to avoid the grimy floor, waiting for Falcon's men to arrive. We remained silent, both lost in our thoughts. The only sound shattering the stillness of the dismal bathroom was the constant ringing of my cell. Every call was from Jamia. I silenced my phone, but still felt the vibration of it against my skin.

"I killed a man." I broke the quiet.

Falcon leaned against the painted cinder block wall.

"You killed in self-defense. He would have killed you first."

I thought for a moment, remembering the man's strange choice of words right before I pulled the trigger.

"I'm not sure he would have. He stopped his attack when he saw me. He told me I was coming with him. I was terrified, and didn't know what to do, so I shot him."

Falcon stood up fast, hitting the wall with his fist. I'd been around him enough to know when he was upset. I knew better than to ask, so I shoved my hands into the pockets of my hoodie and watched him pull a cigarette from his jeans and light up. Aside from his impertinent ways and bad ass exterior, I was beginning to see a real person buried somewhere deep inside. Just a couple of nights ago, at the ram-shackled home, he'd revealed an insightful side. Tonight, I watched him fighting with a passion, killing to protect me, while the hunger for retribution burned in his eyes. When the man grabbed me in the garage, he didn't waste a second. His aim was flawless, his motive resolute. He was a true warrior, yearning for the battle. He'd shown no fear in the fight, yet now, he was anxious. What did he know that he was keeping from me? I decided to tiptoe into the question.

"You weren't kidding about the enemy. Guess I finally saw them."

He remained leaning against the cold hard wall, blowing his smoke toward a small rectangular window near the ceiling. He took another long draw, narrowing his eyes on me.

I shifted my weight on the suitcase, and stared back, deciding to give it another shot.

"I'm glad I didn't do this trip alone. You were right. I wouldn't have survived."

He didn't finish his cigarette. Tossing it into the open toilet, he crossed the small room, and squatted down in front of me. He seemed to be choosing his words carefully. "Scribe, we haven't survived it yet. We left a mess back at the condo. Now we're going to be running from the law as well as Abaddon's men." He paused for a moment, as if he were engaged in an inner battle, fighting the urge to tell me something he shouldn't. My pulse quickened, and for the first time, I thought maybe I didn't want to know. I'd heard and seen enough and if there was something even more dire at play, then I'd choose the bliss of ignorance. He gave me a half smile as if he were reading my thoughts. Patting my knee, he stood. My heart faltered a bit, he'd decided not to say anything.

"Ride's here. Let's move."

Outside the service station restroom, a black SUV sat idling, headlights off, waiting for its passengers. Falcon raised my hood up, placing it over my head. Pulling his gun, he grabbed my arm and led me outside. I took a deep breath, replacing the putrid air of the dirty restroom with the dewy morning breeze.

The passenger door to the SUV opened. All I could see as Falcon pushed my head down was brown leather boots stepping out of the vehicle. Falcon ordered the man to open the back door. Satisfied, he placed his gun back in his jeans and pushed me into the back.

I sunk into the comfort of the soft leather seats, relieved. I was spent, exhausted, not to mention extremely sleep deprived. Raising my head, I lowered the hood shadowing my face and surveyed the two men up front.

I recognized one of them instantly as the man in the garden with Barak and Falcon the night Travis kissed me under the willow tree. He was strikingly handsome as were most of the men I had met from Eden. I couldn't see the driver's face; only his light lavender eyes that continued to gaze at me in the rear-view mirror. The blond man tossed me a bottle of water, "My name's Hawk."

I caught the water grateful for the drink. "Bronwyn, nice to meet you."

Hawk glanced at Falcon, communicating volumes through his eyes. Whatever it was Falcon was debating on telling me back at the service station was the unspoken elephant in the SUV. I didn't care, I was much too tired.

Hawk motioned to the driver, "This is Vulture."

He nodded, still looking at me from the rear view. Twisting the cap off the bottle, I took a long drink, wiped the dribble from my chin, and settled back for a much-deserved rest.

Vulture drove for several hours stopping only for gas. Falcon and I remained in the vehicle, keeping a low profile. Hawk brought snacks out to us along with the breaking news of the slaughter at Ryan Reese's condo. He said it was the subject of conversation everywhere. A wave of dread washed over me. Up until now I hadn't dwelt on the repercussions of the attack. My only thought had been escaping with our lives. My phone vibrated all morning annoying me to the point where I'd turned it off completely. I retrieved it from my travel bag. There was no tracking device on it, despite my mother and Bethany's endless attempts to share a location app with me. I always felt it was an invasion of privacy, so I refused to join their groups. I turned it on. It vibrated instantly with alerts of missed calls and text messages. I scrolled through the list. There were seven from Jamia, ten from my mother, six from Bethany, four from Ryan, two from Lillian, and several numbers I didn't recognize. I could only assume they belonged to law enforcement. The phone vibrated while in my hand, the caller ID on the screen said mother. My heart sank at the thought of what my parents might be going through. I sighed and showed it to Falcon. "Can I answer it? She's gotta be going through hell right now."

Falcon took the phone, "Answer it. Don't tell her anything other than you're alright."

I agreed. He put the phone on the speaker, placing it between us. "Hello."

"Thank God!" Mother screamed, unaware her voice filled the inside of the vehicle, "Are you alright?"

"I'm okay."

"Where are you?"

"I'm okay," I repeated.

"Where? Tell me where and I will come and get you myself!"

"I'm okay, momma."

"It's that all he'll let you say?" Mother's voice was in a frenzy. "This is all his doing, isn't it? I had a strange feeling about him, but I didn't want to say anything for fear of hurting you but now I wish I had. Can you get away from him at all?"

"Are you speaking with your daughter, Mrs. Sterling?" A masculine voice in the background interrupted her. There was a bit of static as the phone changed hands.

"This is special agent Betancourt. Am I safe to assume I am speaking with Bronwyn Sterling?"

Falcon pressed the key to end the conversation.

Chapter 18

I t was early afternoon when the black Suburban exited the main highway, taking a secondary road for at least another eight miles. I figured we were somewhere in New Mexico. I wasn't sure. I'd slept most of the day, waking only for moments at a time when we would stop for gas, or when Hawk thoughtfully brought us food and drink, sometimes surprising me with a coffee. Falcon didn't speak, at least not out loud. So, I slept, leaning against his hard frame. He never moved a muscle, allowing me to rest. In spite of the comforts they all provided me, I was anxious to leave the vehicle and be able to stretch having been riding in the same position for nearly twelve hours. Falcon informed me we were heading to one of the N.E.S.S.T's safe houses. I didn't know what to expect but hoped the place was big enough to shower and clean up the remaining gore, covering my legs and feet.

Vulture turned onto a narrow gravel road cutting across acres of lush pastureland. A herd of wild elk grazed nearby completely unaffected by the approaching vehicle. He drove another four miles before

I noticed a grove of trees directly ahead surrounding an adobe style estate. He stopped at a set of impressive iron gates, waiting for them to swing open. Once they bid him entrance, he followed the cobblestone driveway up to an extravagant two-story villa and parked out front. I emerged from my confined state, stretching, thankful to be standing after twelve long hours.

The late afternoon sun kissed my skin. The warmth felt wonderful, caressing my aching muscles, and thawing out the numbness from the Suburban's overworked air conditioner. The cicadas and crickets composed a grand welcoming song, resonating into a deafening volume, as all of nature came alive with the hums and fragrances of the earth. The place provided a soothing calm, as if all of creation yearned to comfort me during this trying ordeal. I longed to remain outside and enjoy this rare euphoria, but Falcon was already ushering me inside the manor.

The spacious living room offered a warm homey feel, also bringing a sense of calm. Rustic tile covered the floor, connecting to pale olive stucco walls. Dark leather furniture decorated the room, resting on plush throw rugs. A wide staircase led to an upper hallway, surrounding the open room on all four sides. Each side housed four doors all barring entrance to private chambers.

Hawk aimed a remote control at a piece of framed artwork above the fireplace. The scenic painting began rising, disappearing into the wall, revealing a television hidden behind it. Hawk switched the set on and leaned against the stucco wall.

My stomach dropped at the sight of my face plastered across the TV screen. An eager news correspondent stood outside the beach condo, clutching a microphone, informing all America of my personal affairs. Eagerly she spoke of my past engagement to mega star Ryan Reese and the miscarriage, which, in the reporters' opinion, was brought on by my extreme grief over Ryan's involvement with his alluring costar Gabriella Mendez. Just when I thought I couldn't be any more humiliated, the reporter spoke of a scandalous affair involving a married Inn keeper, Travis Colton of Moonshine. The correspondent continued to say that the Dodge Ram pickup registered to Mr. Colton was found abandoned near the Camp Pendleton Marine base in San Diego California, and they fear "the couple" may have crossed the border into Mexico. That bit of news satisfied Falcon, seeing that was his modus operandi in driving south and abandoning the truck where he did.

Mine and Falcon's faces split the screen, showing a picture of me and a composite sketch of Falcon. Before ending her report, the correspondent stated Falcon was considered armed and extremely dangerous. Then, she passed her story over to a news conference where eager reporters stood poised with flashing cameras, anxious to hear what megastar Ryan Reese would say concerning the matter. He'd called a press conference in an attempt to clear any blight on his name concerning the massacre at his condo. Entering the building, Ryan approached the podium, surrounded by his manager and attorneys. I crossed my arms in front of me as he gave his opening statement.

"Good evening," he said, his voice seeping in grief. "It is with much sorrow that I approach my public. I want to state that my deepest concern is with Bronwyn and her family during this difficult time. My prayers are that she is found safe and unharmed. My prayers also go out to the families of the seven men who lost their lives last night." He paused for a moment, biting his lower lip, as if attempting to hold back an onslaught of tears. Looking directly into the cameras he positioned his face in utter distress. "Bronwyn, if you can, please get away from this man who is holding you captive. I beg you." He sighed and turned his face away dabbing at an unseen tear. His emotional pause had the desired effect, drawing longing sighs, sympathy from the reporters and a ton of flashing cameras.

"I still love you babe, I really do, and I told you that less than two weeks ago. I would die if anything happened to you. I will come looking for you myself if that's what it takes."

His final statement incurred a round of applause from his adoring public. I rolled my eyes in disgust, sickened that he would use this to play on the emotions of his fans, trying to heighten his already booming career.

His attorney stepped forward, in a show of taking over for his grief-stricken client.

"I would like to state Ryan's complete innocence in the events that took place at the condo leased in his name. He has not lived at, nor been at the residence in over six months. He is presently working with law enforcement in their attempt to find Miss Sterling and apprehend the guilty parties. Ryan will now be happy to answer any questions that he is at liberty to discuss."

At that point a roar rose from the sea of reporters.

"Were you engaged to Miss Sterling when you became involved with Gabriella Mendez?"

Ryan took over the microphone, "No. We had already broken things off."

Liar.

"Do you know the man, Travis Colton, who Miss Sterling is alleged to be having an affair with?"

"No, I do not."

"Do you know the man she is with now?"

"No, I do not."

"Was Miss Sterling involved with drugs when you were with her?"

"Not that I was aware of."

Of course, I wasn't, you of all people should know that!

"It was reported that you took a trip to the town of Moonshine last week to see Miss Sterling. Any comments?"

At that question, Ryan's attorney took back over the mic. "His visit was strictly business, regarding a screenplay co-written by Ryan and Miss Sterling. The visit has no bearings on the events of last night's massacre."

One last reporter overpowered the sea of voices.

"Authorities claim that Moonshine is nothing more than a ghost town, a modern-day Roanoke. They found no one on their visit. Did you see a functioning town when you were there last week?"

They found no one? A modern-day Roanoke? The room began spinning and I felt as if I might faint. I cast a glance at Falcon. He was unmoved, still watching the report, unaffected by the disturbing statement of the reporter. How could an entire town of people disappear?

Falcon noticed the angst on my face, and finally released a pertinent piece of information. "After we left, Travis led the people underground. It's the only safe haven we have left."

I nodded and turned my attention back to the broadcast. "Ryan was there for only a few hours. He never saw a town, just a small Inn where Miss Sterling was staying." His attorney answered for him. More questions erupted from the sea of reporters, but his attorney had enough of the questions and turned away from the mic ladened podium signifying he was finished with answering speculative questions. Ryan waved to his many fans as he was quickly ushered out of the room. The story was promptly sent back to the newsroom desk. Two anchors, along with their expert guest, eagerly dove into the scandalous story, reporting their personal opinions and assumptions on whether I was indeed a victim or a willing party in the whole ordeal. Falcon aimed the remote at the TV turning it off. The scenic oil painting descended slowly hiding the screen again. An unfamiliar voice interrupted our thoughts.

"No reason to keep her identity a secret anymore, is there Falcon?"

I turned to the sound of the voice. A well-built man leaned against the far wall. He must have come into the room while we were engrossed in the news story. He too was extremely nice looking. His sun-streaked hair was combed away from his face revealing russet eyes. "Seems a lot of work for nothing, wouldn't you say?"

The way the man tauntingly spoke with Falcon put me on edge. He walked up to me, boldly taking my hand and kissed it gently as he bowed his head. "And after all this time, here she stands in the flesh. Our savior, and a beautiful one at that. Who would have thought."

I gave a slight smile as the tension began rising in the room.

"The name's Macaw."

"I'm Bronwyn."

He stared at me for a few minutes, a curious expression covering his face. "My God she doesn't know does she?" His voice bellowed across the room giving way to an amused laugh.

"Watch yourself," Falcon warned, his eyes like daggers on Macaw. His advice was quickly dismissed. "I think we should tell her. She deserves to know. After all, she has put everything on the line for us."

"I won't warn you again Macaw, Travis's orders." Falcon's threat seemed final on the subject.

Macaw wasn't convinced, "Seems Travis may be allowing his personal feelings to interfere." He continued to examine me, taking in my form, and boldly stretching out his hand. He stroked my cheek with his fingers. Feeling threatened, I pushed his hand away and cut my eyes over to Falcon.

"I'm sorry, I didn't mean to be so forward. It was just a touch to make sure what I was seeing was real. Our scribe, our savior in the flesh." He repeated. "One would want to touch that, don't you think?" Macaw moved his eyes from mine and turned his attention to Falcon. "I heard she found the second prophecy. Let's see it."

Falcon struck a match and lit the cigarette clutched between his teeth, "Can't, I burned it."

. "You burned it!" Macaw's anger revealed itself in his face as well as his voice. "Why? Information of that magnitude should be shared with everyone. What happened to accountability? We're supposed to be a team, remember?"

Falcon dismissed the reprimand, "True, but unfortunately I can't trust everyone."

"Is that why you murdered Oren?"

Falcon flicked his ashes in a nearby ashtray, unmoved by the accusation. "Oren switched sides. He knew too much and that made him dangerous. He made his choice."

Macaw wasn't satisfied, "Switched sides according to you. The execution should've been approved by all, not the sole discretion of one."

The tension continued to build. There was an obvious distrust between the two. I wasn't sure who Oren was or where the other men's feelings were on the matter. Hawk seemed to be irritated with Macaw as well. Vulture was harder to read. Others gathered in the room now. Some came from the rooms upstairs and were watching the scene play out from the open hallway. Others came from the kitchen, clad in aprons, wiping their hands on towels or holding utensils, their cooking on hold for now as each person seemed to have a vested interest in what was transpiring.

Falcon took a draw, nodding toward Hawk. "I had Hawk and Barak's approval on the matter, as well as Travis'. Care to dispute it?"

"They approved it on your word alone." Macaw argued, narrowing his eyes on Falcon. "I for one don't think Oren turned. I think he found out some things about you, like where you were all those years you disappeared for stretches of time. I think you killed him before he could disclose the information. Just like I think you burned it because the prophecy had information about the treasure."

Falcon blew a line of smoke into Macaw's face, "It's up to you what you choose to believe."

"I'm right, aren't I?" Macaw wouldn't relent. "It had information on the treasure, and you didn't want anyone else knowing so you burned it."

Falcon took another draw but remained silent. Macaw inched his way closer, "It's hard to trust someone who keeps secrets, Falcon."

I huffed an involuntary laugh.

"Then why do you do it Princess?" Macaw whirled around to face me. "Why put all your confidence in the hands of someone you don't know?"

He was right, in a way, but at present I knew more about Falcon than I knew about him. I shrugged, "I know him more than I know you."

This time Falcon laughed which only provoked him more.

"I think Oren discovered your secret. He knew where you went all those times on your private missions. So guarded, you even kept them from your own men. He was ready to reveal when you had him executed."

"Oren was caught carrying information about her," Hawk offered. "I was there, Falcon's right."

"You have proof to back that up?" Macaw challenged.

"Yes, we do." Hawk dispelled the suspicion.

"And you never wonder where Falcon disappeared to all those years? He comes and goes waltzing back, keeping noticeable secrets and everyone accepts him, open arms no questions asked."

"He had Travis' trust. That's all I needed." Hawk stayed loyal to his leader.

Macaw gave a sarcastic snort. "Abaddon had Travis' trust too and look where that got him."

This time it was Hawk who moved forward in anger, "Watch yourself Macaw, you're bordering on disloyalty."

"Me, bordering on disloyalty?" He shook his head in disbelief. "You've all been deceived." He backed off the accusation for now, taking another route. "I want to know what the prophecy said."

Falcon eyed the others in the room while taking a long draw off his cigarette. Expelling a line of smoke, he began reciting the prophecy; smoke billowing forth with each word.

"Draw your battle lines and prepare for war. The gates are opened, and all dominions have been released." He looked at Macaw as he quoted.

"Be diligent to know the truth and do not be swayed from what you know to be right. For some among you will be influenced by the darkness and join forces with the enemy, threatening your redemption. The betrayers have crept in unaware and are living among you. Wolves in sheep's clothing they are, eating at your tables, and then spying upon you when your backs are turned."

Falcon took another draw, this time cutting his eyes over to me.

"Be careful that you are not deceived. Their words will be convincing, they will offer pleasing and beautiful promises of knowledge and power, yet in the end, the only thing you will get for your allegiance with them is death." I swallowed. The room was quiet as Falcon's final words pronounced a sentence upon the guilty.

"That's it?" Macaw was skeptical. "I didn't hear anything about the treasure."

Falcon continued looking at me, as if he were reminding me of the calling.

"To the Scribe, pen your story. The beginning is yours. Follow your heart and you will preserve life. All depends on your ability to make the right choice. In time you will be led to the secret place. Enter without fear, it is there you will find the third book, and the third prophecy."

Macaw wasn't convinced. "And what about you princess, did you read it as well or did Falcon burn it before you were able to see it?"

Everyone stared at me, waiting for an answer that would sit right with them. A response that would no doubt qualify me or disqualify me for this mission. My reply could exonerate Falcon or condemn him. I shifted my feet, uncomfortable at their gaze. I decided on simply speaking the truth. "I asked Falcon to read it to me because the language was unfamiliar."

Macaw's sarcastic laugh echoed off the high ceiling. "So, neither you, nor anyone else actually read the prophecy, only Falcon? How do you know he interpreted what was on the paper?"

All eyes were on me again. Even Falcon's as he casually leaned against the wall, taking another inhale off his cigarette.

"Like I said, I couldn't read it, he could and if he is as disreputable as you say, he could have slit my throat and taken it anyway." My dislike for Macaw showed in my tone. "I'm kind of going into this blind and right now, he's my guide." Falcon gave a slight grin, watching the scene play out before him. His amusement in the situation angered Macaw. His eyes flashed as he took the conversation to a new level. "And what has he done to earn your undying trust, my sweet lady? Could it be that he too has fallen for you just as his brother did?"

"That's enough!" Hawk warned.

Falcon stood from his leaning position. His eyes flamed with anger. Vulture moved in on Falcon, while Hawk closed in on Macaw. My head began to swim. Macaw noticed my confusion and continued to press his luck. "Oh, let me guess, Falcon didn't tell you about his brother either? Seems there is a lot of information he's kept from you my dear. It's no wonder you trust him. Seems like he makes his own rules just like his notorious twin."

Falcon was eyeing Macaw. Vulture's hold on him was the only thing keeping him from pouncing. I struggled for clarity amid the bizarre accusations. Falcon has a twin? Who? The only person who'd fallen in love with me was Ryan, and he certainly wasn't Falcon's twin. Macaw read my face, "Are you intrigued my dear? I think she deserves full knowledge on the situation."

Falcon crushed the remaining piece of his smoke in anger, "She has no need of full knowledge when she doesn't have the wisdom to comprehend it. She can't know some things. It would be disastrous, not to mention deadly."

"According to Falcon!" Macaw addressed his comrades as if they were the jury and he was delivering his closing remarks. "Falcon quotes from a prophecy only he has read. He chooses to keep certain information from our scribe, deeming her unworthy, criticizing her ability to discern. Why would she have been chosen if she was inept? He is purposely trying to control her for his own benefit no less. We all know his brother betrayed Travis and I believe Falcon is betraying us!"

I paled at his words. His brother betrayed Travis.

Macaw noticed my surprise, "Oh yes. If you've seen Falcon, you've seen Abaddon. They are identical twins. It's quite difficult to tell the two apart. They look exactly the same, except for Falcon's nasty scar."

"I warned you." Falcon pulled away from Vulture and lunged toward Macaw. Hawk immediately moved in, positioning himself between the two, stopping an inevitable brawl.

Thoughts spun like a whirlwind. Macaw's statement caused the peculiar heat sensation to wrap its hot fingers around my throat. I stumbled backward. I'd been with Falcon for the past five days even sharing a bed while we slept, never knowing he was a blood relation to the man who was their mortal enemy. Why hadn't he told me?

"Falcon told me Abaddon gave him the scar." My voice rose above the scuffle. "Why would he do that if they were working together?"

"Abaddon did give him the scar." Macaw confirmed. "I never said they were working together. Disloyalty is in their nature my dear. Falcon made Abaddon believe he was on his side. Made us all believe he was on his brother's side. Then he betrayed him. Abaddon feared he might try and do it again and deceive the people posing as Abaddon himself, so he marked him. Now everyone knows the difference. Falcon is in this for his own benefit, he wants the same things his brother wanted."

I tried to soak it all in, muddling through the madness of it all. If information of this magnitude had been withheld, there would be no telling what other shocking revelations would bombard me over time. Macaw noticed my concern, "Come take a walk with me princess and I will give you all the knowledge you need to write your story. I find it appalling that he has purposely held back crucial information. He fears you having full knowledge. He knows if you were properly enlightened, you might not cling to him as you do." Macaw offered his arm. "What do you say Princess? Take a walk outdoors with me. I will shed quite a bit of light on everything."

The scuffle erupted again. Falcon's eyes narrowed in fury as he pushed against Vulture to get to Macaw.

"Don't go with him, Scribe. You're not ready to hear what he has to say."

"No!" Macaw yelled, "Falcon is not ready for you to hear what I have to say. Beware of those who keep secrets and speak to you in riddles, my love. They keep you confused so you will remain in their custody and place all your confidence in them." He extended his invitation again by nodding his head toward the glass doors leading to the patio. "Don't be afraid, it's just a simple walk my dear and you will know it all."

My mind raced with the possibilities. His invitation was intoxicating. I did want answers. I looked around the room. Vulture stood poised between Falcon and Macaw, his eyes seared into mine, yet his face was unreadable. He remained silent while everyone in the room anticipated my decision.

Falcon continued to push against Vulture, as if he would attack at any moment. His eyes cut into Macaw like daggers, and I wondered what he would do if I took Macaw's arm and headed outside.

"Why didn't you tell me Abaddon was your brother? You had plenty of opportunities. You told me so much of the story, why did you feel a need to leave that part out?"

His eyes flared and he looked at me in a way that took my breath away. "The pain in that confession is too much to bear. Death would have been a kinder separation."

I swallowed fighting the tightness in my throat. His confession resonated with my soul, evoking deep sorrow. I thought of the ram shacked house and how he'd seen it for what it used to be, and then I wondered if it was Abaddon he saw in the rubble. "The broken-down house. You saw him." I whispered. His eyes shuttered and his face went from rage to sorrow.

"Clever answer," Macaw mocked, oblivious to what Falcon, and I shared. He extended his arm to me once again.

I pulled my eyes away from Falcon's and turned them on Macaw.

"I remember a story of another Eden and someone offering a lady full knowledge. It not only destroyed her but everyone else as well. I have no desire to eat from your tree of knowledge Macaw. I'll wait and discover things on my own. And yes, I trust Falcon, I trust him with my life. You would be wise to do the same."

The silence in the room was deafening. Vulture released his grip, and I thought I saw a glint of an approving smile.

"You're making a mistake Princess" Macaw growled exiting the room. "You're all making a big mistake."

Chapter 19

After watching the special news report on TV, Bethany immediately packed her belongings and headed to the Sterling home, deciding to go offer comfort to Madison and Martin and wait with them for any news that surfaced. Now, she sat in the dining room, a small tape recorder between her and special agent Betancourt chronicling every word she spoke. First Detective Delane at her home, and now Betancourt. She'd seen movies where people sat in a small room being interrogated by the police, but never imagined she'd be doing it herself. What could Bronwyn have possibly gotten into? Stating her name for the record, she proceeded to answer all the questions Agent Betancourt hurled her way, starting with how long she had known Bronwyn and ending with their last week together in Moonshine. The forced trip down memory lane only caused her to miss Bronwyn, and the deep friendship they'd shared since fifth grade. Her heart ached at the thought of her missing, hurt or possibly dead.

"When was the last time you spoke with Miss Sterling?"

His question evoked feelings of shame. Bronwyn had wanted to talk with her less than a week ago, right before she left Moonshine, but she'd refused. She was angry, hurt and at that time cared nothing for what Bronwyn had to say. Besides, she wasn't sure she could trust her, feeling as if Bronwyn had been lying to her about things for some time. Now, considering the tragic turn of events, she wished she'd accepted her offer to talk.

"About a week ago, before we left Moonshine. We were on the front porch of the Inn, she took off. I thought she was going for a walk. She said she'd be back later and didn't return till five the next morning."

"Do you know where she went?"

Bethany took a drink of her iced tea. In all the years of their friendship, she'd never ratted out her friend, so to speak. They had covered for each other all through junior high, high school and beyond. In some way, she felt like a traitor revealing top-secret information. She had no desire to betray Bronwyn no matter how tense their friendship had become. Yet, if Special Agent Betancourt could use her information to help Bronwyn, it would be well worth her exposing some of her friend's deepest secrets.

"No, I can only guess. She'd become withdrawn and secretive recently. During our week in Moonshine, she would disappear for long periods of time. She would leave and stay out all night. Then she just up and quit her job without any notice."

"She didn't give a reason?"

"She told me she wanted to take a sabbatical and clear her head. But I think there was more to it than that. I think she wanted to stay in Moonshine because of Travis."

"Tell me about Moonshine."

Bethany sighed. She didn't know why the question bothered her, but it did. She'd become lost in the place, enjoying an unexpected vacation in a forgotten little Norman Rockwell town. In some ways she felt conned, comparing Moonshine to a befriended stranger you invited in, only to find out they robbed you blind while your back was turned.

"I'm not sure how to describe it. It's a strange place, that's for sure. We were all pretty apprehensive at first, but it ended up being one of the best places I've ever visited."

"What did you mean by it being strange?"

"I don't know, we were the only tourists there…it's pretty secluded. Looking back on it, it seems like a storybook town, you know…too good to be true." She sighed again, longer, and louder this time, trying to blow away the pain crowding into her heart. "Considering the turn of events, I guess it really was."

Betancourt smiled sympathetically, "How old would you say their eldest resident was?"

She was taken aback by the randomness of his question and laughed. "I don't know. I never really thought about it." Her mind did a quick scan of the previous week. Travis, Mavis, that Falcon guy all looked in their thirties, early forties, it was hard to tell. She thought of the days they were in town, and the people they interacted with. The manicurists, the waitress at the café, the people at the festival…

Her eyes met Betancourt's, "Come to think of it, there weren't any elderly people there. I'd say the oldest I saw was close to my age or maybe ten years older. That's kind of weird now that I think about it. Is that significant?"

He didn't comment, intending not to lose control of the interview.

"You said earlier you thought Bronwyn wanted to stay because she met someone. Tell me about him."

Bethany sighed, "Travis Colton, he owns the inn where we stayed." She felt dirty for the words but convinced herself she was doing Bronwyn a favor by exposing the ugly truth. "He's the towns' doctor too. He seemed pretty near perfect. You know the type, rugged, handsome, strong, silent, mysterious..."

"You said she would stay out late and sometimes leave during the night. Was she with Mr. Colton during these times?"

"Yes. I think so."

Retrieving a picture from his coat pocket, Betancourt slid it across the table.

"Is this Travis Colton?"

Bethany picked up the composite sketch of Falcon, "No. this is Falcon."

"Do you know him?"

"I never met him, but some of the local women in town said he was some kind of secret agent. I only saw Bronwyn with him once, and that was really weird to me because he frightened her for some reason." Bethany sighed again, dropping her face in her hands. "She told me she saw him kill a man in the garden one night. She said he slit the man's throat with a knife.... I feel bad now that I didn't believe her."

"Why didn't you believe her?"

"I don't know...it all sounded so absurd, and she had been acting so strange.... I just don't know."

Bethany was angry with herself. Why hadn't she believed Bronwyn? She, if anyone knew Bronwyn wouldn't lie about such a thing. Sure, Bronwyn did exaggerate the most mundane events, adding color and excitement to a boring story. It's the way she viewed life, and she described its events the same way. That is, until six months ago, when Ryan broke her heart. After that, she'd lost her edge, lost who she was, and the dramatic flair she added to every occasion was gone. Bethany became so accustomed to it that when Bronwyn told her of the strange goings on in Moonshine, she ignored her, buying into philosophies about the human psyche. "I heard on the news that the town is abandoned... The reporter compared it to a modern-day Roanoke. How could that be? There were thousands of people living there. How could they all leave so quickly?"

Betancourt closed his small journal, replaced the pen in his coat pocket and turned off the recorder before summoning Madison and Martin back into the room.

"That's what I'm trying to figure out.

Chapter 20

Madison and Martin joined Bethany in the kitchen, taking a seat at the table. Bethany's heart went out to the two. In all the years she'd known them, she'd never seen them looking so distraught. Madison was a wreck. She's been awake ever since the authorities called their home, relaying the dreadful news and asking for Bronwyn's whereabouts. From that moment on it had been nonstop phone calls and visits from the police, the FBI, and the media, not to mention their many concerned friends. Bethany felt privileged in the fact she was able to be inside the home with them, seeing they had turned away so many people, asking for complete privacy. Even now, the yard out front was filled with media, and other curious folk, staking out the place hoping for a glimpse of someone or a chance for an exclusive interview.

Bethany took hold of Madison's hand, squeezing it in reassurance. Madison offered a feeble heartbroken smile in return and squeezed back.

Betancourt opened his briefcase and pulled out a soft leather-bound book, laying it on the table. Madison gasped at the sight of it, her eyes wide with alarm.

"Where did you get that?"

"So, you do recognize the book Mrs. Sterling."

"Yes, but how did you.... It had been locked away...hidden...."

"It was left behind at the crime scene."

Madison looked as if she would faint. "How in the world...." Then, the realization hit. "Bronwyn asked if I had any of her old writings, I never dreamed she was speaking of this one...she was supposed to have forgotten."

"Forgotten what Mrs. Sterling?"

Silence...Madison stood abruptly, leaving the table, as if to put as much distance as possible between her and the book. Leaning over the sink, she dropped her face into her hands and sobbed. Martin left the table to comfort his hysterical wife.

Confused at Madison's sudden display of anguish, Bethany glanced at the cover of the handmade book reading the title: Moonshine.

Fear gripped her, she wanted to scream and wake up from his crazy nightmare. Better yet she wanted to give herself a good kick in the ass for sulking, falling asleep and allowing Bronwyn to get lost and drive them straight into the twilight zone.

Betancourt didn't waste a minute, refusing to allow Madison's suffering to delay his investigation.

"Where did your daughter get this book?"

Martin took over for his distraught wife. "Bronwyn wrote it when she was ten."

Betancourt leaned back in his chair, eyeing the Sterling's. No one said a word and the tension grew thick. Opening his briefcase once again, he pulled out another small book encased in a type of Plexiglas box and laid it on the table. The pages were yellow, sticking beyond the border of the antique cover. The worn leather cover bore the faded title: Moonshine. Confusion masked their faces.

"What's that?" Martin asked, guiding Madison back to the table.

"This is the original book of Moonshine, written by an unknown author over six hundred years ago. It's one of the oldest mysteries in the literary world, competing with the Voynich manuscript of the early 1500's. The author remains a secret to this day. The book is filled with cryptic passages identical to the ones in the book your daughter wrote."

He opened Bronwyn's handmade book of Moonshine. Madison gasped in fear when he did. He eyed her suspiciously.

"What frightens you about this book, Mrs. Sterling?"

Madison clutched the tissue in her hand. "You open the book, and you unleash the terrors within it."

Bethany paled at her words. She'd met Bronwyn when she was eleven and never heard of this book. Neither Bronwyn nor her parents had ever mentioned it. She desired to skim through the pages, but Betancourt kept a tight hold on it, thumbing through to the back cover.

Pulling back the soft leather binding he revealed an empty pocket.

"Do you happen to know what was hidden inside the cover?"

Madison and Martin exchanged glances.

"No, we don't," Martin nodded, "We never noticed that before. Bronwyn kept the book to herself."

Betancourt sighed and tapped the glass case protecting the antique book. "So, you tell me Mr. and Mrs. Sterling, how could a ten-year-old little girl write a book, word for word, identical to a six-hundred-year-old novel she has never seen?"

"Bronwyn loved to read; maybe she had read it before." Madison's reasoning was far-fetched.

"Impossible. This is the only copy in the entire world."

Martin cleared his throat, "I know this investigation is not about plagiarism, so you wanna tell me what you're getting at?"

Betancourt's grin didn't quite set right with Bethany. "I think you already know Mr. Sterling. Now... do you want to tell me something about your daughter?"

Madison leaned into her husband for support and closed her eyes. Tired and defeated, she whispered, "Tell him Martin."

Martin held her close, kissing the top of her head. "Are you sure hon? We vowed to never speak of it."

Bethany' took a swallow of her tea, hoping to relieve the tightness in her throat. What secret about Bronwyn could they have vowed to never speak of? Fear gripped her and as much as she wanted to run out the back door, covering her ears screaming, another part of her knew she must hear what they had to say.

Tears escaped Madison 's eyes, trickling down her cheeks along with the little bit of mascara still remaining on her lashes.

"That was before. I don't see how we can avoid it. Besides, if it helps Bronwyn in some way, I think we should tell what we know."

Bethany finally found her voice, "For what it's worth, I think this is off the record. Agent Betancourt purposely left his recorder off. I think maybe whatever you say can't be held against you right now." She looked at Betancourt, "Am I right?"

His eyes sparked at her observation, "She's right. Whatever we speak in this room will never be uttered outside of these walls."

Chapter 21

After Macaw's confrontation downstairs, Falcon escorted me up to the guest room so I could clean up. The room was nice, rivaling any five-star hotel suite, complete with an adjoining balcony, a private restroom with a sunken bath and separate shower. As much as I would love to relax in a tub of warm water and soothe my aching muscles, I decided on a shower. I would scrub off the blood and gore that had long since dried and let the remains of the deceased disappear down the drain.

Grabbing a loofa, I emptied an entire bottle of creamy soap on my legs and with fury began scrubbing at the dried blood, not allowing my mind to dwell on the grisly events of the past twenty-four hours. Neither would I think about Ryan's little press conference or the fact that my private life was now a public spectacle being scrutinized and judged by everyone. Tears spilled from my eyes, mixing with the tepid water as I forced the mental pictures out of my head. Instead, I had something new to mull over and the thought of it intensified my scrubbing. Macaw mentioned a treasure. That was the first time I'd heard about it. Barak, Travis, nor Falcon ever mentioned treasure of any kind. Yet Falcon knew exactly what Macaw was referring to. I hoped this entire quest didn't boil down to a massive hunt for gold with everyone turning into aggressive marauders, killing for their share of the booty. If so, I was out. Even though I stood up to Macaw giving my allegiance to Falcon, there were still doubts, especially since the chilling disclosure of Abaddon being his twin brother. Why didn't he or Travis reveal that piece of information? Something wasn't right, and with the doubt came the memory of Falcon's caution back at the diner.

"I know you don't trust me and I'm warning you now; there will come a time when you trust me even less. If at that time, you react by what you see, all could be lost."

Maybe he was referring to the time when I would find out about him and Abaddon. Sighing, I rinsed the foamy soap from my legs. Trust was such a hard thing, especially when there isn't much evidence to warrant it.

After making sure there were no traces of the gore between my toes or anywhere else, I lathered my hair, clawing my scalp, so as to remove any remaining pieces of gray matter left from the assailant's brain. I shuddered at the thought, nearly gagging in the shower. Following up with a creamy conditioner, I rinsed and then twisted my ebony locks, wringing out the water.

Shutting off the faucet, I opened the fogged door and reached for a towel, only to see Falcon standing in the doorway holding it. Startled, I stepped further behind the cloudy pane to hide my nakedness, although it was too late. I am sure he's seen everything, and there went the trust issue again.

Discreetly taking the thirsty towel, I wrapped my wet body and stepped from the shower. My hair was pulled completely away, revealing the totality of my face. Falcon's attention remained on me as I chose a sweet-smelling lotion from the basket and then gracefully rubbed the creamy substance on my legs; oblivious of how sensual I appeared. He turned away. "Put some clothes on, dinner's waiting on the balcony." He said as he left the bathroom.

A few minutes later, dressed in jeans, a tank, and smelling like sweet potions from the basket, I sauntered out onto the balcony delighted to see a hot meal. Falcon ordered the food from the kitchen while I showered, specifying certain foods so I could eat a healthy meal. I was happy he did. We still had at least two days to go before returning to Moonshine and the safety of the Citadel. I would need nourishment and ample rest if I were to make it back, dodging Abaddon's men, the authorities, and a swarm of media.

Settling down in a comfortable lounge chair, I dove into my dinner of broiled fish and steamed vegetables.

"So, there's a treasure?" I brought the subject up after taking a bite of tilapia.

Falcon nodded while chewing but offered nothing more than a nod of his head.

Cutting the tender fish with my fork, I asked another. "And you never mentioned it because?"

Shrugging he swallowed his water before answering, "Does it matter?"

"Maybe," I stabbed at my carrots. "It kind of puts a new twist on things. I don't mind aiding a cause that will put the proper people back in power. However, I have no intention of putting my life at risk so someone can get rich."

Falcon popped a carrot in his mouth and grinned, "Money means nothing to me Scribe."

I eyed him closely, "Were there clues about the treasure in the prophecy?"

He grinned again but said nothing and I knew I wouldn't get any more out of him than that.

Frustrated, I pushed my plate aside and stood. "I'm done, I'm going to bed."

He caught my arm as I brushed past and pulled me down to his lounge chair, "I thought you said you trusted me."

I let out a sarcastic laugh, "I want to, God, I really want to but..."

"There shouldn't be any buts, Scribe. Trusting is a choice, either you do, or you don't."

"You seriously think you've earned it?"

He swallowed another drink of his water. "I'm not going to perform for you the way you want me to. I have my reasons for the choices I make."

"And I have my reasons for doubting."

"No, you don't."

His audacity appalled me. "Put yourself in my shoes, Mr." My tone was harsh. "My life has just been ruined. Talk about trust...I've more than likely lost the trust of my parents, my friends, people I don't even know. Everyone thinks I've had an affair with Travis..."

"Did you?"

Painful self-consciousness blossomed in my cheeks, turning them a deep crimson. I felt the heat and knew he noticed.

"No, I didn't. I thought he was married to Mavis."

Falcon laughed out loud at that disclosure.

"So, you would have...if you'd have known?"

My cheeks continued to flame, and I knew my eyes could not keep a secret, so I pulled away from his clasp, grabbed my ice water and began chug-a-lugging. I wasn't thirsty, but the glass made a great barrier, blocking my tale-tell expression from his view. Laughing, he rose from his chair, removed the glass from my hand and wiped the dribbles off my chin. Amusement teemed in his eyes.

"So, are you trustworthy? Did you act on your feelings?"

"No, I didn't act on them, it wouldn't have been right."

His impish grin began in his eyes and continued across his lips.

"But Bethany thought you did."

"Bethany assumed. She should have trusted..."

I stopped cold, "should have trusted" my own words firing back at me.

Falcon's grin went from impish to tender, "Assumptions can land you in a world of trouble. Money means nothing to me. There are other riches, however, worth guarding. You, for example, are such a prize. The prophecy did give another clue. It stated that only the Scribe can uncover the treasure, only you will know where to look." He was quiet for a moment and then locked his eyes with mine. "There is already a mark on you, can you imagine the heightened urgency to find you if that information was leaked?"

I lowered my eyes, ashamed until his next disclosure brought them back up even with his.

"When I read the prophecy to Travis, he asked me to burn it. It was his idea...to keep you safe." I felt ignorant, and somewhat like Bethany, annoyingly demanding information, and answers of things too complex for me to understand.

"I'm sorry."

He stared at me for a moment, and I wondered what he must be thinking but I wouldn't make any assumptions this time. Giving me a slight wink, he escorted me back to my chair. "Finish your dinner; you're going to need your strength."

Hawk joined us out on the balcony just as the sun dipped behind the horizon, painting the sky in hues of deep amber. He arrived with a second cart loaded with desserts and hot tea. As enticing as the pastry tray appeared, I bypassed the sweets and offered Hawk my share. Although it was still early, I was tired and ready for bed. I hadn't gotten much sleep over the past few days, and now after taking a relaxing shower and having eaten a hot healthy meal I was ready to turn in.

"I'm going to bed, should I set an alarm?"

Falcon lit up a cigarette. "No, sleep as long as you like. We'll leave tomorrow after we're well rested."

Relieved, I said goodnight and disappeared into the room, throwing myself onto the welcoming bed. I felt completely safe knowing Falcon and Hawk were on the balcony, keeping watch. In a matter of seconds my body gave in to deep sleep.

***

Falcon watched her disappear into the room. Macaw's little display had him on edge and although they were hidden at the safe house, he couldn't lower his guard completely.

Hawk noticed his apprehension. "Don't worry. I'll keep watch tonight. You need your rest too or you'll never make it back."

He was right and Falcon knew it. He was tired, exhaustion was setting in for existing on less than two hours of sleep in the past three days. If he didn't get rest, he feared he might not be able to save the scribe should there be another assault. And he knew there would be, it was just a matter of time. Being at the safe house with a few of his men enabled him to relax some, but still, his instinct wouldn't permit total rest.

"You think Macaw's switching his allegiance?" Hawk asked, lighting up.

Falcon took a bite of his strawberry shortcake, "No. Macaw would never switch sides. He lives for revenge and hurts over Oren's death."

Hawk slid Bronwyn's cake over to him, while clutching his cigarette between his fingers. "He just doesn't trust you or the rest of us for the matter. He's somehow got it in his head that we have started our own regime and that makes him dangerous."

"Falcon blew a line of smoke. "He's talking with someone; they're playing with his mind. Find out who it is."

Hawk agreed. They smoked a few more cigarettes, while discussing the best way to sneak past the media and authorities and deliver Bronwyn safely to the Citadel. The men in the N.E.S.S.T knew the woods well, having survived in them for the past six hundred years. It would be no problem trekking through the Appalachians; the main concern was getting to that point.

Crushing the butt of his cigarette, Falcon poured the tea which they finished off while discussing their plans for the next day's travel. "I'm turning in. My mind is too tired. We'll resume this discussion tomorrow."

Standing, Falcon stumbled, bumping into the patio table, knocking over his empty tea mug. The trees in the distance began circling the patio like a fast-paced carousel, throwing him off balance. Bracing himself against the railing, he tried focusing but his surroundings whirled around him, and his vision began to tunnel.

"Damn it!" He grit his teeth in anger, clutching the rail for support. This was not the result of sleep deprivation but rather a powerful sedative, no doubt, slipped in his tea. Still gripping the banister, he turned to face Hawk who'd brought up the dessert cart, surely...

The tea was having the same effect on Hawk. He hadn't drugged him but that brought little comfort. Someone was working a plan and he feared the outcome. The only consolation was the Scribe hadn't drunk her tea. If she used her wits, she may have a chance. Trying to focus, he stumbled toward the bedroom. Teetering sideways, he bumped into the dessert cart, toppling it over.

"Sh-sh, quiet now or you'll wake sleeping beauty." A sarcastic voice taunted from the doorway. Falcon's lips snarled upward. Elam!

Falcon lunged forward, Elam pulled a gun, shooting Hawk in the chest. The effect of the tranquilizer numbed his senses but the sight of Hawk falling onto the floor, staring up into the night sky, wide eyed in death sent a rage through Falcon rivaling the fury he felt the night his brother murdered Ariston. His rage fought against the sedative diluting the effect long enough for him to ball all his ferocity into his fist, striking Elam in the jaw. Elam recovered quickly, placing his weapon against Falcon's thigh, and fired. It was enough to send him to the ground. Two of Elam's men entered the balcony. One hoisted Hawks body off the ground and the other jerked Falcon to his feet, pushing him into the bedroom. Despite the sedative, pain detonated down his leg, shattering what little strength remained.

"Take them below," Elam ordered his men.

Falcon took a final glance at Bronwyn, sleeping peacefully in her bed. Her hair was swept away, fanning across her satin pillow, revealing the beauty of her face. Her long lashes rested high on her cheek bones, and he wondered what dreams and visions were transpiring behind her soft lids. His lips formed a crooked smile. Behold their scribe; who'd have ever thought? Things were not exactly as he expected and the mystery surrounding her caused many suspicions. He knew what it was like to be misunderstood. He was an enigma himself. True, he could spend countless hours defending himself, giving examples of his loyalty, releasing the secrets of his time missing in action, where he was and what he was doing, but he chose not to. He rather his life authenticate his character. Time would tell his true story and only those who walked shoulder to shoulder with him, looking past the facade would be able to read it.

Scribe's refusal to allow Macaw to enlighten her impressed him and her affirmation of his character was touching. Up until then he figured she loathed him, clinging to him solely out of fear and the need to survive. She was developing in her role of redeemer but in his opinion, still had a way to go. She remained weak and fearful and completely oblivious to the evil ways of the darkness. She didn't understand the spiritual war that fueled the physical one and therefore was apathetic to its power. That, in his opinion, was the most dangerous aspect of the entire quest. She was a good person, yet she never spoke of God or any belief system of any kind. He knew from first-hand experience you can't remain neutral in a supernatural war. When the battle line is drawn across your soul, your heart will choose a side and that side depends on who you really are. Behind the skin, buried beneath the façade of her earthly personality, there was a persona that needed to surface. It would take cataclysmic events for it to emerge. He closed his eyes at the thought. Devastation reveals true character. The decisions a person makes under severe pressure screams of who they really are and is the only thing that will start the transformation. He sighed; her identity would emerge because she would go through hell soon.

"Don't worry," Elam consoled Falcon. "She'll sleep through the entire journey."

Falcon struggled to stay conscious; he was fading fast. Even in his weakened state he could still best Elam, yet he dared not try. Not with

Elam's men in the room and one with the barrel of his gun pointing straight at Bronwyn's pillowed head. Elam sneered, noticing Falcon's contemplation on the matter.

"You make one move toward me or anyone in this room and she's dead. Abaddon will be disappointed but, in the end, I believe he will understand. There are casualties of war you see, and for a while her demise was the objective. Although, being who she is has changed things. Still, if victory demands a sacrifice, then a sacrifice she will be."

The arrogance in Elam disturbed Falcon; he saw the same pride growing in his brother over six hundred years ago. It is a fast-spreading cancer, devouring humility, contaminating the mind and spirit until the person is a hollow shell of who they used to be. It is the prevailing weapon of the darkness. He could only imagine what the city of Eden was like now if that same arrogance was the pervading characteristic in the governance.

"You've changed Elam."

Falcon's accusation guilted his betrayer. His dark eyes were daggers, cutting through Elam's pretense, exposing the cowardice that propelled his friend into settling for the best he could get from the darkness instead of having the courage to fight for what was right, even if it seemed to be a losing battle.

"Times have changed my friend. You either embrace it or you get swept away. It's a shame you couldn't adopt your brother's way of life, the two of you together would have been great. He wanted you as his right-hand man, supporting his cause, ruling with him, governing the masses. You led him to believe you would, but in the end, you betrayed him, and I don't think he'll ever recover from that pain."

The stare down between the two men was intense. Elam backed away first, having the most to hide and fearing Falcon could see into the depth of his tainted soul. Motioning to his men, he nodded toward the door.

"Get him out of here. We're wasting time. Let her sleep, she's not going anywhere."

Falcon kept his cold stare on Elam, all the while knowing it unnerved him almost to the point of remorse. Exposed guilt is a volatile weapon and can be used to your advantage or can backfire wounding the person aiming the missile. In this case Elam's final words on the matter caused it to backfire.

"He loved you once and maybe you could have stopped him before he went too far, instead you left...you left us all."

Elam's pronouncement of guilt hit hard. Falcon spent the better part of six hundred years reliving the what ifs of the situation. He had done what he'd done. His objective was to remove Travis from Abaddon. If Abaddon continued to partake of the tree of life, then he would live forever in his present condition, and that was something Falcon could not allow to happen.

Elam's men shoved him into the hallway, he hobbled, the pain in his leg excruciating. Every agonizing step caused him to walk a tightrope between reality and unconsciousness. If the gunshot wound didn't take him under, the sedative would. Regardless of the haze filling his head he must think fast. He had one last idea. He'd tried it before but to no avail. He was going down and would no longer be able to protect the scribe. Now, with nothing to lose, he tried it again, praying it would work this time. As the men shoved him down the hallway, he tried summoning Bronwyn with his mind.

Chapter 22

Bronwyn is adopted?" Bethany's eyes widened at Martin's confession, "Seriously, she never told me that."

"Because she doesn't know." A look of guilt spread across his face, "We decided never to tell her."

"Why?"

Martin took a sip of his coffee before answering, "Because there is no record of her birth or birth mother."

Betancourt was intrigued. "No record anywhere?"

"No, and we searched for a long time," Madison interrupted her husband, trying to justify their decision. Martin took his wife's hand, holding it in reassurance. "Thirty-three years ago, we took a camping trip to the mountains. On our last night there, a deadly storm hit. It was terrible, unexpected and like nothing we'd ever seen. We hunkered down in our motorhome, praying we'd survive. The next morning the campsite was nearly gone. We hiked around the area trying to retrieve as many of our things as we could."

"That's when I found Bronwyn," Madison interrupted. "At first, I thought she was a toy doll, washed away by the storm. I reached over to pick it up, and to my astonishment she cried. She was naked, abandoned; there wasn't a blanket or anything. She seemed only a few hours old, but there was no umbilical cord, nothing. Other than being covered in mud, she seemed unharmed and healthy. We combed the entire area, it was abandoned. No one was searching for a lost child."

"Madison and I couldn't have children," Martin swallowed, taking back over the story. "We prayed and prayed for a child, but we never could conceive. We figured this was an answer to our prayers. We did an extensive search and still didn't come across any record of her birth or reports of a lost child. She was a mystery."

Bethany shook her head, "This is crazy! And Bronwyn doesn't know any of this?"

"No, we never told her because we didn't adopt her legally. We were afraid if she knew she might want to locate her birth mother and that could have caused us a lot of legal problems."

Martin refilled Betancourt's mug, "We were such a happy family. There wasn't a need to upset things. She was the light of our life, our gift from heaven."

Madison played with the tissue in her hand; and with her head bowed, continued the story.

"It wasn't long before we realized she was extremely gifted. Music came so easy to her. When she was very young, she would sit down at the piano and play the most amazing pieces. I don't know how she did it; without any lessons at all. She was very creative and had a vivid imagination. She could tell the most amazing stories and would entertain us every evening with a new one."

Bethany smiled at the recollection. Bronwyn did have a special way of telling the most colorful stories.

"When she was ten, she told us she wanted to write a book," Martin said. "We encouraged her endeavors realizing that she was truly a gifted child. But as she wrote she became consumed with the story, and in some strange way, it seemed as if the story began to devour her too."

Sorrow hollowed itself in Madison's face. Bethany had never seen her so distraught, and the thought of this family hiding such secrets all these years unnerved her to the point of wondering if she knew the truth about anyone. All these shocking disclosures were taking their toll.

"She began having nightmares," Madison said, still twisting at the tissue in her grip. "She'd wake up screaming and crying. There was nothing Martin or I could do to console her. She kept insisting she was lost and needed to go home. She began to believe the characters in her story were real; people that she was responsible for saving. She began to withdraw from everyone and dwelt only on her story. Her grades started dropping and sometimes she would write in a different language."

Betancourt was leaning across the table now, "What language?"

"It was an unknown dialect. When we confronted her about it, she said she didn't remember doing it, nor could she interpret what she wrote."

Bethany was stunned, not believing what she was hearing, "And you never found out what the language was?"

"Never."

Bethany's heart fell into the pit of her stomach as a haunting terror began growing inside of her. Just when she thought she couldn't take anymore Madison continued, adding to her anxiety.

"Things began to get much worse, so we insisted she stop writing her story. She fought us over it and begged to finish it until other frightening things began to take place."

"What kind of frightening things?" Betancourt asked and Bethany wished he hadn't.

"She began sleepwalking. We found her several times in the attic, in deep conversation with people she referred to as Pravuil, Tiponi and Ha'Amon. Of course, we didn't see anyone there, and when she woke up, she didn't either."

"I did a little research on the name Pravuil," Martin said. "Get this; Pravuil is referred to as one of the seven highest angels. This archangel writes all the deeds of God and is keeper of the books in heaven. He supposedly instructed Enoch of the Bible, and we all know what happened to him."

"I don't," Bethany confessed. "Although I'm not sure I want to know."

Betancourt smiled at her apprehension, "He disappeared one day. No one ever saw him again. It's believed God took him to heaven."

"Like, beam me up Scotty." Bethany tried to release some of the tension.

"More like down a rabbit hole through a portal door." Betancourt spoke as if his disclosure made perfect sense.

Bethany sighed, "Great."

Martin reassured Madison, patting her on the arm, "We're going to find Bronwyn honey, don't you worry."

She shook her head and began to cry. "Martin, the entire damn town has disappeared. They're comparing it to Roanoke and to this day that mystery has never been solved. How are we going to find our daughter?"

Bethany rose form her chair and knelt beside Madison to console her. Betancourt allowed the women to grieve, aiming his words at Martin. "I know it's tough, but we must continue; if we are going to find your daughter, I need all the information I can get."

Martin agreed, "There's not much left to tell. Bronwyn agreed things were out of control, so she stopped writing. She gave the book to us but made us promise we wouldn't destroy it. And personally, I didn't think we should. For some reason, I honestly felt this was some sort of piece to the puzzle of the mystery surrounding her. Instead, we locked it away."

"So, she never actually finished it?" Bethany asked.

"No."

"So how does that compare to the other book? How does it end?"

Betancourt 's eyes danced with intrigue, "They both stop at the exact same place. It was never finished either. That is one of its mysteries... and besides that, the publisher is unknown as well."

Bethany rested her face in her hands for a few seconds before speaking. "My God, Bronwyn never told me any of this and I met her only a year later."

Martin stood to retrieve the box of Kleenex for his wife.

"By then she had forgotten all of it. Honestly not less than two weeks after we took the book away, she was back to normal and never spoke of the story. The nightmares and sleepwalking stopped. We got our lives back. I honestly think she had forgotten all about it. She hasn't spoken of it since the day we locked it away."

Bethany shook her head, "Unbelievable. Wonder what in the hell caused her to remember?"

Betancourt replaced the antique book in his briefcase along with the one Bronwyn wrote. His actions implied the interview had come to an end.

"So, what's next?" Martin asked.

Betancourt snapped his briefcase shut, "I'm headed to Moonshine to do some investigating." He pulled his card from his coat pocket. "I'll be in touch. If you think of anything, give me a call."

Betancourt stood and Martin shook his hand. "I have a question if you don't mind me asking?"

"Go ahead," Betancourt agreed.

"If that's the only copy in the world, how did you get a hold of it? Where did it surface?"

"Off the record?" Betancourt asked.

Martin nodded.

"It's a family heirloom; I found it at my great grandmother's, buried in the spring house on her property. It belonged to my great grandfather, Haytham.

Chapter 23

Scribe wake up! Get out of here, now!"

I stirred, rousing at the command. The urgency in Falcon's voice warranted a sudden leap from the bed, as I feared a reenactment of last night's harrowing escape. The room was dark except for the silvery glow of the moon filtering through the window. I looked around, all seemed calm; Falcon wasn't in the room. I sighed, relieved. I must have been dreaming, reliving the events of last night. My heart quieted. The clock read 10:46 PM, and I wondered where he was. Last I saw him he was smoking on the balcony with Hawk.

Yawning, I opened the French doors leading out to the balcony, welcoming the gentle breeze. The stars were brilliant, scattering across the expanse, like jewels displayed on black velvet. It was dark, quiet, and peaceful. The only sounds were nature driven, a chorus of croaking frogs, chirping crickets and the occasional howl of a coyote, in the canyon below. From where I was standing it was hard to believe I'd been a part of a massacre less than twenty-four hours ago. Yet despite the tranquility of the moment, I felt bedlam brewing not far away. Something wasn't right. And then I noticed the overturned tea cart. Was it overturned? I couldn't tell in the darkness. I tiptoed out on the veranda. Yes, it looked as if it were laying on its side. My foot kicked the tea kettle and my toes slipped in liquid. It was too sticky to be tea. Honey, perhaps. I stooped and touched the substance, then brought my fingers to my face. Blood!

"Scribe!"

I whirled around, but he wasn't there. His voice was loud but coming from no particular direction. I wasn't dreaming. Maybe he was yelling a warning from below. I ran to the railing and slipped in another pool of the sticky substance. My heart raced as I leaned over the balcony and scanned the area, it was empty. I ran back inside, and peeked out the door, over the hallway balustrade and down into the living area.

"Falcon?"

The room remained dark, quiet, and peaceful. Still, I couldn't shake the premonition and despite the calm I sensed a disturbance. Where was he? He'd called twice now, both times with urgency.

"Scribe! If you can hear me, get out of there." I stopped at the bottom of the staircase and whirled around, looking in every direction, every dark corner but came up empty. Where was he? "Falcon?"

Silence filled the empty room; no one was there. My pulse quickened, dread screamed a forewarning, something was definitely wrong. What to do? Falcon's call said to get out of here, but where was I to go, and how? I wasn't leaving without him that was for sure.

"Falcon?" My voice was scarcely a whisper. Again, no answer. He had to be close by. His call was strong, why wouldn't he answer me? I stole across the room. The manor was immense and unfamiliar which put me at a disadvantage. To add to my handicap, it was dark and unlike the others, I did not have the benefit of night vision. A chill snaked up my spine at the thought of the enemy, watching me from the shadows, ready to pounce. I took a deep breath and exhaled slowly, trying to calm my stampeding heart while I contemplated my next move. Think Bronwyn, think! The kitchen was visible from the living area. I'd go there and find a knife for protection...just in case.

Moving quickly, I hurried to the kitchen. It too was oversized, restaurant style. The moon, high in the sky, shined its beams through the massive picture windows, bouncing off the two, spotless, stainless-steel refrigerators, giving a narrow pathway of light. I snaked in between the countertops, quietly opening and closing utility drawers, searching for a suitable knife. Opening the fourth drawer, I discovered my prize; a small, but very sharp paring knife. It would be to my advantage to carry a modest one that I could easily hide instead of a gigantic butcher knife that could be taken and used against me. Closing the drawer, I clutched my defense and continued making my way across the kitchen. Fear gripped me, and I gripped the knife. The thought of having to use it made my stomach knot. I'd witnessed too many throat slicing's back at the condo and considering my abhorrence for blood, I wasn't at all sure I could actually plunge it into the soft flesh of someone, even if they were attacking me. I shuddered, hoping it wouldn't come to that. Slipping past the large island, I kept my back against the cabinetry as much as possible, remembering how shadows emerged from every dark corner at the condo. Each haunting thought kept me on edge.

A small puff of air touched my face as I reached the pantry. The door was open allowing a peek inside. The food cupboard was quite large, extending deeper than I first realized. The corners were deep and dark, the glow of moonlight unable to reach the far recesses. Another shiver raced up my spine stippling my skin, I contemplated turning back but something inside me would not allow it. Call it intuition or plain stupidity but I had a hunch. I needed light however, and the further back into the room I crept, the darker it became. I slipped inside, inching my way past shelves of canned jellies, jars of honey, bags of nuts, beans and rice, and baskets of fresh vegetables along with homemade bread and pastries. The storeroom resembled an old time mercantile, stocked with supplies as well as food; and it wasn't long before I came upon a basket of candles and matches. Laying down the paring knife, I grabbed the necessary articles. Striking as quietly as possible, I lit the wick. I held the light high, lighting the dark corners of the storeroom, then grabbed my knife and took a step forward. A gentle gust of air kissed my cheek, sending my small flame dancing before snuffing it out completely. Panic squeezed my lungs, yet I forced myself to stay calm, and compelled myself to continue my sleuthing. Laying aside my weapon I ran my hand along the shelf searching for the book of matches. I re-lit the wick, this time cupping my hand around it, guarding the flame. Cautiously, I moved further back into the cupboard, intent on investigating the source of the draft. The dancing flame cast twisted shadows on the walls, resembling gruesome faces, each whispering a warning not to venture one step further.

As I neared the end of the pantry, the cool puffs of air became stronger, raging a battle against the flickering candle. Arriving at the final shelf, I raised my candle illuminating kegs of molasses, maple syrup, honey, and agave nectar. The tap of blackstrap molasses revealed a pregnant drip, ready to escape the spigot and fall to the floor. With the tip of my finger, I rescued the drop and placed it on my tongue. I returned my finger to the spigot, closing the tap to prevent additional leakage. As I did, the back wall moved slightly letting in another gust of air. The spigot doubled as a doorknob. I Tugged again at the spout and watched the heavy wall swing forward like the massive door of a vault. Cool air wafted inside, reminding me of the moment in the rustic cabin when the rock wall slid sideways, revealing the dark passageway to the citadel. I peered inside, my candle lit the entrance to what appeared to be another dark tunnel, leading to God knows where.

I took a quick glance over my shoulder and once again contemplated retreating and heading back to the safety of my bed, yet my intuition would not allow it. Plus, there was the mystery of Falcon's call, his warning instructing me to run and get out of there, not to go exploring. Would he be furious if he knew? His call had stopped. I hadn't heard his voice again. Maybe somehow, he knew where I was and what I was doing, and he approved. Or maybe... No, I wouldn't think that, not now, not ever. I remembered the words of the second prophecy, saying in time I would be led to the secret place and to enter without fear. It was there I would find the third book and the third prophecy. I doubted this was the secret place or the location of the third book, but at least it was a rehearsal for the real event. With that thought in mind, I stepped inside the daunting tunnel.

Chapter 24

Bethany stepped from the black Sedan and looked up at the inn. She'd left this place a week ago with no inclination that she'd be returning so soon. But after Betancourt revealed his close relation to the story, and how he'd become obsessed, joining special forces, and spending most of his life investigating the family mystery, Bethany and Bronwyn's parents decided to accompany him to Moonshine. Each of them hoped to uncover more of the secrecy surrounding Bronwyn's birth and disappearance.

The peacefulness of Sandalwood Inn was now replaced with the frenzy of a media circus. News vans, all displaying their stations insignia, were parked all over, littering the beautiful lawn, crushing many of the exotic plants growing in the fertile soil. Standing in front of cameras, clutching their microphones, reporters everywhere embellished stories, speculating on what may have transpired here in the hidden town, all renaming Moonshine the Modern Day Roanoke.

"This is the place," Bethany sighed, calling out to Madison and Martin as they climbed from the car. "This is where we stayed and the last place I saw Bronwyn." Tears burned in her eyes at the tragic disclosure.

The familiar squeak of the screen door was the only welcome they received as they entered the lobby. Approaching the colossal desk, Bethany rang the small shiny bell, hoping Mavis would appear around the corner, missing tooth, and all, welcoming her weary travelers.

Instead, a reporter, recognizing Madison and Martin, eagerly approached, ready for an exclusive. Once Betancourt showed his credentials and demanded to be left alone, the reporter retreated.

Bethany gave her companions a private tour, starting with the room she shared with Bronwyn two weeks ago. Madison attempted to sort through some of Bronwyn's belongings but was stopped by authorities dusting for prints and collecting evidence. A particular item tagged and lying aside caught Bethany's attention, she hadn't thought about the mysterious vial with the puzzling verse until now. She mentioned it to Betancourt who examined the evidence, startling when he read the cryptic message, mumbling that Isaiah 42:9 was written across the first page of the old family Bible. Bethany took one last look before leaving the familiar room. She sighed, wishing she could turn back time, heeding all Bronwyn's warning signs that went unnoticed.

Heading back outside, they took a stroll through the many gardens. The once serene healing grounds were now makeshift studios for the media, reporting their stories, hanging close to the elusive town in case any major developments transpired.

Bethany pointed out the garden where Bronwyn swore, she saw a murder take place. It had all seemed so ludicrous to her at the time. Besides, Lillian convinced her Bronwyn was likely on some sort of meds and was having a post break up crisis. Why had she believed her above what she knew of her best friend?

Betancourt ordered the newly planted tree removed and soil samples taken from the spot where Bronwyn told Bethany the victim bled out. They continued until they reached the final garden. Bethany admitted she hadn't been in this grove because it was always locked. Today, however, the door was open. Following the shaded path, they came upon a group of photographers taking pictures of a lone tombstone, saying it was the only marker of death in the entire town which was quite peculiar. They went on to mention there wasn't a hospital either, only a small clinic. Again, something so obvious yet went unnoticed the entire week she visited. Stepping forward she read the engraved stone.

"Brennan John Colton

Beloved husband,

Amazing father, brother, friend,

Prince of Eden,

On this world but not of it."

She glanced over at Betancourt who was reading the marker as well. "What does that mean; on this world but not of it?"

Walking to the headstone, Betancourt traced his finger over the engraving, and even though he said nothing, Bethany could tell the phrase resonated with him, more than likely affirming his investigation. She marveled at what an enigmatic incident they'd all inadvertently stumbled into. Yet, considering the new revelation on Bronwyn's adoption and the mystery surrounding her beginnings, Bethany had a gnawing suspicion that her wrong turn two weeks ago had been a predestined event.

They left the gardens and continued into Moonshine. The reports were right; it was abandoned, with no hint as to what happened or where the people had disappeared to. Eeriness walked along with her, shoulder to shoulder, mocking all those scurrying around, desperately trying to solve the mystery of the missing people. Every tree, every storefront gave a sneering smile, each knowing the secret of what dreadful thing swallowed this entire town.

They stopped at the café. Yellow police tape forbidding entrance blocked the way inside the small restaurant and to the outdoor dining patio. Betancourt pushed the barrier aside allowing them admission. Littering the tables were plates of half-eaten breakfast. Meals ready to serve were abandoned on the cooling racks, while dirty dishes filled the sink in the kitchen. Betancourt tapped a tabletop with his fingers while scanning the patio; again, his eyes lost in a multitude of thoughts. He was impressive, attractive, and in excellent shape for a man in his early forties. He had an air about him and although he seemed kind, Bethany was certain he was not the type of man you should cross. By his own admission he was obsessed with the mystery of his great grandfather and had been since childhood. He confessed on the drive up that he'd never met his great grandfather but was sure he'd caught glimpses of him from time to time, visiting the old homestead; even after it was rumored, he had passed on.

The secret shrouding his grandfather was that he was immortal, never aging, and lived hundreds of years before marrying Betancourt's great grandmother. Betancourt's father used to tell him the stories his grandmother told him about her husband before her death, claiming he was from another world and one day would return to right all the wrongs of an evil ruler. He'd always considered them as the senile ramblings of a dying old woman, until one day when he overheard his grandfather and his great uncle trying to decipher the puzzle of their missing father. His grandfather swore he saw his dad hidden in the distance at his mother's graveside service. According to him, he didn't look a day over forty, when in fact, if he'd lived, would have been close to eighty-six.

After his great grandmother's death, the homestead became abandoned; there was no longer any reason to visit. The owner of the place let it go, not wanting to invest the money to modernize it and get it ready for new tenants. To this day it sits off the beaten path, somewhere in New Mexico, shrouded in mystery. Betancourt said he visits the place from time to time and on one such visit found the mysterious book, boxed, and buried in the spring house. On other visits he's certain he caught glimpses of his great grandfather roaming the hundred-acre property.

Bethany chilled at his stories.

"Bethany? What are you doing here?" The summons startled her, interrupting her inspection of Betancourt. Turning toward the familiar voice she was surprised to see Lillian making her way over. She had come back, if only to see for herself, if the reports were actually true. It was unnerving seeing the abandoned town when just a week ago they were milling around with the locals, enjoying their unplanned sabbatical. After offering her sympathies to Bronwyn's parents, Bethany introduced Lillian to Agent Betancourt. He asked her the standard questions and then enquired if she had observed anything out of the ordinary during the week of their stay. Lil gave the same answers as Bethany but brought up the night hike to the waterfall. True, the place was somewhat mystical, like a hidden paradise right from the page of an exotic travel brochure. Definitely not your typical mountain waterfall, but other than that, she hadn't noticed anything out of the ordinary.

"What was so unusual about our hike to the waterfall?" Bethany's tone was somewhat accusing. She blamed her for some of this. She had become such a student of her therapy, believing Bronwyn was suffering from the effects of a broken heart, that she totally ignored her cries for help. She reminded herself Lil had never actually been a success as a therapist and life coach which is why she went into acting, which worked, because it was actually her first love.

"I'm surprised no one else noticed." Lil's voice was condescending, a retaliation for Bethany's sarcasm. "When we headed to the waterfall that night Bronwyn had a nasty gash from the night before, when the canoe hit her in the head. On the return hike home, her wound was missing."

"My God you're right." Bethany covered her mouth. "I'd forgotten all about her injury." She shifted her feet, suddenly feeling uncomfortable and wasn't at all surprised when Betancourt immediately asked them to lead the way to the spot. As gung-ho as she was to solve the mystery and rescue her friend, she dreaded making the hike. The picturesque town, once resembling a Norman Rockwell painting, evoking comforting sentiments of God, home, and country, now sat shrouded in a veil of secrecy. Now, a week too late, pieces of a very strange puzzle began taking a predominant place in her thinking.

Lillian led the way to the falls, certain of the direction, admitting that over the course of the week she had visited the place on three different occasions, and then referred to having fun with a couple of the local guys. Bethany rolled her eyes disgusted and fell back, walking alongside Madison. Lillian began recounting all the wonderful things about their week in Moonshine. Unfortunately, while they were in the thickest part of the forest, she remembered Bronwyn making the claim that someone was following them on their way into town. That disclosure catapulted Bethany's thoughts to the night before the festival when Bronwyn fainted and later tried to tell her about cloaked men roaming the surrounding woods. Bethany shivered and even though they still walked by the light of the sun, she switched on her flashlight, bouncing the light through the surrounding trees, lighting the darker thickets. However, the forest was as empty as the town it guarded.

"This is quite peculiar," Lillian voiced her observation to Betancourt. "We should be reaching the falls at any moment, yet I don't hear the sound of rushing water."

She was right, it was quiet and peaceful. The only noise falling upon their ears was the repetitious chirping of crickets, cicadas, and a bullfrog in the distance. There was no roar of a powerful rushing waterfall.

Just as she was about to suggest Lil might have taken the wrong path, they stepped into the clearing of the falls. She stopped suddenly at the sight, a sick feeling snaked its way up, wrapping around her throat and squeezing. Less than two weeks ago, Bethany witnessed these very falls dispense sparkling water in a powerful cascading downpour, now they stood before her dry and empty like parched stones in a desert.

"Oh my God, it looks so different, what happened?" Lillian asked as if Bethany could tell her.

"It's a damn stagnant pond," Bethany said stooping down to feel the water. Without the falls to stir and feed the steamy basin, the mountain pool grew stagnated, allowing a green slimy moss to blanket the surface, creating a film across the top of the water.

"It wasn't like this before?" Betancourt questioned them.

"Nope," Bethany sighed, "It was magical, like a fantastical paradise hidden in the middle of the forest. Now, it's more like an abandoned attraction at an amusement park, shut off and neglected."

"Like the rest of the town," Lillian's voice was soft... haunting.

Chapter 25

I crept down the rustic wooden steps, vanishing into the blackness of the underground tunnel. I edged my way through the shadowy corridor, trying to steady myself against the cold stone wall while cupping my hand around the smoldering wick. It was frigid and damp and smelled of wet earth. The further I descended, the steps changed texture beneath my feet, from crude wood to cold smooth rock, hewn from the underground hollow. I'd descended nearly fifteen feet when I sensed a presence. Someone was following, slinking behind me. Whipping around, I held my candle high. Nothing but shadow. A shiver stroked my skin, sending chills more intense than what the frigid temperature brought.

"Falcon?" I choked out the word, "Is that you?" The only response was the echo of a tiny pebble bouncing down the stairway, skipping past. I leaned against the earthen wall and tried to steady my breathing. Black hovering fog poured into the passageway, snuffing out the feeble flame, leaving me blind in the foreboding darkness. The sudden loss of sight crippled me. I was defenseless against whatever was heading my way. The shadow invading the private chamber was more than the absence of light. It was a tangible presence rounding the corridor, watching me. I hadn't felt this frightened since I was a child.

The wretched vapor boiled toward me, intensifying the darkness, and smothering any feelings of freedom. Had the air not been so frigid, I'd have thought I had descended into the very bowels of hell. The decaying presence hissed a warning to retreat; its breath reeked of sulfur, promising eminent death if I attempted one more step. Then to my horror, the passageway turned icy cold as the sinister presence manifested. My back stiffened at the occurrence, and although I could not see in the thick blackness, I was certain someone was standing right behind me. Whirling around I aimed the paring knife into the blinding darkness; figuring whoever was standing so close would see and back away, or at least feel the impact of the dagger. The presence moved, hovering behind me again and then to my revulsion, an icy finger stroked the side of my face bringing a stinging pain. Spinning around, I backed away, planning to escape back up the stairway, but the darkness was suffocating, and I lost my bearings. The spirit moved up against me, forcing me backward, and then a rough push, sending me sprawling down the hardened clay steps. I plummeted into the dark abyss. Razor sharp stones tore into my skin, slicing into my arms and legs. I desperately tried to grab hold of something, but there was nothing but wet, damp earth. I no longer felt the sharp edges of the steps and figured I'd slipped off the staircase and was now on a mudslide, falling with great speed, to God knows where. I'd read somewhere that underground caves could drop four or five thousand feet. The daunting thought terrified me, and I wondered how long I could survive buried thousands of feet beneath the earth or if I would ever be able to find my way back to the surface. Then somewhere in the hostile darkness icy rain began to pour on my face. Streams of water smacked against me as the mudslide dumped me into an arctic pool. Thrashing in the sub zero waters I fought my way to the top, breaking through the surface, shivering, and gasping for air. Then, a rapturous sight, light glowed in the distance. I scrambled out of the frigid pool, my muscles cramped from the freezing water, making it nearly impossible to walk. I crawled on wobbly arms to the source of the light.

Considering the crudeness of the passageway, I would have never fathomed what lay beyond the colossal stalagmites. Peering around the limestone pillars, was a majestic room. Dumbfounded, I tried taking it all in. A virtual mansion, rivaling any royal palace spread out before me. Grand chandeliers hung from an artistically carved rock ceiling, giving light to the underground fortress. Elegant furnishings spread across a white marble floor, and the arctic waters that engulfed me moments before provided a tributary, cutting along the far edge of the room. This delicate branch of the river offered a pleasing ambiance as well as piping fresh water to the other rooms. Intricately engraved doorways opened up to many other passages, all snaking off to secret locations. Marbled staircases spiraled upward, connecting to a higher level with an open hallway, surrounding the splendid room, much like the manor upstairs.

Shivering, I allowed my body to collapse; relieved I wouldn't spend the remainder of my life as a sightless mole burrowing my way underground. Now what to do? I needed to get warm. I was drenched and shivering uncontrollably. The temperature at this level was bitter cold and being wet only encouraged hypothermia. I must think fast while I can. Obviously, the place was a secret and more than likely off limits to me. Falcon had not mentioned it and felt compelled to leave me in the upstairs house. Should I be discovered here, I'd incur his wrath again, and I wanted to avoid that at all costs. On the other hand, he had called my name while remaining hidden and ordering me to run. Maybe I should have heeded his warning and made my escape. The thought crushed me with defeat. There was only one reason he would warn me to run and that being he was in trouble. He'd instructed me earlier to make my way to Travis should he go down. As much as I wanted to be near Travis again, I couldn't bear the thought of something dire happening to Falcon. Besides, how was I to find my way out of this place, and make it all the way back to Moonshine without being spotted by someone? My face was all over the news. The odds seemed overwhelming; still, I had no other choice. Either I continue on into the cavernous castle or retreat and make my way back up to the pantry. The decision was obvious. There was no way I was ready to face the formidable staircase of doom again.

Grabbing onto a stalagmite, I pulled myself up. The shaking was almost uncontrollable now, as if I were trembling from the inside out. Abandoning my hiding place, I stumbled toward the open room, staying as close to the rock wall as possible. A few more steps and my bare feet touched the smooth marble; leaving muddy footprints as I inched my way across the polished floor, a blatant announcement of my intrusion.

I was halfway across the room when I heard a frenzy coming from one of the hallways. Heavy footsteps, all rushing toward the open area, compelled me to dash for the shadows and take refuge in one of the many passageways exiting the room.

The scowl on the man's face, entering the chamber, was frightening and the men who followed at his heels seemed restless because of it. I counted five and recognized none. Falcon was not with them, neither was Hawke, Vulture or Macaw. A seed of alarm took root; the men were dressed in all black, like those who launched the assault back at the condo, no doubt Abaddon's men.

"How could this have happened?" The angry man spewed forth his venom. "We take Falcon out and still we lose the scribe? I told you to sedate her!"

My stomach dropped. I couldn't breathe. We take Falcon out...Did that mean? No, it couldn't, I wouldn't let that thought take root. Besides, I'd heard him call my name less than twenty minutes ago, he had to be alive. I couldn't make it without him. Tears stung my eyes. As much as I hated to admit it, I'd grown quite fond of him, irreverent ways, and all.

Clearing the tension from his throat, one of the men spoke. "I put the sedative in her tea, and I used the most powerful one at that. I don't know what happened."

Their leader's eyes became daggers cutting into the man's defense. "How incompetent of you to put me in this predicament. This is the most important mission of my life, and you were negligent. I no longer desire your service." With that final word on the matter, he raised a gun, shooting the man point blank.

I covered my mouth at the unexpectedness of the execution and prayed I had not made a noise.

"There is no place for inadequacy in my company," the leader said while putting the weapon back in his jacket. "Search the manor, she's not familiar with it, the rest of you take the grounds, it's dark, she won't be able to see as well as the rest of us. I want her found immediately."

Just as the men were leaving to carry out the orders another man stopped them cold. An evil grin tore across his face.

"No need to go above. She's not there."

To my horror, he pointed at the muddy footprints I'd left across the white marble floor. "The tracks are still wet. She can't be far. They lead over there."

"Find her now!" The leader growled his command. The men sprang into action. My heart seized, leaping into my throat and stealing my breath. My legs weakened, and I remembered Falcon's warning. They will kill you or do things that make you wish you were dead. I thought I might vomit. How could I survive this? There was no one coming to help me this time. Where could I go? What could I do? The men were spreading out, taking every passage, with their leader himself heading my way. It was fight or flight and since I couldn't hold them off, I sprinted down the hallway. It was immense, seemingly running on for miles, with no place to hide other than taking one of the many doors lining the elaborate passage. I limped along; my bare feet numb from the icy cold marble. In a matter of seconds, they would be in the hallway with me. Breathing a quick plea, I tried one of the doors, praying I wouldn't barge into more trouble. My heart fell; the door led to yet another passageway. I thought I might cry. I didn't want to think about what the man said concerning Falcon, yet as hard as I tried, I couldn't keep them from echoing in my head. We take Falcon out...He wasn't here to help me. He wasn't coming this time and I knew it. "I will give my very life to save yours," his words pierced my soul. Slipping through the door I closed it quietly behind me so as not to give them any inclination as to which exit I selected. I glanced down at my feet and was relieved to see I no longer left muddy prints. From here on out they would have to guess what door I chose. This should buy me a little time.

I sighed, doors lined this hallway as well; and I wondered if I should take another or follow the passage and see where it led. I feared if I took too many alternate routes I would be hopelessly lost in the underground labyrinth. The passage snaked along, full of twists and turns and many covert doors all leading to the unknown. I'd had nightmares like this, being chased while lost in a network of doors and passageways, each one leading to another with no end in sight.

I turned another corner and the hallway dead ended at another closed door. Would opening it lead to yet another corridor?

I was freezing, my jaws were clenched, in spite of my chattering teeth. My movements were beginning to get clumsy, and drowsiness filled my head. I wanted nothing more than to lie down somewhere and sleep. I stared at the door, praying there was warmth inside. I could not bear to think of trying to make it down another ice-cold tunnel.

The room was dark, lit only by the ray of light from the hallway. Slipping inside I ran my hand along the wall searching for a switch. As my fingers found the light something wrapped around my wrist, yanking me away from the wall and forcing me to the ground. Instead of hitting the hard floor I landed on top of a person, a still body. The glow from the doorway lit the face of Hawke. His eyes open wide, staring up at the ceiling in death. Before the cry of horror could escape my lips, a hand covered my mouth and pulled me off the body.

"Keep quiet," Macaw choked out. "They will hear you."

By now my eyes had grown accustomed to the dimness. Vulture lay dead near Hawke, along with a couple of other men I didn't recognize. Macaw too was bloody and seemed to be hanging on to life.

"Where's Falcon?"

Macaw's expression reeked of shame. "I'm sorry, I was wrong, I should have..."

"Where is he?" I demanded, screaming the whisper.

Macaw motioned to a bed on the far side of the room. Despite the numbness I felt, I scrambled to my feet, making my way over. Falcon's body was displayed on top of the satin coverlet, blood soaked through his clothing and onto the expensive fabric, he was beaten, like he'd put up a good fight.

My trembling intensified and I struggled to keep breathing. "What...how'd this happen?

Macaw lay on the floor, too weak to follow me to the bed; he closed his eyes, while coughing out the words.

"I gave Elam our location. I trusted him... he was a friend." He choked and blood oozed through his lips. "I didn't believe he'd turned, I thought it was Falcon who had switched sides. When he arrived, he brought an army with him." He gurgled, strangling in his blood. "We didn't have a chance. They butchered everyone ... they're all dead."

My heart crawled in my throat, "Who? Who's dead? Are you talking about the people in Moonshine?" My voice quivered at the thought.

"No," he coughed, exuding every effort to speak. "They killed the entire staff, everyone who lived here at the manor, all stabbed to death in their beds. The women, the children, my family...he killed them all." Macaw was crying now, drowning in his own blood.

I pitied him but couldn't take my eyes off Falcon. More than anything, I wanted to hear him give me a disparaging comment, flash his impish grin, and then light up a cigarette. I wanted to smell his smokey clothes, to scream, to crawl beside him and die too. I was tired, cold, and traumatized and not at all ready to fight my way to freedom. The past twenty–four hours had been nothing but sheer terror, death, and narrow escapes. I was done, I had bit off way more than I could chew. I didn't realize the severity of the situation I had gotten myself into when I agreed to do this. True, they warned me, but I didn't realize how real it actually was. If I escaped this cold tomb, I would call the authorities and turn myself and the entire bizarre story in. Tears escaped my eyes, falling upon Falcon's face. Wiping it away I rested my hand on his chest and noticed it rose slightly. I pressed harder, yes, I could feel it moving. He was breathing! Looking over at Macaw I announced my discovery.

"He's not dead."

Macaw gargled and coughed up more blood, "Not now, but he will be." His voice was barely a whisper. "They're taking him back through the portal to be tried for treason." He grimaced in pain; and despite the frigid temperature, sweat poured down his face. "They plan on a public execution. If you want to save him, then get out of here while you can. Make your way back to Moonshine. Find Travis, he can organize a rescue at the portal."

I crawled over to Macaw, my teeth chattered to the point where I could barely talk. With what little strength he had left, Macaw grabbed my wet t-shirt and pulled my face toward his, "Moonshine will be next. Elam knows where they are, when he's ready, he'll launch his attack, but he needs you first. That's why you must run now, find Travis."

"How can I? I can't even find my way out of here. How am I to find Travis?"

Macaw laughed, and then choked a few more times because of it.

"He'll find you princess... he won't..."

Gagging, he coughed one last time and then... "Turn the shower head to the left... and hurry Abaddon's coming." His voice faded off to silence. "What?" I asked, leaning over him. "What did you say?"

Silence...he was gone. I bit back the tears. I was completely numb; drowsiness was overpowering me, hypothermia taking its course. Had he said Abaddon was coming? He must have been delirious in death. Besides, he'd said to turn the shower head to the left; or was my thinking becoming muddled as well. Then a fleeting thought. A shower meant warm water! Slowly I crawled across the room to the adjoining bathroom, my wobbling arms were scarcely able to support my weight.

Exuding every effort, I pulled myself up and turned the brass knob. Hot water poured over me, I cried out in pain at what felt like a million sharp needles piercing my frozen skin. Peeling off the oversized t-shirt, I allowed the water to thaw me. I wanted nothing more than to sit under it for hours. But time was of the essence; it wouldn't be long before the men came back for Falcon. The last thing I wanted was to be found wet and naked at that. A soft robe hung from a brass knob on the back of the door. I grabbed it to cover my nakedness, wrapped it around me and cinched the belt. Now, what to do? If I retraced my steps, I could make it back to the main room, but I was sure to run into Abaddon's men. Even if I did make it back undetected, I was certain I wouldn't be able to find the staircase that led to the pantry. Besides, I had no desire to put myself in that situation again. Then, a thought...it was worth a try anyway. Stepping back into the bath, I reached for the showerhead and turned it to the left. Nothing. Then I remembered the keg of molasses and how pulling on the spigot opened the door. I turned the nozzle again, pulling this time as I turned. The shower wall moved toward me, opening to a secret staircase hidden behind the wall. Thinking ahead I searched the bathroom and found a decorative candle and some matches. Darting back into the room, I leaned over the bed and kissed Falcon on the forehead.

"Initially I wanted to make this trip without you, I was wrong, I'm not sure I can do this by myself, but you've left me no other choice. If you can hear anything I'm saying, hear this, hang on please, fight like the warrior I know you are..." I wiped away a tear, "Damn it Falcon, I need you, I'm so scared I don't know where to go..."

"Run..."

My heart leaped, "What? Did you say something?"

He continued to lay quiet, unmoving, yet I was sure...I heard his voice.

"Run...down..."

Again, his voice was loud and clear, but he said nothing...his mouth was still closed, and his eyes remained shut. "Run down?" Run down where?

"Run down house.... go to the run-down house."

I whirled around. The voice was loud, like the one that woke me, yet no one else was in the room. Perplexed, I stood there trying to find the source of the voice. Falcon was unconscious and Macaw and the others were dead. Were my thoughts becoming muddled in the place somewhere between sleep and awake?

"Damn it Scribe, run!" Call it premonition or whatever but at this point I didn't care where it was coming from. Bolting for the bathroom I lit the wick and placed the book of matches in the pocket of the robe. Then, with great apprehension, I took the first step.

Chapter 26

The staircase dead ended at a concrete barrier. I lifted my candle and scanned the wall looking for some sort of lever that would open the door. Bloody fingerprints pointed to the device, a brass ring, embedded in a carved-out circle in the middle of the wall. I hesitated before grabbing hold of the ring. The bloody prints were fresh which meant someone had come this way not long ago. What if they were waiting for me right beyond the barrier? Entering would put me at risk of being caught. Still, the alternative would be retreating down the staircase and into the room of death. I turned the ring and pulled. The wall moved toward me, allowing entrance. Cautiously, I stepped into another bath, this one familiar. The staircase led directly into my suite. I wanted to cry tears of relief and fall into the soft bed and pull the warm blankets around me but there was no time to waste. If I were to save Falcon, I couldn't spare another minute.

I grabbed my jeans and Falcon's hoodie and dressed quickly. I would skip the shoes so as not to make any noise. Instead, I tossed them in the travel bag, snatched it up and placed the long strap around my neck before stealing a look out of the door. The house was still and as quiet as before. I figured they were still below searching every passageway in the labyrinth. Now was the time to dart outdoors and make my escape.

I tiptoed down the stairs and snuck outside. I would stay hidden in the trees, follow the dirt road to the main highway, and hopefully hitch a ride without being recognized. At this point, however, I didn't care if I was turned over to the authorities. At least I would be protected from the ruthless men hunting me down.

The moon was high in the sky, giving ample light on this clear night. In fact, there was too much light and I figured I could easily be spotted so I remained hidden in the shadows of the manor. I strained my eyes and scanned the property. Macaw was right. Elam brought an army with him. Men were standing guard; intermittently positioned around the mansion, down the driveway and some in the open field. It would be easier to run through a minefield than to sneak past Elam's patrols.

Plotting a course of action, my eyes fell on the black Suburban that escorted us here only hours ago. Perhaps...there was a chance. Hunkering down I slithered along the shadows and made a quick dash to the vehicle. Crouching by the front tire, I hid and waited. Silence, there was no movement. I'd made it that far. Inching up, I peered into the driver's window. The glow of the moon reflected off the shiny keys dangling from the ignition. I slipped onto the plush leather seat, careful not to slam the door, it would only draw attention. Instead, I would secure it once en route. Pulling it close but not closed, I took a deep breath and turned the keys. As I expected, the sound of the engine drew all attention my way. Black silhouettes moved from their frozen positions all dashing for the vehicle. To my horror the Suburban lurched forward and stalled.

"Damn it! I cursed, not noticing it had manual transmission. Unfortunately, I wasn't too familiar with stick shifts.

The men were closing in; I hit the power locks before starting the engine again. Pushing on the clutch I turned the keys, forced the gear in reverse, and stepped on the gas. Again, I stalled out.

"God please," I begged, while restarting the engine. Another stall. Damn it, why couldn't I remember to step on the clutch? Three men leaped toward the vehicle. One tried the passenger door but to no avail, another jumped on the hood, while the other yanked open the driver's door. I'd never closed it all the way! One last chance, with the clutch engaged I turned the keys and pressed hard on the gas just as the man's hand reached inside for me. The suburban peeled backwards, knocking him to the ground. The front of the vehicle bumped upward as my front tire rolled across him, crushing his body while I backed away. Now to go forward. I thought fast. I needed to keep my foot on the clutch while switching gears. I pushed on the gas, but the vehicle roared in protest, stalling out. What now? I'd mistakenly put it in third gear instead of first. By now two more men pounced on the suburban, while the man on the hood kicked out the windshield. His boot came through, sending pieces of glass showering in around me. I had to get it right this time, it was my last chance. Turning the key, I stomped on the clutch and slammed the gear into first and peeled off, slipping it easily into second then third as I raced down the driveway. I jerked the steering wheel, knocking the man off the hood as I turned onto the dirt road. I slipped the gear into fourth; I was flying now.

I checked the rearview, all was dark. Relieved, I turned the heater on full blast and continued driving in fifth gear stirring up rocks and leaving a cloud of dust in my wake.

Chapter 27

Bethany had been so mystified by the change of the falls that she failed to notice the effect the hike had on Madison. She'd turned ghastly pale, and her knees buckled beneath her no longer supporting her weight. Holding her up, Martin searched the area for a place his wife could sit. Lillian was the first to recognize the dilemma and as usual came to the rescue, grabbing hold of Madison and helping Martin escort her to a nearby rock. One look at her and Bethany knew it wasn't the difficulty of the hike that was taking its toll.

"What's wrong?" She asked, kneeling beside the rock.

"She's obviously suffering the effects of an altitude malady, just like Bronwyn did, remember. Exuding such effort at such a high elevation can have disastrous effects." Lillian began waxing eloquently again; however, Bethany had no patience or interest in her diagnosis this time. Just because she played a doctor once in a show didn't mean she had medical knowledge.

"What is it, Madison?" She asked again, ignoring Lillian.

Madison kept one hand over her mouth while shaking her head in disbelief. Anxiety flooded her eyes and Bethany figured she would faint at any minute. She looked at Martin for an answer. He didn't look any better himself.

"This is the campsite where we found Bronwyn." He whispered the information so Lillian wouldn't hear.

"Are you sure?" was all Bethany could say.

Martin nodded.

"So, you've been to Moonshine before?"

"No, there's a campground probably seven miles down on the other side. We checked in there and then drove our camper up. We never knew Moonshine existed.

"That was thirty-three years ago, how can you be sure it's the same falls?"

Martin smirked, "You don't forget things like that. Besides, it's only been twenty-three years. We came back every summer after that. It was on a camping trip when Bronwyn was ten that she started writing her book." Martin nodded toward the dried-up falls. "She sat right over there, under the waterfall, and wrote its beginnings. We never came back after that trip because things just started going crazy."

Bethany was glad she was kneeling because at this point, she didn't think her legs would hold her up any longer either.

"So, in all the years you camped here you never hiked into Moonshine?"

"No," Martin was adamant in his answer. "We never hiked past the falls. There wasn't a trail back then, or at least not one we ever found."

Bethany looked up at Betancourt who once again was in deep thought; and despite Martin's intriguing revelation, she saw disappointment on his face.

"We better head back while we still have light." He tossed a stone into the stagnant pool breaking through the mossy film. "Whatever was here is gone now, no use hanging around."

The walk back was somewhat slower because of Madison. She appeared tired and sauntered along as if she were in a daze, which Bethany figured she probably was, seeing she felt somewhat confused herself. They made it back to Sandalwood Inn just as the sun was setting. Bethany headed for the black Sedan but to her dismay Betancourt said he wanted to stay at the inn and do some more investigating in the morning light. The thought of sleeping in the new Roanoke unnerved her, so she thought of leaving the mountain with Lillian, but her plans fell short when she realized Lil' was staying up there too; due to various interviews scheduled for tomorrow.

Their old room was still secured pending the investigation, so she took another room. The quietness of the inn had Bethany on edge, and she feared the place might swallow her up during the night as it did everyone else. She had no intention of being alone in the room, so she asked Lillian to stay with her. Lillian was more than eager to accommodate her, seeing her only alternative would be sleeping in her car. They sat on the bed for over an hour discussing the strange turn of events and how they never would have imagined their Bronwyn getting caught up in a scandal of such caliber.

"You know," Lillian said, hugging her pillow as she spoke. "I remember Bronwyn asking a very strange question the day we got our pedicures. She asked Ashley if there was a secret society, a cult so to speak, roaming the woods in black hooded robes."

Bethany was intrigued, "How did the girls respond to her question?"

Lillian shrugged, "They didn't answer, it got quiet and uncomfortable, so I changed the subject. Now I think she might have been on to something."

"No kidding," Bethany was sarcastic. "She was on to something alright. She tried to tell me about a murder in the gardens, but I thought she'd lost her mind. I can't believe she was telling the truth the entire time."

Lillian nodded, "What I'm wondering is what was it that compelled her to stay behind, especially since she was so frightened by everything? Do you think she was forced, you know, being black mailed by something?"

Bethany thought for a moment, she knew Bronwyn would risk her life for theirs if it came down to it. What if she stayed behind to save them? Bethany's stomach twisted in knots. "The last time we really talked was on the Sunday after the festival. She seemed normal, told me about watching the fireworks with Travis, later we cleaned up the room, did some laundry and then that evening after Mavis questioned her about the firework show, she took a walk. She didn't come to the room until five the next morning."

"I remember," Lillian picked up the timeline. "When we got back from breakfast she was gone and then showed up later with Falcon. That was a big surprise seeing she was terrified of him."

"You're right, it made no sense at all; but nothing does..."

"Then Ryan arrived, and we all found out about her pregnancy." Lillian shook her head, "Unbelievable she kept such a secret. She must have lost it right before she started writing the last novel. No wonder she was quiet and distant all the time."

Bethany felt ashamed. She'd been a bad friend, becoming angry and pulling away just because Bronwyn kept her secret shame to herself. She sighed, "She left with Ryan and that was the last we saw her until right as we were leaving. She wanted to talk but I was so upset I told her no... ...you're right Lil, what could have possibly compelled her to stay?"

They sat in silence for a few moments, both lost in thought trying to imagine what could have possibly been transpiring right under their noses. Bethany stood from the bed breaking the silence, "I'm starved. Wanna go raid the fridge?"

Lillian yawned, "No I'm too tired to eat; besides it's too late, anything I eat now just turns to ugly fat. I need to get to bed anyway. My interview is early in the morning."

Bethany shook her head, "Why did you agree to an interview?"

Lillian grinned, "We're talking Good Morning America here Bethany. I'm an actress, I could use the publicity."

Bethany rolled her eyes, "I'm getting some food."

Betancourt was in the kitchen making a sandwich. He offered to make Bethany one when he saw her. He looked delicious, so did the sandwich so she agreed. Laying out two more pieces of bread he motioned to the coffee maker.

"I made a pot, but I better warn you, it's strong."

"Just how I like it," she said, grabbing a mug from the cabinet and filling it. "As tired as I am, I doubt anything could keep me awake."

She sipped her coffee, he was right; it was strong, a little too strong so she made her way into the pantry looking for the creamer. It was quite large and much deeper than she first realized. It was ample size for stocking everything you need to run a small bed and breakfast, even the back wall was lined with kegs of maple syrup, honey, and black strap molasses. Bethany smiled remembering the amazing waffles Mavis served up every day and thought it might be a nice gesture to make Madison some in the morning. Locating the creamer, she joined Betancourt back in the kitchen. She watched him spread egg salad across the bread, then layer it with fresh cut tomatoes, lettuce, onions, and pickles. He tossed in a few jalapenos before closing it with the second piece of bread. Placing the sandwich on a plate he carried them outside on the porch, offering her a seat on the swing.

"Thank you," she said and then bit into her late-night snack. "I was starving. I've been too upset to eat and didn't realize how long I'd gone without food until a few minutes ago."

He smiled, "Well there's a lot of food in this kitchen, and it'd be a shame to let it go to waste."

Bethany nodded and swallowed, "Mavis was a great cook; I had a lot of delicious meals here." She sipped her coffee, "You know, agent Betancourt, people who plan on going away usually clean out their fridge. By the looks of it, Mavis never planned on leaving, neither did the people at the café. So, what's your take on it all? Where do you think they disappeared too?"

Betancourt smiled, "My name's Jacob, you can drop the agent Betancourt."

Bethany tried to suppress her smile. She was glad he felt comfortable enough to be on a first name basis with her, but she didn't want him to know it. Instead, she tried acting indifferent and continued on with her question.

"Alright Jacob, what do you think happened to everyone?"

He sighed, "I wish I knew. I have my suspicions, but that's all they are. Years of investigating, and the more I find out, the more mysterious it gets."

"How long have you been investigating?"

"Since I was a kid but started it seriously at the age of nineteen. That's when my great grandmother passed and my great uncle swore, he saw my great grandfather in the distance at the graveside. Since he was supposedly dead, I became curious."

Bethany sipped her coffee and wished she'd put in more creamer, "What do you mean supposedly? Wasn't there a funeral when he passed?"

"Yes, but the casket was sealed. No one ever saw the body."

She was intrigued, "Ever think of exhuming the casket?"

Jacob took a swallow of his coffee. "Of course, I did... it was empty."

She shivered at his blunt confession. "Whoa, why would it be empty?"

"Because he's not dead. They just wanted us to believe he was."

"Who ordered a sealed coffin?"

"My great grandmother, she said he'd been burned badly in an automobile accident. She wanted him to be remembered for the way he was before. No one questioned her at the time."

"So, she was in on his secret?"

He nodded, "they say she loved him with a passion, and he loved her too, that's why suspicion began sometime after his death. She wasn't that shook up over it. Then there were reports of them seen together. Of course, she denied it, and it was a touchy subject since he was gone. What got me interested was a picture of a man in the distance, at her graveside, standing in the trees. It was too far to make a positive ID, but my uncle swore it was him. Not long ago I had the picture blown up and analyzed. It was him alright; he hadn't aged a day, when in fact he'd have been eighty-seven."

Bethany shook her head, marveling at the mysteries of the universe. And at that moment, just when she wondered how many inexplicable secrets go on all around us undetected, the lazy tune of the dulcimer began wafting through the trees. She sat up straight.

"Someone's still here...whoever is playing that dulcimer...they're still here!" her voice trembled at the eerie thought. "Someone played that same tune almost every night the week we were here."

Jacob set aside his coffee and walked off the porch, Bethany shivered, staying close on his heels. Reporters, and law enforcement officials came out of their campers, and tents; all milling around, looking up past the tall pines and into the starry night sky, spooked by the song.

Jacob ordered some men to take to the hills and investigate the source. The group immediately armed themselves, like soldiers, taking off into the woods.

"Tell me about the song," he asked.

Bethany rubbed her arms to keep from shivering. The night was warm but still a chill stroked at her skin. "Not much to tell. It played almost every night. It was soothing. I always pictured some mountain man sitting on his porch, rocking, and playing his dulcimer while smoking a pipe. I never thought much of it."

Jacob looked up into the sky, "It's a signal. They're communicating which means they are close, and I have a suspicion they are hiding right under our noses."

Bethany trembled and looked around, wondering if Bronwyn was close by too, watching her. "So, what are your suspicions?"

He grinned but didn't answer the question. "They say my great grandfather played a dulcimer."

Bethany forced a smile, the eeriness of the night taunting her. "Really? So, do you have a picture of him? Maybe I should know what he looks like just in case I see him walking around here in Moonshine."

Jacob reached into his shirt pocket, pulled out a photograph, and handed it to her.

"Meet my great grandfather, Haytham Elwell."

Bethany paled, "Oh my God, that's...."

He smiled, "I know."

Chapter 28

I had been driving for half an hour when I exited off the main road. As far as I knew I wasn't followed. However, I wasn't going to waste time worrying about a run of good luck. Making a left hand turn I pulled onto a narrow country road. I had no idea where I was going. I was simply following my instincts; and being good at directions I could usually find my way back to a place if I'd been there at least once. A half a mile further and I'd succeeded. The headlights illuminated the ram-shackled home. I wanted to keep them on but feared I would only draw attention to my whereabouts if I did. I killed the engine and shut them off. I kept the doors locked, but wondered what good it would do, seeing the windshield was gone.

The place sitting before me was intimidating, like an old, haunted house that everyone avoided because of the harrowing stories told about the residents and how they had been murdered and walked the halls not knowing they're dead. I shivered, trying to control my vivid imagination, and then remembered Falcon's take on the place, and how he'd seen the beauty of what once was. I forced myself to think of it in that light.

Taking a deep breath, I removed the keys from the ignition and tossed them into the travel bag. Rummaging through the glove box, I found a flashlight. Biting my bottom lip, I climbed from the safety of the driver's seat.

The front door was locked so I entered in through a broken window, being careful not to cut myself on the remaining shards. I switched the flashlight on, bouncing the beam around the open room. Several pieces of furniture remained. They were faded, and soiled from being subjected to the elements, due to the broken windows and leaky roof. The cushions on the couch were torn, the fluff pulled out, revealing rusted springs; no doubt the work of squirrels and other wildlife burrowing to find material to make a nest. A thick layer of dust carpeted the hardwood floor, along with scattered dried leaves, sticks, and broken glass.

I refused to think about my situation, alone inside the old house, out in the middle of nowhere. It was like the beginning of a horror movie, nothing about it seemed right at all. The only reason I had come here was the voice back in the caverns had said, run down house. I wasn't sure if it meant to run back to the house, or if it was telling me to make my way to this God forsaken place. No matter, I was here, and as harrowing as it may be, it offered a place to hide for the rest of the night or until I could figure out how to make my way back to Moonshine without being spotted.

Taking every precaution, I mounted the staircase, making sure each step was secure. The condition of the second floor was much like downstairs, covered in dust and dirt. A branch from a nearby tree had long since crashed through one of the bedroom windows, offering a passage inside to all the woodland creatures that cared to relocate.

Searching the room, the beam of light caught the glowing golden eyes of an owl sitting high in the ceiling rafters, staring at me. His inspection stopped me cold, and I gasped at the eerie sight. It prompted me to think of the red glowing eyes in my nightmare which did nothing to ease my fearful mind. I retreated, quickly making my way out of the bedroom and into the next.

This one surprised me. It was in much better shape than the rest of the house. The room was well-kept, as if someone tended to it, much like a person would a graveside. I wondered if whoever preserved the room was close by, possibly in the house now, watching me intrude on the sacredness of their sanctuary.

Scanning every corner as a safety measure, I made my way over to the four-post bed and ran my hand over the beautiful hand-stitched quilt lying on top. The bed faced a stone fireplace and two large portraits hung above the mantle. I shined my beam on the pictures, ready to see who once inhabited the run-down house. If the hidden owl hadn't stolen my breath away, one of the two faces staring at me from the vintage photographs would have. Casting the light on the mantle I noticed a smaller framed picture of the same two people. Flipping the frame, I tore off the back cover, removed the old-fashioned wedding photograph and read the inscription on the back. "Haytham and Carleene Elwell 1925. Falcon's real name must be Haytham Elwell. I sat on the bed, dumbfounded. The picture was nearly a hundred years old, and other than the clothing; Falcon still looked the same. He was right; they didn't age, not like everyone else. I walked the room and collected more photographs, noticing Falcon hadn't aged in any of them, and after a while there were only pictures of the woman, Carleen. The last picture of her, she looked to have been in her eighties.

Exhausted, I lay across the bed. Despite the crudeness of the place, I felt safe in this room. Perhaps it was because Falcon's face stared at me from the wall making me feel as if he were here, protecting me. I sighed, wishing he were, so I kept the light on his face. I wanted to sleep but the urgency of what I should do kept me from it. I needed to make my way to Moonshine and find Travis, so he could intercept Falcon at the portal. But how was I to get to Moonshine? The Suburban had a busted-out windshield, and I couldn't make the drive without one. Neither could I stop to have it fixed or I'd be recognized. Then I thought, perhaps there was a car in the detached garage. It was possible, after all, someone or something had instructed me to come here. It was worth the look, yet, I had no desire to leave the safety of the room and venture out in the dark of night again. Besides, if a car were indeed in the garage, would it even run? Still, the thought of Falcon unconscious and bleeding compelled me to swing my legs over the side of the bed and get moving. As my light left the old brown and white portrait of Falcon, it highlighted a particular stone in the fireplace jetting out a little further from the others. Curious, I crossed over to examine the crude rock and ran my hand over the stone. I grabbed the protruding corner and jiggled. It moved at my interference. I stopped and looked around. No walls were moving and if they were, I definitely had no intentions of following another passageway down into hell. I pulled at it again, this time it began sliding out of its home, revealing a hidden compartment somewhat like a safe, but with no combination lock. Lowering the heavy rock, I aimed the light into the cubby hole. A single box lay inside accompanied by a lone envelope. I grabbed both. I opened the letter first and shined my light on the paper. It was a death certificate. According to the document, Falcon passed away in the year 1949. Hmmm, I opened the lid to the antique box next and discovered several old journals, all belonging to Falcon. Fascinated, I carried the crate over to the bed. Finally, an introspective look inside the life of the cagey man. Settling onto the mattress, I positioned the flashlight for perfect reading and lifted the first book from its hiding place. I opened the cover and read the handwritten words on the first page.

The adventures of Abaddon and Haytham

My memories of a beloved brother, who once walked in the light of peace and was good.

I read through pages of stories about Falcon and Abaddon; some were humorous while others were tender and compassionate evoking tears. I was impressed, Falcon was excellent at penning his thoughts and I figured maybe he should have been chosen as the scribe instead of me.

His deep admiration for his identical twin was evident, but as I switched journals and began reading his memories of Abaddon's treachery, the esteem he held for his brother switched to contempt. The pain in Abaddon's betrayal had taken its toll on Falcon as if his very soul had been ripped from his body, leaving a hollow cave inside of him, filled with echoes of his hatred. The devastating disappointment in what Abaddon had chosen turned to bitterness. This bitterness became a cancer, eating away at him, transforming his own character into an insolent rogue with an ill regard for his own life. The fruit of his resentment produced a dangerous rebellion that if he weren't careful would catapult him into a world as dark as the one his twin inhabited. The last page in the journal was Falcon's final say on the matter.

And so, with part of me missing, what then shall I live for if not revenge? My passion is not to destroy my brother because of his wickedness, for even though it pains me to admit, it was his weakness that allowed the invasion of the darkness. I cannot fault him for this flaw for it dwells in every one of us. It's the fissure in the resolute wall of our convictions. This tiny crevice is the keyhole that the enemy unlocks with promises of fulfillment; and yet we are not fulfilled. So, in time the tear in our spirit divides, separating us from what is good until the gap is so wide, we can no longer return. Is there a way back? What then will fill this void so we may cross back over?

I closed the journal and was much more educated about Falcon and my nemesis. Yet, with the knowledge there came great sadness. Abaddon was no longer the evil ruthless ruler, but the brother of a friend, taken captive by a much darker adversary. Did this wickedness have a name, a face? What were my chances of going against the pervading darkness? Could I in my quest rescue both Abaddon and Falcon? And what if this impious spirit knew of my weaknesses? I had many. Could I too unknowingly fall prey to its promises?

The crunching of tires, moving into the gravel driveway, interrupted my thoughts and signaled the approach of a vehicle. I gathered the journals and placed them back into the box. Looking out the window, I saw a car approaching without the use of headlights. My heart seized, whoever it was intended on a surprise attack. Scrambling, I placed the crate back in the cubby hole and with trembling hands lifted the heavy stone, securing it back in place. Killing the flashlight, I crept back into the bedroom where the owl sat in the ceiling rafters. If critters could use the tree branch as an entrance perhaps, I could use it as an exit. Besides, now would be an excellent time to check the detached garage for a car. I placed the strap of the travel bag around my neck, and climbed on top of the hefty limb, inching my way down and stopping where it made a Y shape, connecting to the trunk. Maybe I should just wait in the tree; I doubted they'd look up there, but I wasn't going to take the chance, especially remembering what happened back in Moonshine when I hid in the tree from the cloaked man. I slipped down another branch and made the jump. I was on the far side of the house and either needed to make my way to the Suburban or the backyard where the garage sat, several feet behind the house. Crouching in the overgrowth,

I crawled toward the front. The Suburban was out of the question. A burly looking man stood guard, preventing me from escaping that way again. To the garage it was. Staying hunched down, I snuck to the back.

"She's been inside!"

The announcement coming through the broken windows caused my heart to skip a beat.

"Her footprints lead upstairs, check it out."

I forced myself to stay calm. Taking a deep breath for momentum I dashed from the bushes, darted across the back lawn, and slid up against the side of the garage and peered inside. Empty. Now what to do? I needed to move. The garage would be one of the first places they looked should they search the grounds. With nowhere to go but the surrounding woods I made my escape. Fortunately, there was a crude little path, not too overgrown, so I was able to make my way down it, picking up the pace, separating myself from the thugs looking for me. Without much light I couldn't see the change in the surface of the footpath and suddenly felt myself slipping, sliding in ankle deep mud. The unexpectedness of the change threw me off balance, sending me plunging into shallow water bubbling out from under the rustic wooden door of a turn of the century spring house.

"Damn it!" I cursed this time out loud. How many times in one night could I fall off a path and land in frigid water? At least the temperature outside was warm, and for that I was thankful.

The spring house resembled a wooden shack. It had a weathered roof, a barricaded door in which the pieces of plywood had been pried away, and one small window near the back with glass so filthy it would be impossible to see through. The place looked as if it hadn't been used for years. Switching on my light, I examined the door, looking for the best possible entry and was unnerved to see claw marks scratched into the weathered wood. What kind of animal would make such hideous scrapes? The area didn't seem conducive to grizzlies... mountain lions perhaps. Great, just what I needed, something else to add to the terror of this long night.

Prying open the door, I held my breath hoping I wasn't barging in on a family of wildcats. Waving the light from wall to wall I saw the spring house was empty save for the rising water bubbling up with such force that it created a wading pool in the bottom. Before fully committing to entering the moist hideout, I flashed the light into the water looking for snakes. Not finding any I slipped on inside, closing the door behind me. Safe inside I kept my flashlight lit while wading across the frigid pool and then took a seat on a concrete slab. I would wait here until they gave up and left. They may have been able to follow my tracks on the dusty floor inside the house but there was no way they would know I had taken off into the woods. I felt safe, at least, until the light began to dim and then went out completely.

"No, not now, stay with me... please don't do this to me." I whispered; but despite my coaxing the light dimmed and then faded out...darkness.

I was too tired and frustrated to curse this time; besides, I had a suspicion the batteries hadn't simply died but that a force beyond my control extinguished my light. For the first time in several days, the intense heat sensation invaded my body, a warning signal that something wasn't right. I dropped the flashlight and rummaged through the travel bag until my hands touched the cold metal of my cell phone. I pulled it out and turned it on, notification bells began sounding immediately, deafening in contrast to the silence surrounding me. I quickly put the phone on vibrate and contemplated my next move. The battery bar was red. I could possibly make one call before it died. I could call 911 and tell them my location. When the police arrived, they would have Abaddon's men to deal with, giving me a chance to escape. I would wait in the springhouse until the ruckus was over and then hike my way back to the main road. It seemed like a good plan until my phone went black. This time I cursed, and the darkness became tangible, crawling upon the concrete slab with me, blowing its scorching sulfuric breath against my neck. I bristled at the presence; I'd sensed it before. It was the same evil existence that manifested in the passageway, tearing its finger into the side of my face, and sending me tumbling into the murkiness of the underground cavern. The same presence swept through Moonshine my first night, tossing me into the angry waters of the lake, trying to drown me. It was this all-encompassing evil that stole the virtuous spirit of a much-loved brother, enslaving him to do its bidding as a murderous, malevolent enemy. This was my adversary, and what my book of redemption must annihilate.

The angry marauder beat against the door shaking it, demanding entrance. Holding my breath, I pulled my legs up on the concrete slab, and hugged my knees. The fear was overwhelming, ravaging my body and at this point I'd rather face a thousand of Abaddon's men than this heinous apparition.

A gust of wind blew through the room blowing open the weathered door allowing the sinister wraith to enter. The moist chamber continued to shake, rocking from the foundation upward as a vexed howl filled the room, screeching its hatred for me, hissing its intent in words I couldn't comprehend. My desire was to run from the dark tomb, yet my body wouldn't move. Whether it was intense fear or a force the demonic spirit inflicted upon me, I was paralyzed. My eyes searched the darkness for a glimmer of hope. What could I do? My mind went back to the night at the falls where I had a similar experience but this time, I knew Travis was not coming to my aid.

I closed my eyes, trying not to panic. I desperately searched for peaceful thoughts to counteract the fear and slow my accelerating heart rate. I pictured Travis. His chocolate eyes, his perfect face, the stubble outlining his chin. His lips, and the way they felt when he kissed me under the willow tree. I thought of his strong neck and his broad shoulders and his sculpted, rippling chest. His bulging biceps and the veins that traced around them. I pictured his arms holding me. A strong tower of safety where this horrid presence could not find me. "Please," I whispered. "I am so lost in all of this. I have no clue what to do. I need guidance. I am willing but lost." The heat continued to rise within as the faint voice of a woman began to sing. The voice was soft and melodic. The music flowed delicately from the unseen woman's mouth directly into my soul. The lyrics of the song were in the unknown tongue, yet they somehow stirred the spirit within me. A brilliant white light invaded my thoughts bursting through all the confusion and panic. Rays of blue and lavender burst forth from a magnificent sphere, making me think the room was aglow with fireworks; yet I kept my eyes closed for fear of interrupting the vision. The woman continued her haunting song singing as a mother would to her child. The white ball of light burst, exploding into tiny fragments, each miniscule piece spiraled upward. I felt my innermost being soaring through the atmosphere beyond the confines of the dilapidated roof. A gentle breeze tenderly pushed me along, as the glow of the moon cradled my body. The tiny orbs of light encircled me as I flew across the great expanse. One by one the orbs collided with my body, exploding, each having a unique effect. Some calmed me, some were empowering, some filled my soul with longing, some offered courage and inspiration, and some offered feelings of emotion I could not comprehend. The explosions became addictive as I anticipated each encounter. Then, a memory; it came suddenly, flashing across the screen of my mind and in that moment, I saw it all, everything that had been stolen from me. At the vision, an anguished scream tore from my lungs, coming head-to-head with the vexed howling of the sinister spirit. My spirit rose into battle with the opposing force. I screamed repeatedly, my torment colliding with the vicious rage spewing from the darkness. When my voice could no longer scream, I fell into the cool dark water. In the distance I heard the weathered door swing open and heavy footsteps enter. The small building shook as another vexed howl filled the room and then suddenly faded away as the threatening presence dissipated. A euphoric feeling of love surrounded me. This love empowered me, giving me more inner strength than I had ever experienced. The enraptured feeling was consuming, filling me with peace. The orb of light began to fade, the song of the woman drifted off to silence as the bubbling waters swirled around me. Someone was splashing their way toward me. They lifted me from the waters and carried me outside.

Chapter 29

Bethany woke early and joined Lillian in the adjoining restroom to get ready for the day. Even though she'd stayed up pretty late, talking with Jacob, she had no problem getting out of the comfortable bed. She had an incentive. Jacob had asked her to meet him at sunrise for a hike back to the falls. He said he had a suspicion and since she was dying to know what it was, she agreed to go with him. Besides, he was hot.

"Where are you off to so early?" Lillian asked while putting a second coat of mascara on her lashes.

Bethany applied a thin layer of gloss over her lips before replying. "Just doing some investigating with Jacob, I mean Agent Betancourt."

Lillian lowered the wand and stared at Bethany in the mirror. "So, we're on a first name basis with the man, now, are we?"

She grinned, "Well, Agent Betancourt is a mouthful; Jacob is so much easier to say."

"Uh huh," Lillian was sly, "Bethany Betancourt is a mouthful too."

She laughed and then felt guilty for her giddiness. She had only met Jacob because of the tragedy that had befallen Bronwyn. Lillian's next observation didn't add any comfort.

"You're like Bronwyn was a couple of weeks ago, staying out late and then venturing off with a mysterious man. Maybe it's the magic of this place." Grabbing her purse, she headed out the door, "Be careful Beth," She gave a haunting whisper, "We wouldn't want you swallowed up in the secrecy of the unknown."

She left the room and Bethany shivered.

Jacob was waiting for her on the front porch; he looked much more approachable in jeans and a T-shirt than he did in his intimidating black suit. Tiny lines creased around the corner of his mouth when he smiled, and she thought it added to his attractiveness, and that when he grinned, he favored his great grandfather, who despite his rough exterior was also a hottie. He was sporting a backpack, which he informed her carried their breakfast and a thermos of hot coffee they could enjoy once they reached the falls. Her heart skipped a beat at the thought.

They made the hike in record time, making small talk about the beauty of the place. Bethany told Jacob detailed stories of her stay last week and how, other than the fact that no one else was visiting the hidden town, everything seemed normal. It was when she mentioned normal that he chuckled.

"The best disguise," he said, "Is appearing normal."

She'd never thought about it that way, but he was right. Whatever secrets the town was hiding were veiled in the ordinary.

"Not one of us noticed anything unusual the entire time we were here, except Bronwyn." She sighed, "She wanted to leave right away, went hysterical on us during lunch our first day, saying she was being stalked by men in hooded robes roaming the woods... no one believed her."

Jacob moved aside a low branch blocking the path. "If she was so frightened what caused her to willingly stay behind when you both left? She must have found something enticing, something worth staying for."

Bethany laughed, "She did, and his name is Travis."

Jacob disagreed, "Then why is she with my great grandfather?"

Bethany stopped walking and looked at him. "I don't know. That is the question of the hour. She was afraid of him, or so she said, and then she showed up on the back of his bike like they're dating or something. Next, she takes him to her parents' house in Texas and introduces him as someone named Dakota, calls him her boyfriend, and fabricates a story about him having her on contract to author a book. Then a blood bath happens at her condo, and they disappear into thin air. You tell me, you're the investigator here."

He smiled and motioned for them to continue walking. They'd reached the clearing and he pointed to the rocky staircase leading to the top of the falls. "Let's have our breakfast up there."

Bethany wasn't used to rock climbing and became a little winded with the intensity of the climb. Jacob, however, was in excellent shape, scaling up the rocks like a deer with hind's feet, moving easily across the uneven terrain of this mountainous landscape. She felt somewhat embarrassed for tiring so easily and her inability to maneuver through the stony path. The climb was steep but not too treacherous and without the water cascading off the rocks, there was no fear of slipping. Still, she was grateful when they finally reached the top.

Opening his backpack, he pulled out a thermos and two mugs. The aroma of the coffee, combined with the scents of spruce and pine, was the perfect morning blend, invigorating her senses. He uncurled a paper bag and retrieved two large egg and cheese biscuits.

Bethany was surprised, "You cooked?"

He grinned again, "I was too excited to sleep so I got up early."

She wondered if his excitement stemmed from the investigation or meeting her for the walk. She hoped it was the latter.

"Okay Jacob," she said, biting into her biscuit. "Don't keep me waiting. I wanna hear your suspicions."

"It's simple really," he said while chewing. "You got a town of people who never age, hiding out here for hundreds of years, with a deep secret."

Bethany grinned this time, "You think they have the infamous fountain of youth?"

He shook his head, "No."

His answer surprised her, "No?"

He took a sip of his coffee, "If they had access to the fountain of youth, my great grandfather would have shared it with my great grandmother. They loved each other dearly, why would he continue to stay young and allow her to age?"

Bethany shrugged, "Ever read Tuck Everlasting? Maybe she didn't want to live forever."

"Maybe," he said, "But then I think my great grandfather would have refused the potent water and aged with her. What's the good of immortality if you live alone?"

Bethany nodded, "True."

"Besides," Jacob continued, "A group of random people who discover buried treasure is more than likely to turn on each other in time, or at least one member of the group will spill the beans, leaking the secret. And then there's the issue of money. Someone would betray the secret to get rich. So, what is it about this assembly of people that allows them to exist up here for years in unity and pull off this facade flawlessly?"

Bethany shook her head, "I don't know. You got me there."

He smiled and took a deep breath. "My suspicion is they are guarding the Tree of Life."

"You're serious?" She laughed. "You mean the Holy Bible Tree of Life? The one Adam and Eve weren't supposed to eat from?"

This time it was Jacob who laughed, "You need to study your Bible more, young lady. That was the tree of knowledge, not the tree of life."

She blushed at her ignorance, "Sorry I'm no Bible scholar."

He grinned at her and that caused her to blush even more. "Well let me give you a little Sunday school lesson then. Once they ate from the tree of knowledge, they were banned from the Tree of Life. He made them leave the garden and then he put the tree in another dimension."

Bethany's eyes were wide now. "You think God put the tree here?"

Jacob shrugged, leaned back against a rock, and sipped his coffee.

She thought for a moment, "I wonder why? Why would God not want them to have knowledge?"

Jacob sat aside his mug and wiped his mouth with his arm. "I don't necessarily think knowledge was forbidden. I think it's all-encompassing knowledge that he didn't want them to know. It's not always expedient to know everything. Wisdom, however, is different from knowledge. With life comes wisdom, so eating from the tree of life must have given wisdom and wisdom is better than knowledge. You can have all the knowledge in the world but if you do not have the wisdom to use it, then that's where you become dangerous and maybe that is what God was trying to prevent."

Bethany shook her head in disbelief, "Wow, and I never took any of that as literal."

"Most people don't."

"So, things like that really exist?"

Jacob took a deep breath, "Bethany my dear, the organization I work for is a special secretive branch devoted solely to incomprehensible mysteries. I'm just saying; nothing is impossible."

She sighed, "As adventurous as I thought I was, I think I'd rather exist in normalcy. There are some things I'd rather not know."

Pouring the last of his coffee out on the rocks, he began loading the backpack, "That's too bad. I'm leaving today, heading out to the old homestead, there's something there I need to check on and I was going to invite you to come. But if the mystery is too much for you..."

She smiled, intrigued at the invite, "I'd love to come."

Chapter 30

I was too tired to open my eyes. My head throbbed and when I swallowed it felt like a million pins were sticking in my throat. I tried to think but my mind was cloudy. I'd been to so many different places in the past week, existing on hardly any sleep, my rest was always interrupted by a desperate run for my life. Where was I? Was I in danger? Should I run now? Think. The fog filling my head moved aside just enough to remember the ram shackled house...Falcon's journals...the springhouse...the footsteps! I sat up fast and looked around. The room was dark giving me no clue as to where I was.

"Hello?" My voice was hoarse.

Someone stirred in the far corner. A dark silhouette moved from the shadows making its way toward the bed. Then, the sound of a striking match echoed across the room, the tiny flame dispelled the gloom of the dark chamber. I took in a quick breath, "Falcon!"

Relief flooded over me. He was alright. He'd escaped Abaddon's men and come to my rescue once again which was amazing considering the condition he was in the last time I saw him. Travis must have received word and rescued him at the portal and then healed his wounds. If so, Travis must be here too. Things were looking up already.

"I thought you were dead. How'd you..."

He smiled, turning up the wick of a small lantern. The calm I felt only seconds ago shattered. Something wasn't right... something about his smile... No, that wasn't it...I gasped again, backing away, the scar beneath his eye was missing!

"Please don't be frightened of me. That would distress me so."

The voice was different too. It was smooth, polished, and eloquent; and even though he'd asked me not to be frightened, terror gripped at the realization."Where am I? Where's Falcon?"

His smile didn't grow but remained the same. His eyes, however, skewered directly into me, searching to the point where I had no other choice than to look away. When I did my eyes fell on a strange vial hanging around his neck and the white stone pendant that said Ariston. The sight of it brought added unrest. Icy fingers touched my chin, lifting my face back toward his. He tilted his head and stared at me again. His eyes narrowed and seemed to pulse from green to a clouded seafoam and then back to green. "You are safe, in the city of Eden. Haytham, or Falcon as you know him, is being well taken care of; I can assure you."

Eden? His declaration was paralyzing. Terror stunned me to speechlessness and although I wanted to question him profusely my body would not allow it.

"I am no one for you to fear," he continued, "And yet no one to trifle with as well." His eyes clouded for a second and then cleared. Contrary to what you have been told by those who plot my demise, I am not your enemy." He poured water from a pitcher into an ornate goblet and handed it to me. I didn't reach for it, so he sighed and sat it back on the table.

"You are very lovely." He touched my hair, brushing it away from my face. His eyes clouded as he hungrily took in my form. "By what name are you called?"

"Abaddon?" I choked. His eyes cleared and he held the goblet to my lips and forced the drink. "What a coincidence, that is my name as well." He grinned. I swallowed the water. It felt heavenly against my parched throat and his playful response lifted some of my fear.

"My name's Bronwyn," I said, wiping the dribble from my chin. "How did I get here?"

His eyes narrowed and impaled me once again. "You located the second portal my love, transportation was quite simple after that."

"Are you going to kill me?"

His smile faded and I wished I hadn't asked.

"It grieves me that you think so ill of me. As I mentioned before, you need not fear me. If it were my intention to kill you, I would have ended your life when I found you lying helpless in the shallow pool. Besides, I usually do not make it a habit to slay the innocent."

"Then why did you bring me here?"

He didn't answer. He tilted his head again as if he didn't know why I was here. It was as if he were fighting some inner turmoil, all the while his eyes continued to swirl from the pure green to the milky seafoam. After a minute or two of uncomfortable scrutiny, he stood and made his way to the door. He was identical to Falcon minus the scar and the clothing choice. He was dressed casually yet elegantly in dark linen pants, a light gray pirate type shirt, opened in the front revealing the strange vial. He accessorized with a scarf draped once around his neck, the fringed ends hanging open and a wide leather belt cinched tightly around his waist. His pants were tucked into knee high soft suede boots. His hair was long, and the same length as Falcon, it too was brushed away from his face and fastened in a ponytail. His eyes were the same emerald, green, yet vacant.

He stopped at the door and pivoted on his heels, facing me once again.

"I will send my personal attendants in to care for you. They will honor any request except the one to leave. You are confined to the castle and the surrounding gardens for your protection."

"Protection?"

He brushed back a strand of hair that had fallen into his eyes and allowed them to bore into mine one last time.

"Beautiful Bronwyn, there are many in this world who do not wish your book to be written. Given the chance, they will kill you."

Chapter 31

Abaddon's personal attendants flooded the chamber only seconds after his departure which made me believe they had been hovering outside the door waiting to do his bidding. There were seven altogether, five women doing the serving and two men standing guard. All were silent as they went about their task of drawing a bath, brushing my hair, laying out clothing and serving me refreshment. They only spoke when spoken to, and then used as few words as possible.

After a tranquil bath in milky sweet-smelling waters, I received a relaxing manicure and pedicure. Halfway through the foot massage I began feeling somewhat anxious knowing Falcon was lying in prison, hurt, and possibly hanging on to life. Even though I needed the bath and relished the pampering, I felt it was an extreme waste of time considering the urgency of my situation. I longed to see Falcon and planned on asking Abaddon on their next encounter. The terror I felt for Abaddon was gone, replaced by wild curiosity and a spark of adventure.

I would not allow my mind to mull over the fact that I was in another dimension. It was too much to take in and I knew dwelling on it would only bring on extreme anxiety and handicap my judgment. My best defense would be to remain sharp and alert to my surroundings while gaining all the knowledge I could. That, I felt, would be the key to my return.

The ladies finished off my nails with a pink gloss, painted my eyes and lips and added mascara to my lashes. Then they dressed me in a strapless, pale yellow, Athenian style gown. I gazed at my reflection wearing the form fitting bodice, that revealed too much cleavage, and thought the attendants must have performed some kind of magic, transforming me into a tantalizing goddess. For the first time in a long time, I felt beautiful.

They slipped a pair of ankle strap sandals on my feet and then stood back to survey their work. It was then one of them spoke without being prompted.

"Dinner is being served in Abaddon's private dining room. He has requested your presence. Hamza and Conall will escort you there."

The beefy guards gave a slight bow of their heads acknowledging their assignment and swiftly escorted me out of the isolated chamber, down a broad hallway, and then descended a wide spiraling staircase. We made our way across the floor of an exquisitely furnished sitting room and through a set of double French style doors. Stepping outside, my delicate sandals clicked along a cobblestone walkway bordered by flowering bushes, hedges, hanging ferns and moss-covered trees.

The sun hung low in the sky, still radiating its warmth, while birds scattered across the soft violet expanse finding their rest in the massive branches of nearby trees. Other than my unfamiliar surroundings, this world proved no different than my own other than the time period being ambiguous. The manor grounds resembled a small renaissance city, quaint and simple yet surprisingly modern all the same. Many people scurried about, all staring at their infamous visitor, much like the citizens of Moonshine on my first day in town. These people, however, did not share the same excitement as the Moonshiners. In fact, I noticed my presence seemed to bring a much different emotion and it was difficult to discern whether they were saddened by my arrival or angry. In any case I was grateful for the guards.

My escorts led me to a neighboring structure with enormous wooden doors. Grabbing the brass handle, Hamza swung open the heavy gates allowing me entrance.

The place was breathtaking, and in all of my travels I'd never witnessed anything as lavish. Cathedral style, stained glass windows surrounded the room, the top of each pointing high to the third-floor dome ceiling. Plush sofas, divans and soft rugs littered the floor of the colossal area. Rectangular tables, no higher than a foot, formed a three-sided open square in the center of the room, allowing the waiters easy access. Lush decorative loungers surrounded the outside of the low-lying table allowing the diners to recline while eating. Ornamental fountains occupied the open area as well, offering a soothing ambiance to the reclining guests along with a small band of musicians pacifying the listeners.

Unsure of the situation, I held a nervous breath. I was the last to arrive, all the other diners were already at the table lounging and drinking from ornamental goblets. At my entrance the idle chatter dissipated, giving way to curious stares. One of the servers quickly made his way over to me, promptly escorting me to the settee nearest Abaddon. His stoic expression melted into a pleased smirk as I took to the comfortable couch, reclining on my left side.

Leaving the others, the servants congregated around me, tending to me alone. They dipped my hands in a bowl of warm water, and then wiped them dry with a soft cloth. A servant filled my goblet with drink, while another brought me large portions of food, laying out a spread of broiled fish, rice, cheese, nuts, fresh fruit, a variety of bread and creamy sauces for dipping. Once they'd served me, they brought food to the rest of the guests. There were no utensils on the table; everyone used their hands dipping into their own personal bowls. I watched the others eat, spellbound by the eccentricity of it all.

The musicians continued playing, their melody evoking a greater sense of lonesomeness, and although I was the obvious guest of honor at a prestigious dinner party, I felt isolated. Each note of their heart-rending tune brought with it suffocating thoughts of being trapped in another dimension far from Travis, never being near him again. I wondered if he had any way of knowing my situation and figured he didn't since I had no idea where he was either. My heart nearly ruptured at the thought and tears burned in my eyes with every stirring note the orchestra played. I wished they would stop or at least change the dirge to a livelier tune.

A cold substance touched my lips, breaking my trance and interrupting my mournful thoughts. Abaddon held a piece of bread covered in a cold creamy sauce to my mouth. "Eat, beautiful Bronwyn. Tonight's banquet is in your honor, each dish prepared specifically for you and while you are a delicate specimen of true loveliness, I fear you have become somewhat emaciated. Tell me, when was your last decent meal?"

I opened my mouth, accepting the offered morsel, leaving a trace of pottage on my lips which Abaddon promptly wiped away with his fingers. My stomach tightened at his touch, and I tried to keep from shuddering as a new dread began manifesting inside. I dipped into my bowl and began eating so he wouldn't feel the need to feed me again. And although I kept my head bowed, concentrating on my food, I felt his gaze upon me, and my cheeks burned hot because of it.

After a few minutes of painful silence, the dining guest began chatting again and even though they spoke in the foreign dialect their body language was easy to understand. Each one trying desperately to outshine the other while attempting to gain the favor of their esteemed host. Abaddon, however, appeared apathetic to their triviality concentrating only on me. I tried keeping my eyes low but every now and then they would glance up, and each time, I found his eyes fixed solely on me. I tried looking at the other diners but received in return, scowls from the women and looks of distrust and loathing from most of the men. There was one lovely woman however, who kept silent during most of the meal. She too seemed disgusted by the showy antics of the group and offered me a soft comforting smile when our eyes met. The meal continued for what seemed like hours and sometime during the whole of it, the sun set, and no longer filled the colorful stained glass with light. The room grew dim and soon dozens of candelabras sitting in various locations around the room lit magically. The orchestra continued playing, the diners continued to gorge and chatter, and Abaddon persisted in his unrelenting inspection of me. I sighed. Of all the tumultuous events of the past week; this occasion was proving to be the most torturous.

With the main course finally over, the servers cleared the table making way for trays of delectable desserts. The platters they laid on the table were laden with puddings, custards, fruit tarts, cakes, and an assortment of pastries.

Abaddon spoke and when he did, the room resonated with his voice. "Before we bring our next guest into the room, I request the language of choice be English to accommodate the lovely Bronwyn. I will now dismiss the musicians and the servers, and all women except Bronwyn of course. Your desserts will be served in the starlight chamber.

My stomach knotted at his announcement and the seed of fear attempted to take root once again.

The room cleared quickly; the chatter gone leaving an unnerving silence. This time I kept my eyes on Abaddon. His composed demeanor seemed to change as he drank from his goblet. I wondered what malevolent thoughts were invading his consciousness. He poured more into his chalice, savoring the drink, moving his tongue across his lips, like a serpent sniffing into the air. His pupils dilated as his eyes stared into the open room, focusing on nothing.

The heavy doors clattered open. I gasped at the sight. Two brawny guards shoved Falcon into the chamber. Blood oozed from his nose and lips. The eye above his scar was bruised and swollen shut. His hair was matted in blood, sticking to the front of his face. A blood-soaked bandage was wrapped around his right thigh. He wore a brass collar fastened tight around his neck with chains clasped around his wrist and ankles. His clothes were gone, only a loincloth of sorts covered his nakedness. His skin was shredded.

I stood, making my way over to him but a harsh command from Elam stopped me. "I'd stay put if I were you sweetheart."

I turned to face the arrogant man who gave the unwanted advice. I'd seen him before; in the underground cavern, leading the revolt. He was the man who easily gunned down one of his own; no doubt the one who ordered the massacre, killing Vulture, Hawke, and Macaw.

"Well, you're not me," I bit back, my anger for Falcon's condition fueling my courage. With determination I made my way toward Falcon. Elam's pride interfered once again.

"Stop her!" He gave the order directly to Hamza who moved away from the wall and caught me by the upper arm, pulling me back away from Falcon. I attempted to yank loose, but his tight clutch would not allow it.

"Sit!" Elam ordered as if I were a misbehaving dog. My disgust for him would not allow me to sit, so I stood in defiance, staring at him with eyes like daggers. Elam nodded to Hamza who with one effortless tug slammed me back onto the plush divan. Fury boiled inside, giving way to a spirited rebellion. In retaliation I grabbed the edge of a dish filled with warm custard and hurled it toward Elam; the contents splashing into his face and covering his expensive attire. The room grew deathly quiet, the tension hung thick in the air, all eyes on Elam and me. Even Abaddon sat unmoved watching the battle of wills. Not to be shamed in front of the men, Elam stood abruptly, and in one swift move pushed me flat on the settee then clinched his hand around my delicate neck. His fingers circled around my throat much like the brass collar Falcon wore, and then he squeezed enough to steal my breath. I gasped for air. He climbed on top of me pressing his face close to mine.

"The plan was to kill you on sight. Your life has been spared due to unforeseen circumstances. Still, it's better for us if you're dead so I wouldn't press the limits anymore. You understand?"

I couldn't swallow let alone make a sound, and for the first time since my arrival I suffered. The wickedness of the enemy was now set in motion and the seed of terror began to grow.

"You understand?" Elam asked again, tightening his grip around my neck. He wanted my submission and I refused to give it. From where he was positioned, I could easily raise my leg and knee him, but wasn't sure if I could get enough momentum to do any harm. If I made the attempt and it fell short, he might end my life right there. He tightened his choke hold again and I wheezed. The light in the room seemed to dim and, in the distance, I heard Falcon say, "Submit for now Scribe, it's your only chance."

Before I could acknowledge Falcon's request and give in to Elam, Abaddon's voice resonated across the room.

"Enough!" At his command, Elam loosened his grip but finalized his disapproval with a hard slap across my face. Against my unyielding resolve, I rolled on my side, gasping for air, and cried out in pain.

Leaning forward, Abaddon cupped my head in his hand and fed me drink from his goblet. The sweet nectar mixed with the copper taste of blood oozing from my split lip. I stifled at the taste of it. After drinking a few swallows, Abaddon again wiped my lips, cleaning the blood with his fingers. Expressionless, he stared into my eyes and then licked the blood from his fingers. Shuddering I looked away, horror flourishing inside of me.

He faced Elam, "We've wasted enough time and I needn't remind you that time is no longer on our side." He picked up his chalice and returned to his reclining position, "Give your report."

Elam wiped the custard from his clothing the best he could before turning to the table. He glared at me and in some strange way I almost feared him more than I did Abaddon. His arrogance fueled his ambition, and a prideful man desperately trying to advance his influence is dangerous; especially when there is no integrity or morality to channel his lust.

He cleared his throat. "My strategy for the most part has been quite successful. However, as in all best laid plans, there are unforeseen circumstances that slow the progression of the operation. I was able to cast suspicion in the hearts of a few of Haytham's men. They unwillingly gave up his location and as I suspected he had the prophesied scribe in his keep. The identity of the scribe, however, was one of those unforeseen circumstances and my directives were changed because of it. I complied with our Lord's wishes and now we have in our possession the scribe and Haytham. What we still lack is Travis, and the book of redemption which was unfortunately left in the other world. However, we have the Scribe so that ensures that we will get Travis. And, a wordless book, without the author, is useless."

For the first time since my arrival, I thought of my travel bag and the book of redemption. Where was it? Had I left it behind in the spring house? My heart raced at what I had already written and the consequences if anyone were to read it.

"It's not wordless." I found my voice, interrupting his report, inciting alarm on the faces of the men.

"I began the story already." Abaddon's eyes cut over to Elam, no doubt reprimanding him with his mind and in the deafening silence Falcon raised his eyes and flashed me a concealed grin.

Elam made light of my announcement, "What does it matter? So, she began the story, she couldn't have written much. They've been on the run for the past week; at best she penned two or three pages." He gave a confident smirk. "I'm right, aren't I? You were only able to pen a couple of pages?"

I returned the sneer, "It matters not how many pages were penned, what's important is the power of the words written." I lifted the chalice to my lips, carefully avoiding the painful split. "Ever heard of the Latin term in medias res?"

He hadn't and so I swallowed the sweet nectar before enlightening him.

"It's a literary narrative technique where the story begins at the conclusion, rather than the beginning and then backtracks." I smiled savoring his pained expression.

"I'm quite good at it; I adopted that writing style some time ago. Who knows, I may have begun the book of redemption in that manner, if I did, then I'd say your fate has already been sealed."

There was silence for about ten seconds before the room turned to chaos. Elam's voice rose above the uproar, "She's bluffing."

I raised my eyebrows, challenging his accusation, "Why would I make that up? The second prophecy said the beginning of the book was mine and if I followed my heart, I would preserve life...so I did."

At the mention of the second prophecy the clamor intensified. Elam tried to regain control but when Abaddon stood the bedlam stopped.

"It sickens me to see the elect become rattled and lose all restraint at the slightest hint of hostility. If our fate was already sealed, would we be here at this hour with two of our most notorious enemies as our prisoners? It's a disgraceful regime that accepts defeat in their hearts before the war is finished being waged. Any of you who accept subjugation on circumstantial evidence will be executed immediately. Am I clear on this?"

The men shifted on their chaises, self-conscious of their esteemed leader's disapproval. Even Elam wore a shameful expression, which switched to bitter hatred when he looked my way. I'd humiliated him in front of Abaddon, and his own men, somehow, someway he'd make me pay. Abaddon was my only chance of escaping Elam's wrath. For whatever reason he seemed to like me, but then again that could be to my detriment as well.

Abaddon returned to his chaise, resting on his left elbow. He patted the open space next to him, and then extended his arm to me. My heart thundered against my chest. I'd displayed amazing nerve going up against Elam in a battle of wits but feared my spunk might take a beating under his heinous plotting.

I swallowed and remained frozen on my personal sofa. I had no desire to cozy up next to Abaddon. He'd touched my lips twice already, even licking my blood from his fingers and the thought of his unwanted advances turned my stomach.

His eyes bore into mine, then tilting his head; he patted the area beside him once again. I remained frozen still yet made the mistake of glancing toward Falcon. I didn't know why I did it but wished I hadn't. Abaddon noticed, and a slight nod was the only instruction needed for the guards to club him in the back of his legs, sending him to his knees. It was then I noticed the deep lashes cut into his back. It was when the guard lifted his club again poised to strike that I made my move, jumping from my settee and joining Abaddon on his. I didn't recline but sat in the offered space which seemed to please him. Leaning high on his elbow he stroked my hair, while touching the softness of my cheeks. His hands lingered where his eyes did, running down my neck and across the top of my breast. I closed my eyes and held my breath. "Don't hurt him...please. He doesn't deserve to be treated that way."

Laughter erupted from around the table followed by opinionated comments of the legends surrounding Falcon. Elam's sarcastic voice launched a pathetic rebuttal.

"The punishment for high treason is death and I believe that holds true in the world you come from as well."

"If that is the case then all of you should be sentenced first. For it is my understanding that Abaddon led the rebellion that dissolved the allegiance with the three governing princes of Eden."

At my words a hush fell across the room, the silence so stark that the sound of the trickling fountain seemed like a massive waterfall. No one spoke, not even me, although my mind raced with a million reprimands, I dared not utter another, not yet anyway. My candor surprised me. It had been some time since I'd been this gutsy. The breakup with Ryan had changed me, stripping me of my spirited personality and sense of adventure. Bethany had been right; I had changed and hadn't noticed it until now. Maybe it was traveling through the dimension, or the frequent rushes of adrenaline in the fight to save my life that jolted me back. Whatever the case, there was a sense of freedom in being myself again.

Abaddon removed his fingers from my breast and raised himself to a sitting position. He wrapped his arm around me, drawing me close. Avoiding my swollen lip, he placed a lingering kiss on my neck before whispering in my ear. "Do you love Haytham?"

My stomach constricted at his touch, and I fought to stay calm. I didn't want to display fear, for if Abaddon knew of my faintness, he'd use it to his advantage. I turned my mouth to his and whispered back, "Like a brother."

He paused. His head tilted as if he were hearing something in the far distance. He tilted it again and seemed lost in thought. He laughed and his eyes danced, switching to the deep emerald green. He backed away from me, as if he were frightened, then stood abruptly and headed for the exit.

"We're done for tonight." With those words he stormed out through the massive doors leaving everyone baffled.

Chapter 32

The soft rap on the chamber door startled me. Had I been sleeping I wouldn't have heard it. But ever since I returned from the dining room, sleep would not come. I'd laid in the regal bed for some time, contemplating my situation, the sexual advances of Abaddon, Elam's loathing of me and Falcon's physical condition. I figured he was alright. Emotionally, he was strong-willed, and determined. Besides, the grin he'd displayed confirmed he was still his wayward self. I had no doubt he was planning his escape and the criminal beating of the guards holding him. I'd spared his life for now, insinuating to Abaddon that I didn't love him. There was only one man I truly loved, and he was worlds away. My heart burned at the thought of him, and I wondered if he was thinking of me, and if he was concerned that I was missing in action. He probably figured out by now that Abaddon's men had captured us, and I hoped he didn't think I was dead. I'd been away from him, for as long as I'd known him, and I wondered how I could love a man I'd only known for such a short amount of time. It was crazy, but I couldn't help it. The love I felt for him was like nothing I'd ever experienced before. And just as traveling to the new dimension had renewed my self-awareness, it had also heightened my longing to be with him.

The rap at the door sounded again and my stomach tightened, hoping Abaddon wasn't coming in with certain intentions. Maybe I should feign sleeping and my clandestine guest would go away. Another soft knock and I figured Abaddon being who he was would just enter and not wait for an invitation. Whoever was outside was knocking softly so as not to call attention to themselves. Figuring it might be important; I climbed out from under the silk sheets of the magnificent bed. I unbolted the door and opened it just wide enough to see the beautiful woman from dinner with a soft smile.

"Please, may I come in?"

Curious, I bid her entrance.

"I do apologize for waking you from your slumber."

"Actually, you didn't. I haven't been able to sleep."

"I can empathize with that," the woman's words were tender. "It's not surprising considering the dramatic turn of events after dinner, still the hour is late and for that I apologize."

I wondered how the woman knew what happened after the evening meal since she had been sequestered to another room. "So, you heard?"

The woman smiled. "News like that travels fast, even if it does transpire during a covert meeting. Bedside's Elam's soiled clothing sort of gave it away." She laughed delicately and touched me on the hand. "You've got spunk honey, hang on to it and keep your wits about you, it will help you survive."

I relaxed. Finally, a friend, possibly someone to confide in, and enlighten me on how to stay alive in this dimension until I could find a way to return home. And as if the woman could read my mind, she offered just that. The expression on her face grew serious as she moved close to me and motioned to the outdoor veranda.

"Have you smelled the fragrances of the evening? They're quite delightful and therapeutic. The aromas will aid in relaxing you so you can sleep."

This was her secret way of luring me onto the balcony so we could talk without the fear of being overheard, which suddenly made me paranoid, wondering if there were listening devices or cameras hidden in my room.

The night air was balmy, a soothing breeze stirred through the trees, mixing the fragrances of the flowering plants, delivering the pleasing aroma onto the upper balcony. I inhaled and smiled. The perfume brought a euphoric feeling. I'd smelled this bouquet before and recently, but where? The scent desired to take me back to a particular event, a blessed memory that I had forgotten. My heart skipped, longing to unlock the memory, it was there, close, within the reach of my fingertips. I inhaled again and my mind went to Travis.

"Smells heavenly, doesn't it?" The woman interrupted my dreaming.

"It does."

The woman moved in closer and spoke in hushed whispers.

"Time is not on our side so I will get to the purpose of my late-night call. I do apologize for my ill manners. I have yet to introduce myself to you. My name is Kenalycia, and they say you know my Travis."

My cheeks burned a crimson red and although my heart dropped into my stomach it raced while doing so.

"Is he well?" Kenalycia asked, tears burning in her eyes at the question. My throat tightened preventing me from speaking so I shook my head instead.

Kenalycia sighed, and then took a deep breath. "Has he waited for me, or does he love another?"

I forced a smile, holding back the tears that were pooling just behind my eyes. My heart thundered and suddenly I felt extremely exhausted. The first time I saw Ryan on the cover of a magazine with Gabriella could not compare to the way I felt now. I swallowed, and bit back the emotion. I didn't want to cry, not in front of her but I wasn't sure how much longer I could keep my tears at bay.

"The rumor is his heart belongs to only one person." I worked hard at keeping my voice from quaking. "He's waited faithfully."

Kenalycia dropped her face into her hands and began weeping. She was a beauty, ivory skin, ebony hair, and emerald, green eyes. Her lips were full, and her lashes fanned wide across her lids, giving her such an innocent look.

"It was such a wicked thing that happened. We were robbed, separated by evil, never having the chance to live our life together. Abaddon led the revolt the night of our union. He kidnapped me and had me confined to the palace. After Haytham helped me escape through the portal, Abaddon's men found me right away and brought me back. My recovery was top secret, Travis never knew. The day he went through the portal without me was the day I died inside. After Travis was gone Abaddon made me his wife. I've survived only with the blessed hope that I will be with my dear Travis one day. And now...you're here and it seems possible again." She hung her head, "I hope he will have me even though I've been with Abaddon."

I looked away and let the breeze dry my misting eyes. I took a deep breath. "I'm sure his love for you far surpasses that."

"Will you take me to him?" Her question surprised me. My first reaction was to say, "Hell no! Not on your life sweetie, finders' keepers, I have the key to the portal and I'm heading back alone". Instead, I thought of the joy it would bring Travis if I showed up with his love in tow. But could I do it? I loved him myself with a strong powerful love and although I couldn't explain it, I knew it wasn't a lustful crush. There was a painful depth to it. But then again, wasn't that the true love Travis had defined so beautifully that night in the garden? Could I give him away, knowing I would never experience him, but he would experience all he'd ever dreamed? I could if my love was for him and not myself.

"I'm a prisoner here, same as you. I am not allowed to leave."

Kenalycia moved in closer, "For years I have been plotting my escape. The one problem was that Abaddon controlled the portal. Now you have control too. So, with your help I will be able to put my plan into action."

I offered my second excuse, "I don't know how to use the portal. I'm pretty sure I came through by accident. Besides, I don't think I have control."

"Yes, you do control it, you came through it alone. Abaddon found you here, lying in the shallow pool at the falls."

I came through alone? I fought through the haze of that night. I remembered hiding in the spring house. The rest was a blur. I faintly recalled something terrifying coming into the darkness, scratches on the door, then the song of the woman, the intense heat, the moon, the tiny orbs of light...it was all coming back! There was a memory...something I'd forgotten about, something very important, what was it? And just as the memory began to take root, Kenalycia touched my shoulder, interrupting the revelation, leaving the events of the night just as hazy as before.

"Are you alright dear? You seem perplexed."

"It's all just a tad bit overwhelming," I said, frustrated at her intrusion. Kenalycia's wide eyes locked on mine, "I understand completely, but we must make haste if we intend to make it to the portal before sunrise."

"Leave now?" Her anxiousness was understandable, but I never fathomed she meant to escape immediately. She seemed somewhat pushy, and it annoyed me, and I wondered if my irritation stemmed from jealousy.

"Yes, now. My dear, take it from one who knows, by tomorrow night you will be in Abaddon's bed. He is quite captivated with you, and he has no qualms about taking what he wants. As a matter of fact, I am somewhat surprised he hasn't had you escorted to his bedchamber already. I saw the way he looked at you."

I shuddered at the thought.

She noticed my fear and gave another warning, "And it gets worse. Some of the women here are ruthless. They all desire to be intimate with Abaddon. Given the chance they will hurt you. You should have heard their plotting during desert."

Leaving sounded like the thing to do but then there was the matter of Falcon. It didn't feel right leaving him behind.

Excuse number three, "I can't leave without Falcon."

Kenalycia looked puzzled, "You have a pet bird?"

"Haytham...I meant Haytham. I can't leave without him, especially since Abaddon plans on executing him. He saved my life so many times, it wouldn't be right to abandon him."

Again, Kenalycia's lips melted into the soft smile. "You are so lovely, no wonder you were preordained to be the Scribe. I can imagine the stories you have penned are filled with sacrificial love. It's beautiful really, something so foreign to our world, especially during these days of Abaddon's rule."

For a moment it seemed Kenalycia had disregarded the urgency in her mission as she gazed across the veranda, staring into the starlit sky, as if she were reliving cherished memories once forgotten.

"No matter," she said, breaking her own trance. "Rescuing Haytham at this point is suicide. But don't be troubled, Abaddon will not kill him anytime soon. He'll need him. Like you, Haytham has information about the other world and the whereabouts of my Travis. Besides, the execution will be a grand deal. Abaddon will want everyone in attendance. Including Travis." Her knowledge of the matter seemed reasonable; still it seemed cruel to leave him behind.

"Please," she was losing patience, "if we're to accomplish this we must leave now. The two men guarding your door are my friends. They will accompany us there safely, but we must make our escape now, otherwise it will be too late."

"And what will the punishment be if we're caught?"

"We won't be caught," Kenalycia was adamant. "I believe it's mine and Travis' destiny to be together, we were stopped before; we won't be again. You have arrived and now the promises are being fulfilled. Besides we have Hamza and Conall with us. They are the two highest ranking guards in the entire city of Eden. No one will question us if we are seen with them."

I sighed, heavy-hearted and tried to think of another excuse to delay their expedition but there wasn't one.

"Okay, let's go."

I dressed back into the Athenian gown wishing I had something more appropriate to wear, but the servants had taken my clothes, leaving me with only the dress and the silk see-through nightgown I was wearing. Of the two choices, the dress seemed the most appropriate. When I finished changing Kenalycia gave a soft rap on the door. Hamza opened it and nodded acknowledging all was clear. Kenalycia squeezed my hand and together we stole behind Hamza and Conall down the splendid spiraling staircase across the sitting room and out through the double French doors.

Once we'd made our way out of the main castle and across the grounds, it was only a half hour walk to the portal. They didn't talk much; and when they did, it was usually in the other language. I didn't care; I didn't have a lot to say anyway. I purposely kept my mind off the subject at hand, but as hard as I tried not to think about it, I found myself unwillingly rehearsing what I would say to Travis.

Hi honey, I'm home and I brought you a souvenir from Eden.

That wouldn't work. He probably would be offended if I referred to his lifelong love as some kind of vacation knick-knack. Maybe...

Hi Travis, I'm back and would you look at what the cat drug in.

No, that seemed too disparaging, like I was comparing Kenalycia to a disheveled dead rat. How about bearing my soul?

Hello Travis, I went to Eden and met Kenalycia, and I brought her to you because I know having her back will make you happy. Even though it kills me to hand her over to you, I will do it because for some reason I love you. I can't explain why my heart is so drawn to someone I've only known for a week. It makes no sense yet the first time my eyes looked into yours that stormy night on the bridge, my soul connected to your soul, and it has not rested since that moment. It longs to be near you, aches at the thought of you, yearns for your touch and tries to remind me of something I have misplaced and need to find. To be honest, I feel adrift without you, and I never realized how lost I was until I stood before you that night, and for a brief fleeting second, I felt as if I'd come home after having been gone for years...I know you do not share the same feelings for me, so I guess I do know what true love is after all. Tears pooled in my eyes, spilling over, and trickling down my cheeks. I was glad the early morning hours remained dark, that way no one would notice the pain etched in my face.

The morning air was heavy with dew, soaking the tall grass; and even though I held the hem of my dress high, it still absorbed the water. The misty air wreaked havoc on my hair as well. I glanced over at Kenalycia who resembled a fragile goddess; her perfect lips were pursed in an anticipated smile, no doubt conjuring up the romantic welcome that awaited her. Her thick mane of hair seemed to come alive with body, and the tiny dewdrops clung to her ebony locks like miniature stars in the midnight sky. I no longer felt beautiful in my Athenian dress.

Hamza stopped abruptly, speaking to Kenalycia and Conall in a foreign tongue and then retreated away, disappearing into the trees.

I wished they would clue me in without me having to ask, and again I felt annoyed and hoped it didn't show in my voice.

"What's going on?"

"My apologies for our rudeness, I forget you do not speak the language. Hamza is making sure no one is following. It is possible for hitchhikers to sneak into the portal making the trip through the dimension. Once the portal opens, it remains accessible for a good seven minutes allowing easy access for any stowaways. That is what happened during my escape. Everything turned into chaos. Haytham and Travis were so engaged in fighting off the enemy; they never saw the men jump into the portal and come after me. I was apprehended in no time and brought back through the vortex." I sighed, "We're trying to keep that from happening again."

I had a desperate idea that would keep me from the pain of seeing Travis welcome back his love. "Why don't I open the portal and send you through with directions on where to find Travis. That way I could remain behind and guard the door, so no one follows you."

And if it were possible, Kenalycia's eyes widened even more, "Oh my, you are such a dear. I'm overwhelmed at your kindness to a complete stranger. Forgive my emotions but it is a rare find these days. To be honest I haven't had a real friend in years, not one I could trust anyways."

Shame punched me in the face. My offer wasn't birthed from kindness but rather from my heart's self-preservation. In any case it didn't matter, for Kenalycia would not hear of me remaining behind. It was much too dangerous. Hamza returned, barked a few words in the unknown dialect, and we continued.

The portal site resembled a shrine. A giant ornamental structure had been fashioned around the entrance. Two soldiers guarded the entry to the underground waterfall at all times. Two burning torches stood at the opening giving the passageway to the underground portal a primeval look. Hamza went on ahead and spoke with the two guards. After a few minutes he motioned for us to come. Following Hamza, we descended the steep decline into the underground cavern. Beautiful lights had been placed into the rock walls, illuminating the shallow pool, and falling water, giving it a mystical appearance. The waterfall seemed almost identical to the one in Moonshine. I sighed at the memory of that night and the supernatural encounter I'd had at the top. The recollection of Travis touching my face and placing my hand on his chest was now almost unbearable. I forced the thought from my mind and as I crept along behind the falling water, nervousness clawed at my stomach. I was anxious to see Travis, there was no doubt about it; but the eagerness was crowded out by knowing I was not the one he'd be thrilled to see. Tears wet my eyes so I kept my head down so Kenalycia wouldn't notice. I'd hate to explain how much I loved "her" Travis. I took a deep breath as I stepped on the polished rock behind the falls. Kenalycia moved in beside me and when Hamza and Conall crowded in on both sides, Kenalycia gave an affirmative nod.

"I'm sorry; I don't know what to do." I admitted.

"You simply say two words. They can be any of your choosing."

Before I could say anything, somewhere in the distance the haunting song of the woman began ever so softly. I paused to listen; the melody summoned me, trying to remind me of something long forgotten. It was the same with the opulent scent on the veranda; it too tried to unlock a forgotten secret. What was it I couldn't remember?

"Please," Kenalycia seemed anxious, "We must leave now, I was followed once before and do not wish for it to happen a second time."

I nodded and closed my eyes, "For Travis." It was a whisper, but still I said it. And then... the vision. Under the falling water Travis reached for me, and just as I reached out to him, I fell into the blackness.

Chapter 33

The only turbulence during the flight to New Mexico took place in Bethany's stomach. The fact that she agreed to accompany Jacob to the homestead after knowing him for only a few short days surprised her. It wasn't like her to take off in reckless abandon without sitting down and making out a plan first; let alone with a man she hardly knew. And to make matters worse, he was kin to Falcon and as far as she knew, it was Falcon who had put Bronwyn in peril. Or maybe Lillian was right, and the peculiar town of Moonshine had a strange effect on unsuspecting women; luring them into surreptitious relationships with shadowy men who enticed them into precarious situations. Now, sitting thirty thousand feet in the air, jetting toward an abandoned house, shrouded in secrecy, she wondered if she hadn't lost her mind somewhere in the fallout of what happened to Bronwyn.

August was winding down. September would be here soon. A month ago, she would never have imagined all of this. It's funny how life will take a drastic turn without giving any warning at all; and suddenly you find yourself catapulted into situations beyond your control. Like the time her mother picked her up from school, and instead of driving home, they hit the interstate and drove for hours until they arrived at a rundown motel in Texas. It's hard for a fourth grader to understand why her mother would leave her father and put that many miles between them. It was also difficult to fathom why she wasn't allowed to say goodbye or even go home and get her favorite things. Her mother had packed only what she thought was necessary, leaving behind Bethany's most treasured possessions. It was that turn of events however that eventually allowed her and Bronwyn's paths to cross...a treasure she had no intention of leaving behind this time.

Swallowing back the tears she looked out her window. The earth below resembled a green and brown checkerboard, with each square of land perfectly measured and set with boundaries. Even the streets intersected at precise times, all life controlled by the human mindset of parallel lines and boxes. This pattern continued on for miles, repeating itself until a river snaked its way through the checkerboard, interrupting the plan with beautiful twists and turns.

The picture below reminded her of a blog she read once. In the article the writer mentioned this very scenario; comparing it to how we as humans live our lives, spending our time and effort trying to put the whole of life and God in our little boxes of understanding. "Little by little," she said, "We create a world without the beauty of mountain ranges or rivers; and although the flat land is boring to us, we prefer it because it's safe and seems to make sense." And as Bethany's eyes followed the river she wondered if this entire turn of events was God's finger, interrupting her carefully laid out plans. And if that was the case, then maybe some good was to come out of this too. With that thought, the turmoil of her mind gave way just enough for her to settle back and sleep the remainder of the flight.

The plane hit the tarmac just as the sun hit the horizon. Since it would be futile to try and investigate after sunset, Jacob suggested they go out to dinner instead and get an early start in the morning. He chose a nice restaurant, requesting a table outdoors so they could dine under the starry sky.

Through the first half of dinner, they talked about his career and the fact that he had never submitted to holy matrimony. He confessed he was pretty much married to the job; and that, combined with having to keep secrets of his whereabouts and activities, usually ended up running off all the women he dated. Then he complimented Bethany on her sense of adventure, saying the fact she dropped everything to accompany him to Moonshine and then on to New Mexico impressed him. She relished the compliment but thought the impulsive decision was birthed more from her innate curiosity than a daring spirit.

"Bronwyn always sparked my sense of adventure," She admitted to him. "I probably wouldn't have done half the things I did, had it not been for her prodding me along."

Jacob sipped his wine, "She's been a good friend to you?"

Bethany nodded, "The best. I love her, she's like the sister I never had."

Taking another sip of his wine, he narrowed his eyes on her. "How far would you go to help her?"

His question unnerved her and the look on his face added to the alarm.

"What do you mean?"

"Exactly what I said, how far would you go to help her?"

This time it was Bethany who grabbed her glass and drank. The wine warmed her inside, relaxing the panic-stricken butterflies in her stomach. What was he up to? Clearing her throat, she tried to stay composed. "Why?"

Resting on his right elbow, Betancourt leaned over the table, "Because Bethany, Bronwyn is part of something that will be hard for you to wrap your mind around. What you learn could change the course of your life forever."

She must have looked bewildered because he continued. "I'm not sure what belief system you subscribe to, or if you believe in God. All I'm saying is if you have any faith at all, what you learn during this investigation will test it. I just want to make sure you're ready for the challenge?"

She laughed brushing the warning off, "My mother got upset after reading The Da Vinci Code; said it shook her faith. I read it. So, what if Christ was married. Marriage isn't a sin? Would being married make him any less the messiah? I figure, if a fictional novel could shake your faith, well it wasn't that strong to begin with."

"True," Jacob said, "But what if the information has the opposite effect. What if it not only proves the existence of God, but of other entities as well?"

"Are you implying that Bronwyn is an extra-terrestrial? If that's the case, why doesn't she just phone home?" Bethany laughed at her own joke; hoping humor would lighten the anxiousness she was feeling.

Jacob didn't miss a beat, "Not extra-terrestrial my dear, but extra dimensional. Do you realize that almost all paranormal activity is caused by breaks into other dimensions?"

Bethany squirmed in her chair feeling as if she'd just entered the twilight zone. She'd never been one to delve into the paranormal, the subject frightened her.

"What are you saying? You think Bronwyn is in another dimension right now?"

"She could be, I don't know, but I do believe she came from one. How, or for whatever reason I don't know."

Bethany took another sip of her wine. Martin admitted there was no record of her birth, no missing child report, nothing. Then there was the strange language... it was all so bizarre. To think her best friend was from another dimension was too much to take in. And if she hadn't heard enough, he continued.

"Bronwyn's special Bethany. I think she was hidden here, on our earth, for a purpose."

Goosebumps tickled her skin, racing up her arms and stirring her hair.

"What purpose?" and as soon as she asked the question, she wished she hadn't. True, sometimes it was better off not knowing things, but not knowing didn't make it any less real. The issue was, could she handle the knowledge she was soon to receive? And then, there she was, standing at the tree of knowledge, wondering if she should take a bite of Jacobs's apple.

The dinner conversation robbed her of sleep. Lying in the hotel bed, she watched the news, listening to eerie stories of Roanoke and Moonshine. The latest accounting coming across the wire was that the whole thing was a publicity stunt for Ryan's new movie. It was amazing what some people choose to believe. Speaking of believing, she'd pulled the Gideon Bible from the drawer but didn't really know where to begin reading. After skimming through Genesis, and trying to make sense of Revelation, she closed the book and muted the TV. Picking up her cell she aimlessly hit Bronwyn's number. As she figured, it went straight to her voicemail. She let it play, enjoying the sound of her friend's cheery voice. At the tone all was silent, and as the light emanating from the TV cast shadows across the room, she mulled over Jacob's answer to her question and finally drifted off to sleep.

Chapter 34

Hamza jimmied open the springhouse door, it was early morning, the sun was just beginning to rise in the early September sky. I had no clue as to what day it was, or how much time had passed since I'd been away. The days switched over in a blur of confusion; my only hope was that things had calmed down and we would be able to make it back to Moonshine undetected. The authorities were no doubt still searching for me and Falcon. The thought of him chained and in prison, worlds away, caused pain and I wondered if he would approve of what I was doing.

I led the way down the long-crooked path to the ramshackle house. The Suburban was still parked out front along with the car that arrived the night I sat upstairs reading Falcon's private journals. Fortunately, Elam had left the keys in the ignition, so at least our transportation problem was solved. The recollection of the journals spawned an idea so before climbing behind the wheel, I left my companions with the car, and went inside to retrieve the books.

The front door was ajar, so I entered that way, thankful I didn't have to climb through the broken window in my evening gown. The early morning sun pierced through the shattered panes casting a golden glow across the dirty floor. The rays filled with floating dust created a haze, obscuring my vision; but a creak on the steps brought my attention to the form of someone standing on the decaying staircase.

"Bronwyn?" My heart raced at the familiar call. I shielded my eyes from the glowing rays and stepped past the light. My vision cleared for a moment until the tears pooled, blurring my ability to see once again.

Travis bit down hard on his jaw, closing his eyes and then reopening them like he did the first night I met him on the bridge. He stood still, gazing at my form outlined by the golden light. I smiled at him through my tears, thrilled to be in his presence yet sickened at the thought of passing him over to Kenalycia. Pushing through the emotion, I choked out a greeting.

"What are you doing here?"

His voice was quiet yet determined, "Falcon said I would find you here."

I laughed through the tears, "Well you did."

He stared at me, taking in my form in a way I had yet to see him do. "You've been to Eden?"

I nodded, "I have." I looked down at my clothes and ran my hand down my dress smoothing the mess. He stepped off the staircase, making his way toward me. He touched my split lip and looked me over. I thought my heart would literally rip right in two. As much as I desired his touch, I stopped him by nodding toward the front door. Although I'd rehearsed what I would say nearly the entire trip, I could think of nothing other than, "I brought you back something."

He looked at me puzzled. I nodded to the outside of the house. "Go ahead, take a look."

He gave me a lingering gaze, before stepping into the glowing rays of dust where I could no longer see him and headed out the door. No matter how self-sacrificing the act was, I couldn't bear to watch. I had to leave. Rushing out the back door I bolted down the porch steps, tore across the overgrown yard and headed toward the crooked path. I didn't hold back the tears, but rather allowed them to pour down my face. Once deep in the woods, far away from everyone, I stopped running, collapsed against a sturdy tree, and sobbed.

I cried without stopping, my heart mourning the extravagant loss; and while I gave into the pain of sacrificial love, I neglected to hear the footsteps skulking down the path, stopping directly behind me. Yet in the face of my inner grief, I sensed the opposing spirit, a manifestation so sinister, my skin chilled in the warm morning sun. Turning around slowly I jumped to my feet, terror pulsating through my veins at the sight of Elam's manic smile.

Chapter 35

Bracing herself, Bethany grasped the door handle while Jacob sped into the front yard of the run-down house. Bumping across the lawn, he drove over the broken sidewalk, stopping only a few feet from a dead man lying in the grass. Blood marked the path of his demise, splattering across the porch and ending in the puddle where his lifeless body lay. Two men were engaged in an intense knife fight, tumbling over the two parked cars and across the overgrown yard while a beautiful woman watched the battle. At their arrival Bethany watched her disappear into the darkness of the abandoned house

"That's Travis," Bethany gasped, recognizing one of the men, while bracing against the intense bumping.

Jacob slammed on the brakes and then pulled a gun from his jacket, inserting a round in the chamber. "Call the police."

Pulling her cell from her purse, she dialed 911; her fingers trembling with each punch. While she waited for the operator, Jacob jumped from the car, aiming his gun.

"Freeze!"

Paying no attention to the command, Travis continued his fight, slashing his razor-sharp knife across the chest of his latest victim. Weakened, Hamza stumbled, giving Travis the opportunity to grab him, and with the same prowess as Falcon, slit his throat and tossed him in the dirt.

Horrified, Bethany screamed into her phone, telling the operator what she had witnessed.

Travis turned to Jacob, peering at him through the tatters of hair sticking to his face, wet with perspiration. Bethany shuddered; she'd never seen such ferociousness in him; he'd always appeared as such a gentleman. She never figured him to be the blood-soaked savage standing before them.

"Drop your weapon now!" Jacob ordered cocking back his gun.

"There's no time Jacob," Travis panted. "Bronwyn's in trouble."

Guarded, Jacob kept his gun aimed but softened his tone, "How do you know who I am?"

"Your great grandfather is my friend."

Travis' disclosure confirmed Jacob's suspicions. He grinned pleased for now, "So he is alive."

Travis' agitation rang in his voice, "Alive yes, but in serious trouble and needs my help. The longer you detain me you seal his and Bronwyn's fate."

Jacob narrowed his eyes on Travis, contemplating the situation. "This is a high-profile case Mr. Colton. I can't in good faith just let you walk away. It's my duty as an agent of special forces to take you into custody."

"I'm sorry but I can't let you do that," Travis was resolute, his eyes burrowing into Jacob's.

Jacob grinned, somewhat amused. "Pretty bold words seeing I'm the one holding the gun."

"True," Travis agreed. "But I'm the one holding the secrets you've been searching for all these years. You want to know where Haytham Elwell is, I'll tell you, but only after I have Bronwyn safe with me. Now I'm going after them, shoot me right here, right now or bring that gun of yours and help. It's up to you." Travis didn't wait for Jacob to make up his mind. He took off running around the back of the house faster than Jacob had ever seen anyone run. He couldn't have shot him if he wanted to.

Jacob took off after him. "Here goes fifteen years of faithful service."

Chapter 36

Grabbing a fist full of my hair, Elam pulled my face up against his. "You didn't really think I'd be so lax as to let my most valuable prisoner escape her first night in captivity, did you?" His scalding breath burned against my skin as he laughed. "I do want to thank you for leading us right to Travis. What you thought was an act of true love will imprison him for the rest of his life."

In spite of the pain, I struggled against his grip, hate fueling my fight. Then, to add to my anguish, I heard footsteps rushing down the path.

"Trav...."

Elam's hand clamped over my mouth, muffling my warning.

"Bronwyn!" Travis called out, urgency ringing in his voice. My chest heaved in panic. In my eagerness to see him again, and reunite him with his long-lost love, I had inadvertently sealed his demise. I struggled against Elam, stomping on his foot, and trying to land a backwards kick to his groin. He tossed me to one of his burly guards who held me in a constricted hold.

"Keep her quiet!" Elam snarled and the beefy man slapped his thick hand over my mouth covering my warning.

"Be prepared," Elam instructed his men. "Travis will be ours today. We carry this out and you will live in extravagance for the remainder of your lives."

As the footsteps grew closer, I screamed muffled warnings. The man pressed his hand harder across my mouth, worsening the split on my lip. Pain, mingled with sticky blood, oozed from the fresh wound.

Elam pulled his pistol, pulling back the trigger; but instead of aiming it at the sound of approaching footsteps he burrowed the barrel into the side of my head. Poised for victory, he sneered delighted to be in control. Travis stopped at the threat.

"Make a move and I'll kill her."

My heart thundered. Travis was alone, Kenalycia wasn't with him, and his blood-stained clothes gave reason to believe something dreadful had happened. The cold barrel pressing into my temples didn't frighten me as much as the ferocious look emanating from his eyes. And if it were possible, I thought his glare alone would annihilate every living thing around him. The man holding me must have sensed the same for he slowly released his hand, unveiling my blood-stained face and an oozing split lip. "I'm sorry," I mouthed the words despite the pain. "I didn't know...I would have never..."

Travis' jaw tightened; his eyes fell on Elam detonating in rage. "You've caused much pain today. I will kill you because of it."

Elam smirked, but fear revealed itself in his countenance. I remembered Falcon's accounting of the night of the revolt, and how Travis went into a rage taking out ten of Abaddon's men with ease. The only thing that stopped him from killing Abaddon was his threat of the immediate execution of Brennun and Mavis. I figured the story of that fight had spread over the years, no doubt inciting fear in Elam. And now, seeing Travis standing before him, soiled with the blood of his fallen men, was proof he'd singlehandedly taken out Hamza and Conall, two of the fiercest guards in Abaddon's militia.

A strong wind stirred out of nowhere, pushing through the forest, bending the trees, and flattening the tall grass. Ominous clouds boiled across the sky, stirring up a mighty wind, whipping my hair into my face, obstructing my view. A chill fell into the air, threatening the warmth of the September sun, bringing a sudden end to the morning serenade of the birds and cicadas. An eerie silence hung like an omen that something was about to go terribly wrong.

The sound of approaching footsteps seemed deafening in contrast to the unnerving stillness. Elam's attention left Travis for the moment and focused on the two people running toward the standoff. Not able to use my hands to brush away my hair, I tossed my head, clearing my view and was stunned to see Bethany running behind a man carrying a gun. How in the world had Bethany ended up here and for that matter, who was she with?

"Freeze!" Jacob stood poised, ready to shoot. "Drop your weapon now!"

Elam sneered in defiance.

"I said now!" Jacob ordered pulling back the trigger.

Ignoring his demands, Elam directed his words to Travis. "I could care less who this man is, or what organization he's with. I'm in control here and I will kill her unless he drops his weapon."

Raising his hand, Travis signaled Jacob to back off but kept his eye on Elam. "Abaddon will kill you if you end her life and you know it."

"True, Abaddon wants her alive for reasons I am sure you well know." He taunted as a sensual perversion glowing in his eyes. "However, it's my opinion that we all would be much better off if she's dead, so I have no qualms about killing her. Abaddon would eventually get over the loss and be better for it. She produces a weakness in him that results in poor decision making."

"Is that so?" Abaddon stepped past the trees, joining the group. His unexpected appearance tore a look of horror into Elam's face. Thunder echoed in the distance, applauding his arrival, adding to the ominousness of the moment.

I shivered at his presence, as an abominable dread manifested, filling my spirit with imminent doom. I feared for Travis more than myself. It was no secret Abaddon demanded I be kept alive, why I didn't know. Perhaps it had something to do with the treasure. Travis, however, was Abaddon's key to eternal life and would be taken alive as well. But what worried me was Travis not succumbing to the demands of his mortal enemy. This would result in unspeakable acts of brutality that would be unleashed on both of us.

"Behold, the long sought-after prince Travis," Abaddon leered at Travis. "It's been a long time my friend, and may I sincerely say it's good to see you."

Travis didn't respond to Abaddon's greeting and revealed nothing in his expression. His dark eyes burned into his enemy, searing a mark of vengeance on his betrayer's soul.

The wind whipping through the trees, wailed a heinous dirge, circling the confrontation. Dead leaves blew up in a small whirlwind spinning across the dirt path. Again, my hair became a blindfold, hindering my view of what was soon to transpire between the two. I twisted my arms, hoping to free myself from the thug's tight hold. Annoyed with my struggle, he yanked my arms, nearly pulling my elbow out of socket. A cry of pain escaped my lips prompting Travis to cut his eyes into the man. The strength of his stare intimidated him to loosen his grip.

Abaddon, however, glared back, unmoved, and unafraid; and with an attitude of superiority grabbed me from the guard. Stroking my hair, he brushed it away from my face, and continued with his heinous plot.

"Well done, Elam, your plan played out just as you suspected it would."

Elam gave a nervous smile, hoping his last comments would be forgotten amid their victory.

"Thank you, my Lord, it is my pleasure to conduct the task. Might I add that your presence is a welcome surprise?"

Ignoring the phony gratitude, Abaddon surveyed the group, his eyes stopping on Jacob. "Who are you?"

"I'm your great grandson," Jacob introduced himself, still poised to shoot. "And I want to know what the hell's going on here."

Abaddon laughed, "My great grandson? Now that is interesting. You no doubt are mistaking me for my disreputable twin, Haytham."

"I've called for backup; the police will be arriving any minute and this place will be surrounded; you'd do best to surrender to me right now." On the heels of his announcement, sirens sounded in the distance, accompanied by the low rumble of thunder.

I had been dodging the authorities for days now, however, being taken into custody would be a welcoming event in light of our present situation.

White lightning dropped from the sky, ripping its way down the gray canvas, falling somewhere near the old house. A deafening pop echoed across the property, immediately followed by an explosion, shaking the ground, vibrating up through the soles of our feet. Abaddon's lips pulled into a fiendish grin, as if he'd directed it where to go. "Looks like we have a direct hit."

Fire roared from the decaying house as the wind whipped the flames high into view. Not intimidated in the least by the threat of police thwarting his plan, Abaddon turned his attention to Elam. "Clean up, it's time to leave."

In one swift, unexpected move, Elam removed his gun from me, immediately shooting Jacob in the chest. He slumped to the ground as a horror-stricken Bethany screamed. The split-second incident was all Travis needed to throw his knife, sinking it into Elam's throat before he could do the same to Bethany. Elam's hands curled around the blade as he collapsed to his knees, gurgling, struggling to pull it out.

Abaddon kept a tight hold on me, unmoved by Elam's misfortune. A sinister calm resonated in his voice as he continued to call out orders, not once contemplating the possibility of defeat. "Use the tranquilizer on Travis, get him to the portal, I have help waiting on the other side." One of the guards pulled a handgun, aiming it at Travis, just as Abaddon yanked me onto the dirt path pulling me toward the spring house.

I fought hard against him, but his strength was too much for me. The sound of an exploding firearm caused my heart to plummet. I struggled against him, trying to turn my head to see what had become of Travis. Abaddon jerked me back, but from the corner of my eye I saw him, dashing directly toward us, madness burning in his eyes. Lunging, Travis took us both down. We collided with the hard earth, knocking the wind from my lungs. Pain invaded every inch of my body as I struggled to catch my breath under the men's crushing strength. Travis regained his footing first, pulling Abaddon off me and slamming him up against a nearby tree. Using his elbow, he forced a punch to his gut. Abaddon doubled over, taking the blow, and then retaliated by pulling a knife and charging Travis. Like a possessed man, Abaddon flew through the air, his eyes white with rage. I screamed, cringing at the sight.

Spinning on his heels, Travis kicked the knife from Abaddon's grasp, sending it flying into the air and then catching it with ease. Six hundred years of indignation discharged from his fist as he brought the blade down slicing into Abaddon's face, cutting deep beneath his eye. Stunned by the blow, Abaddon stumbled backward, losing his balance. Travis lunged forward kicking him in the jaw, sending him sprawling to the ground. Abaddon moaned, struggling to hang onto consciousness.

The sirens were deafening, most of the vehicles having arrived at the ram-shacked house. Fire engines pulled onto the property. The fire was raging now, consuming the dried overgrown grass. The wind tossed the embers into the trees, igniting them like torches.

Leaving Abaddon writhing in pain, Travis turned his attention to me, helping me to my feet, "You, okay?"

I wasn't but nodded anyway.

"We need to move fast." He made his way to Bethany who was sobbing while holding Jacob's gun and leaning over his lifeless body. Travis pulled the gun from her hand, and then grabbed the one lying next to Elam. Placing both guns in his belt, he grabbed Bethany by the elbow. "Let's go."

My heart went out to her. I knew firsthand the terror she must be feeling. All my previous annoyances melted into compassion for my distraught friend.

Just before making the dash to the springhouse, Travis pulled his knife and sliced through my dress leaving the hem line high on my thighs. Then he made a quick stop, kneeling beside Abaddon who was struggling to stay conscious.

"I won't kill you, not today; instead, I'm leaving you here, just as you did all of us. I'm going back to rescue Haytham and then reclaim Eden. I will bring the royalty from Moonshine back to their homeland while you remain here and pay for Haytham's crimes. I will secure a place in Eden for the story of redemption to be written, sealing your doom. I will eventually come back for you, so you better hope you die in prison; it will be a better fate than what I have in store for you."

Having said his peace, we bolted for the spring house just as the rain began falling in torrents, extinguishing the blazing trees.

Ignoring the authorities' command to freeze, we dodged bullets and striking lightning, running blindly through the rain, veering between the trees, and leaping over fallen limbs and debris. All the while I wondered where Kenalycia was, and why she wasn't coming with us.

Lightning struck just yards in front of us, the bolt splitting a tree in two, sending half of the trunk to block our path. "This way," Travis pulled us both on a quick detour to the other side. The rain was falling in torrents now. The worry of being consumed by the jumping flames was extinguished by the downpour; my only concern was being shot or burned to death by a powerful bolt of electricity. The rain pelted us so violently that sometimes I feared I'd been hit by flying bullets.

A few more feet and we arrived at the portal. Travis kicked open the door to the spring house and we darted inside, splashing through the ankle-deep water and heading toward the cement slab in the back. It was then I noticed my travel bag, hidden in the far corner, and partly submerged under water. Grabbing it, I ripped it open, pulled out the precious book and held it close. Taking my hand, Travis pulled me to him, "Abaddon has men on the other side, armed and ready to attack. You and Bethany stay down, take shelter behind the rocks."

I nodded, wide eyed.

The wind howled, shrieking through the forest, shaking the distressed wood of the spring house, ripping the worn roof from the walls, and tossing it through the air like cardboard. The small shack collapsed around us like dominos. In the distance I saw Abaddon, hobbling toward the spring house, blood poured from his wound, mixing with rain, giving him the appearance of a possessed madman. Shuddering I reached for Travis, and although I could barely see him in the driving rain, his face indicated the severity of our situation. As I reached for him, the heat sensation exploded inside of me. This was my vision. The one I'd had since I first met him. And as I fell into the blackness of the portal something told me this wasn't the first time it had all happened.

Chapter 37

The men were waiting, just as Travis predicted. What Elam had hoped would be an ostentatious escort through the city of Eden, was suddenly transformed into a face-off between the returning Prince and the men who orchestrated the coup that abolished the reign of the three princes. The sight of blood-stained Prince Travis arriving without Elam or Abaddon rattled the small group and at first no one seemed to know what to do. It wasn't until one of the men, Blaine, spoke up over the roar of the waterfall, that things began to escalate.

"Where's Elam and Abaddon?"

Travis eyed the assembly, "They're not coming."

A murmur resonated through the men.

Blaine spoke again, taking the opportunity to advance himself among the inner circle.

"You arrive without an army and expect to take over what we have built for the past six hundred years." His voice thundered over the rushing water, "A new regime is in place, you have no authority here. Your days of reigning were over some time ago."

Motioning to the small militia, he barked out his orders. "Escort Travis and the women to prison."

The armed men moved into position, surrounding the rocky plateau situated behind the falling water.

My heart hammered against my chest as I looked out over Abaddon's personal mercenaries. They were men fighting only for individual gain and the approval of their malicious leader. Their kind had no conscience and would do unspeakable acts just to advance themselves to a place of significance.

Travis surveyed the men, only fourteen of them were armed, the other six stood to the side; devious politicians and not warriors ready to engage in combat.

"Get down and stay down," he pushed us deeper into the cut-out cavern "Keep hidden behind the rocks as best you can. Let me fight them off. They won't kill me, but they will you."

I grabbed Bethany's hand and pulled her down behind a row of large boulders. She wore no expression and appeared numb, as if she were in a hypnotic trance waiting for the snap of fingers to wake again. There was no time for me to console her or try and explain any of the craziness that was transpiring and for the first time ever, she asked no questions.

Once safely behind the rocks, Travis drew the pistols from his belt, simultaneously pulling back on the guns. His gaze lingered on me, stealing my breath much more than the panic squeezing in.

The men froze at the sight, not sure of what to do. Should they fire, they might kill him, thus sealing their doom, yet if they advanced, they would surely be shot. So, the stand–off ensued. No orders were voiced audibly, only transmitted through the mind so as not to give away the tactic. Two men covertly, backed away from the rest, and began advancing around the back side of the falls. Another two took to the opposite side while two others darted around the back, preparing to scale the rocks and then descend into the cavern shielding us. The remaining eight faced off, aiming directly at us. Their directives were to maim Travis enough to disarm him and take him prisoner. But by no means was anyone to kill him. Blaine along with his five cohorts waited in great anticipation but seemed somewhat at a disadvantage without Elam or Abaddon. Neither one of them was aware that their greatest defeat would transpire among themselves, each one trying to usurp authority over the other, taking command of the throne until Abaddon returned.

Travis fired the first shot. The victim fell from one of the higher boulders on the left side of the falls, his body crashing into the jagged rocks below. The men in front began firing at will, bullets zipped through the falling water buzzing into the hollowed-out cave like bees swarming their hive. More than anything, I wanted to see how Travis was faring, yet I dared not lift my head into the line of fire. As long as he continued moving and discharging his pistols, I knew he was okay.

Bing...a bullet hit the rock, barely missing my hand. Another exploded on top of the boulder gouging out a small hole, detonating a dust cloud into the air. Another hit the rock wall sending loose stones cascading down upon us. I covered my head with the book, and hunched down further, my heart accelerating with every firing of the weapons.

Travis continued shooting. Each deafening blast echoed in the small cavern. That, combined with the roar of the falls, was earsplitting and left no way of knowing if anyone was stealing around the sides ready to ambush.

The gunfire began to lessen; I could only hope the reason was that Travis had taken out most of the mercenaries. Then a sinking sound... the click of an empty gun. I raised my head just enough to see him toss his weapons aside. Out of ammo, he pulled a dagger from his belt just in time to engage in a knife fight with an assailant slinking around the sides. Then to my horror, another aggressor was skulking up behind him. Thinking fast I snatched a rock and hurled it with all the strength I could muster. I'd never been great at sports and spent most of my childhood in the theater or piano recitals, yet I landed the rock to the back of his skull with such accuracy that he doubled over, grabbing his head in pain. Recovering fast, he whirled around. With fury ablaze in his eyes, he charged my way, and as he did, I threw another stone. Dodging it, he pulled his knife and yanked me from behind the rock. I grabbed another rock and hit him hard at close range, before landing a swift kick to his groin. Growling like an animal, he spun me around and pressed the blade against my neck. Bethany's scream drew Travis' attention to the skirmish. Two mercenaries crashed in from above. One jumped on the man holding me, allowing me to escape. The other fired a round into Travis' shoulder.

Scrambling out of the way, I retreated against the wall. The barbaric mayhem continued to play out before me, and I wondered how long Travis could continue to hold Abaddon's men off. It didn't matter how many he slew, with each that fell another was summoned to take his place. Now he was without ammunition and a grisly wound shattered his left shoulder. My spirit faded at the sight. Yet despite the agony etched on his face, he continued to fight. The mercenary, who took down my assailant, fired a shot into his comrade, killing him.

Travis lunged toward the man, jerked the gun from his hand and pressed it into his forehead.

"Who are you?"

"My name's Cenric, I've come to help you."

Travis pulled back on the gun. "Why?"

"Because I have been praying for the return of your reign, vowing if I ever have the chance to put you back in power, I would take it."

"I don't trust you!" Travis grunted through the pain.

"I speak the truth." Cenric spoke up over the roar. "Two men will be charging across the waters any minute now to divert your attention from the person poised on the rocks to your left. He has a direct line of fire to the two women."

Keeping his gun aimed at Cenric, Travis glanced at the rocky ledge on his left. Cenric was right. A shadowy figure moved along the stalagmite catwalk. Travis fired, sending the stalking culprit toppling over the ledge to his death.

Raking the hair from his eyes, Travis aimed at the rocky bank and shot the two revolutionaries charging the falls. With the death of these last two Travis had incapacitated the small army leaving only the six unarmed representatives of Abaddon's inner circle. Still not sure whether he trusted Cenric, he pulled him close to his face.

"You're coming with me." Biting through the piercing pain he ordered us to stay put. Then with a running leap, he soared through the falling water, taking Cenric right along with him. Storming across the shallow pool, he grabbed Blaine and pushed him up against the rock wall. Wrapping his fingers around his neck, he knocked Blaine's head hard against the stone. With his other hand he pulled back on the gun, and at the same time shoved the barrel directly beneath Blaine's chin.

"Since you seem to be calling the shots among your contemporaries, you can send the order to release Haytham."

Gasping for air, Blaine choked out his objections, "I have no authority to order that release. Haytham is being held for high treason, Abaddon..."

"No excuses, do it now!" Travis growled, shoving the gun deeper under Blaine's chin. "Have Haytham brought to the landing at the east shore. Secure us a boat. Once Haytham is in my care and we have a safe passage, I will set you free. Otherwise, you can join your fallen men in death."

"You're the giver of life, you won't take mine." Blaine audaciously challenged the once reigning Prince,

"That's where you're mistaken," Travis clenched his teeth to mask his pain. "Sometimes you must take one life to preserve others. Just so you know, I find no joy in this." Having said what he did, Travis pulled the trigger spraying parts of Blaine's head across the granite wall. Then like a mad man he grabbed the next cabinet member of the inner circle, shoving him up against the place where Blaine once stood.

"I'll execute every one of you if I have to."

The rough barbaric actions of Travis were shocking. I'd never seen this ferocious side of him and could only attribute it to the possibility that since Kenalycia was not among them that something dire happened to her. That would no doubt explain his wild possessed behavior. My heart ached at the thought, especially after remembering Falcon's accounting of the anguish he'd already suffered. Now after remaining true to his love and waiting for six hundred years could she be gone? As much as I desired him for myself, I regretted this turn of events, feeling my impulsive decision to reunite the two may have caused the tragedy. I only hoped he could forgive me.

After Blaine's execution, the remaining members of Abaddon's council agreed to his demands. Bethany and I walked in silence, following Travis, Cenric, and the hostage. Bethany hadn't uttered a word since we came through the portal, and this concerned me. Travis was quiet too, focused on the task at hand. The blood from his wound soaked through his t-shirt but I couldn't tell if his behavior stemmed from pain or controlled fury; and for the first time since I met him, I felt somewhat frightened. He hadn't informed me as to what we were doing or why Cenric was accompanying us. But in all reality, he never gave reasons for any of his actions back in Moonshine either. His life was a total enigma; I consoled myself with this reasoning.

About a half hour later we arrived at the banks of an enormous lake. Several large fishing boats floated in the water along with sailboats and a few other smaller vessels anchored near the docks. Old-world buildings seemed to grow from the ground and sat nestled near the shoreline, creating a picturesque little fishing village. Fishermen milled around, tending to their boats, making last minute preparations before setting sail for a long night of fishing. At the arrival of the battle-weary party, the quaint village came alive with curiosity. Shopkeepers left their stores, fishermen stopped mending their nets, everyone gathered in the cobblestone streets eager to see what historical turning event was transpiring.

Cenric ran ahead and in no time was back pointing out the boat we would be traveling on. Not letting his guard down for a minute, and keeping his gun buried in the back of his prisoner's head, Travis climbed aboard the vessel and checked every compartment making sure it was unoccupied so there wouldn't be any surprise attacks. Once he deemed it safe, he told Cenric to bring Bethany and me aboard.

I felt the stares of everyone as I climbed the ladder into the boat. I could only imagine what they were thinking. What a sight I must be in my torn, dirty evening gown, and sporting a busted bloody lip. Would there ever come a day when I would be clean, dry, and well-dressed again? A day where I wouldn't get hurt, bleed, and have to make a mad dash for my life?

Cenric offered his hand when I topped the ladder and helped me board. Bethany boarded next leaving Cenric waiting as if he were expecting someone else. I wondered who we were waiting on but decided not to ask. Travis still had a strong hold on his hostage and remained quiet like he did when he was communicating mentally with someone. That was it, possibly the reason for his extended silence. He was back in Eden now; maybe he was in contact with old friends trying to elicit some help.

A ruckus from the crowd drew my attention to a small group on the street headed toward our boat. Stumbling along, surrounded by four guards and two of Abaddon's men, was Falcon. My heart rocketed at the sight. Travis must have taken the man hostage to bargain for the release of Falcon. My heart warmed at the thought, increasing my admiration for him. In the midst of losing Kenalycia he still had the fortitude to save Falcon.

"Remove his chains," He ordered from the deck.

Without an argument the guards unlocked the collar and shackles binding Falcons, wrist, and ankles. Despite his weakened battered state, his eyes danced in mischief as he lifted his head and tossed the hair from his face.

Bethany gasped at the sight of him, not knowing there were two. Noticing her confusion, I touched her arm, promising to explain later.

With much effort, Falcon made his way to the boat. The crowd grew quiet as he staggered along. I pitied him for the unwarranted brutality he suffered at his own brother's command; and as I watched him teeter along, making every effort to climb up the ladder, my heart burned with an all-consuming hatred for the enemy.

Running to his aid, I reached him just as he topped the ladder and collapsed onto the deck knocking me down with him. Rolling off me he gazed up into the blue autumn sky and flashed an impish grin.

"Looks like you and I were invited to the same party, Scribe. Glad to see you've survived. I taught you well."

Smiling through my tears, I reveled at the sound of his voice. Even in weakness, he stayed true to form, choking out his sarcasm.

"Get the boat underway," Travis ordered Cenric, who immediately obeyed by pulling in the ladder and scurrying about the deck, pulling in the lines, preparing the boat for departure.

Travis bound his hostage and pushed him to the ground. The man protested vehemently reminding Travis of his deal to set him free once Haytham was released and safe in his company.

"I'll set you free once we're underway, Travis snarled, "You can swim back."

I remained by Falcon, as the boat left the shore. I watched Travis haul in the lines and chart our course. I was able to relax some, feeling confident now that I was with Travis, and Falcon was safe. I wasn't sure about the Cenric fellow but figured if Travis trusted him enough to have him along then I would too. After all, he did save my life.

Bethany still leaned against the railing disoriented and staring into nothingness as if she were under hypnosis. My heart went out to her. As soon as things calmed down, I would console her and try to help her mind grasp what was happening.

Leaning against the deck wall I stared up into the pure autumn sky. White fluffy clouds drifted along with the boat, as birds raced with the wind, gracefully gliding along the deep blue expanse. The late afternoon sun warmed my skin bringing with it a gentle breeze wafting onto the boat, stirring my hair, and drying my damp dress. I inhaled and enjoyed its fragrance. It smelled like freedom.

Chapter 38

Madison carried in the vegetables from the garden and placed them in the basket on her kitchen counter. She was up earlier than usual. Sleep wasn't coming easy these days. She spent the better part of every night waking suddenly and checking her cell just to see if Bronwyn had called. Lying in bed, staring at the ceiling, only brought dire thoughts. So, she got out of bed, even though she was still tired, and busied herself, trying to give her mind something else to dwell on.

"It's going to be another hot one today," she said, taking her frying pan out of the cupboard.

Martin joined her in the kitchen after having retrieved the morning paper from the front lawn. Placing his reading glasses on the tip of his nose, he removed the daily from the narrow plastic bag.

"Oh No!" he groaned after seeing the headline.

Leaving the bacon sizzling on the stove, Madison joined him at the table, reading over his shoulder.

"Agent Betancourt is dead! But how? And Bethany was with him, does it say anything about Bethany?"

"Call her." Martin said, skimming the front page.

Grabbing the remote, Madison turned on her small kitchen TV before dialing the phone.

"Put it on CNN," Martin told her, still scanning the front page.

Holding the receiver with her neck she changed the channel.

Sure enough, the correspondents were discussing the latest developments out of New Mexico while aerial footage of a burning house and emergency personnel tending to slain and wounded victims covered the screen.

"What you're seeing here is footage from yesterday's carnage at the old Elwell property right outside of Cedar Crest New Mexico. At approximately 7:36 yesterday morning a call was placed to 911 operators alerting authorities of an attack taking place on the property. The caller identified herself as Bethany Baker of Los Angeles California. Miss Baker is a longtime friend of Bronwyn Sterling. Miss Baker told the operator that she was in the company of special agent Betancourt and was requesting police back up. Here is a recording of the call."

Martin laid aside the paper, "Turn it up dear."

The printed version of the call appeared on the screen as Madison and Martin listened to Bethany's frantic call.

Operator: "911 Emergency."

Caller: "My name is Bethany Baker and I'm with Agent Betancourt of special forces. We are three miles off Penny Lane at the old Elwell property. He needs back up." (Woman screaming) "Oh my God! He just killed someone! Oh my God, Oh my God! He just stabbed him."

Operator: "Calm down ma'am, I need you to calm down. Who got stabbed?"

Caller: "I-I-I don't know, some man. Travis killed him...."

"And that's where we lost the call," The anchor took back over the story.

Madison hung up the phone, a look of despondency etched on her face. "It went straight to her voice mail."

Before introducing her special guest, the newscaster recapped the events of yesterday's mysterious bloodbath. "Yesterday's massacre left five dead, including agent Betancourt, and two wounded, one critically. The dead men carried no identification which is consistent with all the deceased in this baffling case. An unidentified man survived the attack and was taken to Baptist Memorial Hospital with a knife wound to the throat. The fugitive by the name of Dakota was taken into custody. The caller, Ms. Bethany Baker, was not located, neither was Ms. Sterling found at the scene. Her whereabouts are still a mystery."

Madison clicked the remote, turning off the TV.

"Call the police, Martin and tell them we want to talk to Dakota. I want to know what he's done to my daughter."

Chapter 39

The cabin creaked as the boat rocked in the peaceful waters. The rhythm relaxed me, to the point where I could barely keep my eyes open. I'd gone below after Travis equipped his hostage with a life preserver and tossed him overboard telling him to swim toward the horizon and eventually, he'd see land. I'd heard of men having to walk the plank but never actually seen it in action until now.

Leaving Cenric to navigate the boat, Travis went below and went to work making the best use of the crude conditions.

He cut into specific parts of plants he collected on the walk to the village, steaming some and crushing the others. He cooked them to a thick oily paste and set them aside to cool.

With other ingredients he found in the galley, he mixed up an elixir and gave the concoction to Bethany. It took effect immediately, soothing her troubled mind and putting her to sleep. It was when he removed his shirt, withdrew the dagger from his belt and offered it to me that I snapped from my stupor and became alert.

"I'm going to need you to remove the bullet."

I was wide awake now. "I'm not sure I can, I might hurt you more."

"It's not very deep, you will feel it if you probe a little. Once you remove it, I can heal myself."

My stomach constricted at the suggestion of probing the wound. I'd always had a strong aversion to blood, nearly fainting at the sight of it, however I'd seen enough of it in the past week to make me immune to such a phobia. Besides, this was Travis, how bad could it be? It was his chest, his blood, his wound, and nothing about the man repulsed me. This was an opportunity to be near him, to touch him and maybe have a conversation, so I could find out what happened to Kenalycia back at the ram shacked house. With those thoughts tumbling around in my head, I took the dagger. "I'll do my best." I swallowed back my fear and dug the knife into the small hole only to pull it back out when I noticed pain take residence in his eyes.

"Don't look at me," He said, "Or you won't be able to do it. Just concentrate on the wound." I nodded and placed my left hand flat on his chest and with the other I stirred the knife around, stimulating more blood to ooze from the puncture. My mouth began to water, and my stomach squeezed. Just when I was ready to tell him I couldn't do it, the blade hit a hard object.

"That's it," he said quietly but I heard the discomfort in his voice. "Try to get behind it and scoop it out. I pressed my lips together, despite the fact they were swollen from the split lip, and cut around the object, digging it from the hole and catching it in my trembling hand.

"Good job, now if you don't mind, will you apply the paste to Falcons wounds while I take care of mine."

Again, I nodded and said nothing. Grabbing the pot of cooling balm, I stole a glance at Travis, who was sweating profusely while mopping up the blood from his chest. Picking up a thin piece of gauze I dipped the fabric in the mixture and dabbed it on each slash in Falcon's back. He sat slumped until the balm brushed his wounds, then he arched his back wincing at the touch.

"I'm sorry," I whispered, keeping my voice low.

"It's okay," he groaned through the pain, "You owe me one anyway."

I smiled, lifting my eyebrows, "Only one?"

He grinned, "What I'd give for a damn cigarette."

"It's a fishing boat, I'm sure I can rummage some up, somewhere on here."

"You do that Scribe and I take back everything I ever said about you."

I laughed this time. "I'm glad you're okay. I missed you."

"I missed you too. I was proud of the way you handled Elam at dinner. You showed a lot of courage. You did good...really good."

"Not so good," I lowered my voice and glanced over at Travis. I doubted he'd hear me anyway. He seemed to be engaged in some sort of healing ritual. His eyes were closed. One hand was pressed against his wound while the other was placed against his heart. His body trembled and perspiration dotted his forehead, rolling down his face.

"I messed up. In my hurry to right a wrong, I may have caused Kenalycia's death."

Falcon cut his eyes up to mine, "How so?"

"She asked me to take her to Travis. She had it all planned out, the guards helped us escape to the portal, but somehow, we were followed. I think they might have killed her."

Falcon didn't show any signs of surprise, let alone remorse, his only reaction to my dismal news was a reprimand. "What's the one thing I kept telling you Scribe?"

"Not to trust anyone but you."

"Uh huh," he gritted his teeth in pain. "I also told you you'd come face to face with the enemy and it wouldn't be what you expected."

I dabbed the moist goo, stirring it up; the aroma somehow soothing my own aching muscles.

"I'm not quite sure I'm following you."

Falcon propped his leg on the table allowing me easy access to his wound.

"I think you should talk to Travis about it."

"Maybe," I said and then began applying the ointment to his leg.

"Looks like your friend managed to stick her nose in a little too far."

I glanced over at Bethany who was curled up on one of the bunks asleep.

"That's for sure. I don't know how she managed it, but she shows up with a man claiming Abaddon is his great grandfather."

"That was my great grandson, Jacob." Falcon said, pointing to an abrasion on his pectorals. Rolling my eyes, I applied the mixture. "I'm sorry, I guess you know…"

He sighed, "Yes."

Travis joined us, taking over for me. I was fascinated to see his wound had all but disappeared. He moved along silently, and although his injury was gone, hurt still showed on his face. Too ashamed to look him in the eye, I stepped aside allowing him to do his work on Falcon. With a heavy heart I excused myself, leaving the confines of the cabin for the deck.

Cenric had dropped anchor but remained on watch for safety measures. I smiled at him, and he nodded, returning the silent greeting.

The night was cool and peaceful. The moon reflected off the waters creating a silver path all the way to where I was standing. The breeze wafted over the water touching my face and tousling my hair. The night was serene, the water tranquil, and the weather pretty much perfect, a stark contrast to the past several days. I fought back the tears pooling in my eyes at the thought of what my parents might be going through. They probably thought I was dead by now. How could life take such a drastic turn in such a short amount of time? Just a month ago my major source of anxiety was getting over Ryan and trying to salvage a poorly written manuscript. I shook my head thinking about Bethany. In a way I was glad she was down below in the cabin. Having her along brought some sense of normalcy to this bizarre experience, although I'd never seen her in such a traumatized state. As soon as she woke, I'd console her and try to explain some things. I sighed. Falcon suggested I talk to Travis about Kenalycia. The conversation was inevitable, I knew that; but how to go about it was what unnerved me. I thought back to the craziness of it all. I'd come through the portal with Kenalycia, Hamza and Conall. I'd left them by the car when I went to retrieve Falcon's journals. That's when I ran into Travis. The thought of that moment made my heart ache. He was happy to see me, I could tell. He had walked towards me, but I had stopped him, sending him outside. That's when I bolted from the house only to run into Elam. Could Elam have already killed Kenalycia? No, there wasn't time. Something wasn't right. Perhaps Hamza and Conall betrayed her, killing Kenalycia to get to Travis. That sounded more plausible. Whatever the reason, I was to blame and hoped somehow Travis would forgive me for my part in the whole tragedy.

The feel of a soft blanket being draped over my shoulders inter-rupted my thoughts. Travis stood beside me at the railing. My heart hammered against my chest at the sight of him. Would this ever stop?

"Thank you," I said, pulling the blanket tighter around my shoul-ders. "How's Falcon?"

"He's doing much better, should be back to his rascally self within a few hours."

"Bethany still sleeping?"

"Yes."

I smiled, "And what about you? Are you okay?

He nodded and looked out over the railing, watching the water."

I continued with the questions, trying to dispel the awkwardness, and delaying the inevitable reprimand for my carelessness. "So, what's next? Where do we go from here?"

"It so happens Cenric has been forming a small army, over the years, in hopes of starting an uprising. When Falcon was in prison, he was able to communicate with some old friends; all of which knew about Cenric and his plans. Some of his men are on a boat headed our way. We will join them and sail to their secret location where we can hide and plot out our next course of action."

I nodded and everything became quiet again. I couldn't think of another question other than asking what happened to Kenalycia. And as much as I wanted to know, I didn't have the courage to ask. Despite the awkwardness of the moment, I refused to go below but continued to stand alongside the man of my dreams, staring out over the water. The rhythmic waves splashing against the side of the boat only accen-tuated the silence.

"Bronwyn," Travis broke the quiet. "That wasn't Kenalycia. You were set up. They tricked you."

The swaying of the boat, combined with the shock of his statement, nearly caused me to topple backwards. Had he not grabbed hold of me I'd have fallen.

"Oh...really, that's great... I think... I didn't mean to disappoint you or get your hopes up... I mean it's great she's probably still alive...wait... I'm sure she's still alive, I didn't mean to say probably it's... when she wasn't with us, I thought she had been killed. Not Kenalycia but the woman I thought was her. She lied to me...I didn't know, I just believed her, and I shouldn't have. Falcon told me not to trust anyone, but he wasn't there and all I could think about was you... anyway you and the real Kenalycia still have a chance to be together." My mouth was rambling as fast as my heart was beating.

"I need to ask you a question?"

I quieted my incoherent and long-winded speech and nodded.

"Why did you run off? After you sent me outside, to who you thought was Kenalycia, why did you run away?"

Color flooded my cheeks and despite the darkness of the night I knew he saw. I turned away from him and looked out over the railing, focusing on the shimmering path that led to the moon, and wishing I could follow it to some sort of Neverland and avoid his question. He surprised me by turning me back around to face him. "I need to know. Did Abaddon..."

"No," I interrupted, not allowing him to finish. "He didn't."

"Then what?"

I held my breath trying to prevent tears, but it didn't help. They came one by one trickling from my eye and rolling down my soft cheeks. I dropped my head.

"I..."

If I were to tell him, I needed to look away, but he held my chin in his fingers, so I had no other choice than to look, and lie.

"It was your reunion. I didn't want to intrude." I took another deep breath. "I thought you would want privacy."

He kept holding my chin and my gaze. His eyes were dark and unreadable, but in the depths, I could see he knew I was lying. He dropped his hand from my face. I didn't have the courage to look at him, so I kept my head bowed and kicked at the dirty nets on the deck.

"I'm sorry Travis; I didn't mean to upset you anymore than you already are. I wish I had brought you the real Kenalycia. In my rush to make you happy, I didn't think, and I never meant for...."

"You wanted to make me happy. Why?"

Color flooded my face and I turned to the railing allowing the sea breeze to cool my humiliation. "Remember the night in the garden, when you told me what true love was..." I didn't wait for him to acknowledge. I am sure he remembered so I continued. "Well, that hit hard, and I wondered if I could do it. So, I was trying to give you away, knowing I would never experience you, but you would be happy, having what you wanted."

"Are you saying you love me?"

I wanted to jump over the railing and swim all the way to where the sky met the horizon. I should have known I couldn't explain it without revealing my affections. So, I went down another road of denial. "I barely know you..."

He stiffened.

"I can't explain why my heart is so drawn to you. It's ridiculous I know, and I apologize. It's just that my soul hasn't rested since the moment I met you. I was going through a lot but never realized how lost I was until I stood before you that night. And for a brief fleeting second, I felt as if I'd come home after having been gone for years."

My heart thundered in the silence that followed my admission. My face burned hot and a part of me wished I hadn't confessed, but I had, and it was too late to take any of it back. I wanted to sneak a peek at him but dared not turn my head, not until the color left my cheeks anyway.

He stroked the side of my face, running his fingers along my lips, he stopped at the swollen split.

"Is it painful?"

I shook my head, "It hurts like hell."

"I can fix that." He said, and then pulled my face towards his and placed his mouth over mine. I inhaled, devouring his breath as his lips caressed mine. The rush of heat detonated inside me, and the tears poured out, the saltiness mixing with the sweet taste of his lips. He pulled away gently and smiled, searching my eyes. I laughed softly through my tears and when I did, he leaned in and kissed them dry. This time I returned the affection. Holding nothing back, I kissed him with more passion than I ever thought capable. He lingered savoring the taste of me before pulling away.

"Bronwyn, I've kept a secret from you..."

Epilogue

Taylor thanked the UPS driver and carried the small box to his kitchen table. Laying his cigarette in the ashtray, he grabbed a knife and cut into the taped box. It was an eerie feeling to receive a package from Jacob, five days after his death.

Pulling back the cardboard flaps he lifted out an envelope addressed to him and an airtight Plexiglas case and set both objects on the table. Inside the container was an antique book titled Moonshine. On the far end of the casing were two holes, with gloves made of a thin nylon fabric. Slipping his hands through the openings and into the gloves he carefully opened the cover of the book and thumbed through the pages.

After a few minutes he removed his hands, took a draw off his smoldering cigarette and opened the envelope. Pulling out a letter he read,

Dear Taylor,

I'm sending you the book. Put it in safe keeping. I believe it to be very important; especially the letter hidden in the cover. I'm heading up to Moonshine to do some investigating. There is a chance I may disappear for a while if not for good. There are some things we are not meant to know and once one possesses the knowledge then the universe must deal with them because of it. There is a reason God told us not to eat from the tree of knowledge. I have nibbled and fear I will pay the price eventually.

One day people will come for this book. Protect yourself and protect it. Another world's survival depends on it. Only release it to Bronwyn Sterling, she is the author, and the cryptic letter is for her.

Sincerely,

Jacob Betancourt

Afterword

AN EXCERPT FROM BOOK THREE, THE STORY-TELLER'S SECRET

The boat creaked, swaying gently as the water swelled, pushing against the hull. The peaceful rocking was hypnotic, a perfect sedative, but despite the soothing tranquilizer, sleep would not come. I gazed up through the porthole, and stared up at the night sky, while fumbling with a carton of cigarettes I'd found up on deck. They would be a gift for Falcon once he woke. I turned the box over in my hand, and contemplated smoking one myself. Perhaps it would calm me some, take away the jitters and dull the confusion crowding my mind. Yet I wouldn't dare replace the sweet taste of Travis' lips with tobacco. He'd kissed me and it was rapturous, freeing my spirit from the cold prison of loneliness, releasing me to love again and find rescue in the arms of the one who held me. Yet, his kiss did not prepare me for the secret he revealed soon after, and now lying in my bunk, I stared into the black night, and felt more alone than ever.

"You alright Scribe?"

I took my time before responding, not knowing how to answer Falcon's question. I wanted to believe I was. I'd been strong, determined, surviving so much already. Losing myself at this point would make all my efforts seem in vain. Yet that is exactly what happened tonight, on the deck of the fishing boat, I became a stranger to myself.

I rolled onto my side and faced the bunk parallel to mine. Moonlight streamed through the open portal, reflecting the sympathy in Falcon's eyes. I reached across and offered him the carton of smokes. "Got something for you."

He rose on his elbow, ready for conversation. "You wanna talk about it?"

"Only, if you can explain it to me."

Lying back on his bunk he knocked the carton against the weathered ceiling, hanging a few inches above his face. "I wish I could," he said, pulling a cigarette from the box. "I've been trying to find a way, ever since you stepped out of that car."

I let the silence hang in the air, while contemplating his words, allowing them to take me back to that fateful night. Beth's wrong turn, the blown engine, none of it was accidental. I'd never thought much about destiny before. I'd always been a life's what you make it, type of thinker. But there was no denying, I was not in control that night. Either God or some dominant force predetermined a set of events for me. I sighed. This was more than a set of events. True, I believed their story but this... this new revelation was unfathomable.

"I think you're all wrong." I launched my defense. "Maybe I just look like her. I can swallow the notion that I am some prophesied scribe but telling me I am someone, other than who I know I am, is where I draw the line.

The boat rocked with more intensity, causing the beam of moonlight to dance about the cabin, losing the light on Falcon's face. But even though I could no longer see him, I felt his eyes on me.

"Stop basing everything you believe in logic and listen to someone who knows. There are powers at work here, you know nothing about."

"Listen?" I argued, trying to dismiss the disturbing notion of mystic forces messing with my life. The thought was unnerving, taking me back to terrifying, paranormal events from my childhood I had long since forgotten. "Listen to what? You never tell me anything."

"I do, but you don't hear me." He reprimanded me again. "I told you the night we read the prophecy you had forgotten who you were." His voice was haunting and from the darkness of the cabin it caused my skin to crawl. I remembered that night. In the shadows of the room, he called me a storyteller. Had he been giving me hints all along and I completely missed them? Maybe he was right. Had I been so busy trying to prove him wrong that I never noticed all the little breadcrumbs he was leaving on the path, so I could find my way home?

"Why wasn't I told the night at the Citadel, when Barak convinced me I was the prophesied scribe? He could have dropped all the bombs at once."

"Travis asked him not to."

My stomach knotted. Why wouldn't he want me to know? Why would he keep that information from me? This was the question I'd neglected to ask him, earlier tonight, when he told me I was Kenalycia.

"Why?"

This time it was Falcon who let the silence linger. "Because Scribe, you were in love with someone else."

About the Author

About the Author

Denise Parton is described as one of the purest storytellers of all time, pulling of romance, suspense, and a touch of the supernatural, all in the same piece. Born and raised in Tennessee, Denise Parton sets her stories in the Deep South and her natural southern style charms all her work.

In addition to writing, Denise enjoys directing for the non-profit, Inner Light Family Theatre, that she and her daughter, Brittany founded. She has brought many wonderful stories to life on stage. To Denise, there is nothing more thrilling than bringing characters to life, whether on stage, sitting around a campfire or in the pages of her books.

In her free time, she enjoys spending time with her four daughters, watching fireflies in the evenings, dreaming up her next story and inspiring others.

Denise's books include, *The Secrets of Moonshine*, *The Secret in the Rubble* and *The Storyteller's Secret* all a part of her Moonshine series. She is currently writing, *The Final Secret*, the last book in the Moonshine series.

Thirteen For Dinner, a historical time travel romance and *The Haret*, the first book in The Haret series.

Love is the New Pink, a non-fiction book on love and social accep-
tance.